MAGGIE BLUE
and
THE DARK WORLD

GUPPY
BOOKS

MAGGIE BLUE
and
THE DARK WORLD

ANNA GOODALL

**GUPPY
BOOKS**

MAGGIE BLUE AND THE DARK WORLD
is a GUPPY BOOK

First published in the UK in 2021 by
Guppy Books,
Bracken Hill,
Cotswold Road,
Oxford OX2 9JG

Text © Anna Goodall
Illustrations © Sandra Dieckmann

978 1 913101 312

1 3 5 7 9 10 8 6 4 2

The rights of Anna Goodall to be identified as the author of this work has been
asserted in accordance with the Copyright, Designs and Patents Act 1988.

All rights reserved. No part of this publication may be reproduced,
stored in a retrieval system, or transmitted in any form or by
any means, electronic, mechanical, photocopying, recording or
otherwise, without the prior permissions of the publishers.

Papers used by Guppy Books are from well-managed
forests and other responsible sources.

MIX
Paper from
responsible sources
FSC® C020471
www.fsc.org

GUPPY PUBLISHING LTD Reg. No. 11565833

A CIP catalogue record for this book is available from the British Library.

Typeset by Falcon Oast Graphic Art Ltd
Printed and bound in Great Britain by CPI Books Ltd

For Juno

PART ONE

1

WEST MINCHEN

Maggie was sitting in Sol's café, a cup of tea cooling beside her, only a few crumbs left of the huge slice of chocolate cake she'd just devoured. Beyond her flowed the dull afternoon bustle of West Minchen's high street: its pound shops, gambling shops, restaurants and newsagents. But Maggie didn't notice any of that. She was staring at someone. Her eyes were even wider than usual and a deep crease of concentration streaked down the middle of her forehead.

A woman was telling off her little boy for knocking over her coffee. Her voice was all agitated and angry, and the boy was crying. But the woman wasn't really angry about the coffee. If anyone had been taking any notice of Maggie – but then adults don't generally think kids can be doing anything of interest to them – they would have seen that the crease between her eyes got even deeper. She was trying to understand.

It wasn't the churning, wild anger Maggie had sensed in her mum when her dad left them. It wasn't really anger at all, or not entirely. It was more like the woman was overwhelmed. And suddenly, with a weird click somewhere in her brain when a piece of knowledge rose up to her so certainly, Maggie understood, she felt it. The woman had lost a friend, or someone very close. They'd argued or fallen out . . . or something. Beneath her anger the woman was feeling very lonely. It made tears well up in Maggie's eyes.

'What are you looking at?' The woman had noticed her. Maggie's mouth opened but no sound came out – how could she explain? Maggie felt sweat cluster under her armpits and blood rush to her cheeks as she flushed bright red.

The woman put her arm round her son. 'Stop staring at us like that. It's rude.' They were united now, the two of them against her, their fight forgotten.

And then Maggie felt that other familiar red begin to surge through her. Why did people have to make you feel bad? She'd only wanted to help. Maggie shoved her chair back so hard when she stood up that it was only stopped from falling by an adjacent table. Then she stalked out of the café slamming the door behind her, but not fast enough to miss the woman mutter, 'Weird kid.'

Maggie hurried back through the darkening streets, past all the terraced houses squashed together with yellow light spilling out. She was late. Not for her Aunt Esme, who didn't care when she got home or what she did or why, but for her mum. For their weekly phone call: five p.m. every Thursday.

She cut through the alleyway down the side of the church emerging onto the crescent of identical fancy houses that led back onto the main road and to Milton Lodge. It was a big haunted-looking place set back from the road by a moss-covered gravel drive where water often gathered in huge pools after the rain. Her aunt lived here in a one-bedroom garden flat. Maggie trudged up to the door.

Winter darkness had fallen very suddenly, like it always did, and the Lodge's welcome light had stopped working. But she could still make out the contented fat lump of the one-eyed tabby cat who seemed to belong to no one, but who often sat on the doormat of the Lodge.

Maggie touched his warm fur as she went past. The old cat purred briefly but powerfully, and looked up at her, hopeful she'd allow him indoors and out of the cold.

'I'm sorry, cat. You know Esme hates you. *I* would let you in.'

It was weird because Esme seemed relaxed about everything *but* this cat. He was a battered-up old beast, a retired street fighter by the looks of his torn scraggy ears. But because of his one eye, it always looked like he was winking at her in a jovial sort of way. And she swore that sometimes she could hear him humming a tune beneath his purr, like a little jazz melody. But then she often imagined things that weren't real.

'Maybe tomorrow.'

This seemed to satisfy him, and he lowered his rotund head and went back to watching the cars race past on the dark narrow road beyond.

As soon as she got into the drab dusty hallway, Maggie heard the phone ringing.

'Damn!' She rushed to unlock the door of Flat 1. But there was a knack to jiggling the key in the lock and in her haste it got stuck. Meanwhile the rings seemed to get shriller and shriller. She could hear her mother's thoughts: *I can't rely on that girl for anything. She's useless.*

Finally the door flew open. Maggie raced into the living room and picked up the old black dial phone, probably the only one still in use and not in a museum.

'Hello?'

'So you are there? I didn't think you were going to pick up.'

'I was . . . having a bath.' Maggie wasn't sure why she lied, but she often did to her mum. It was a habit, self-preservation.

'You know we talk at five p.m. every Thursday. It's the only thing I ask.'

'I didn't realise it was so late.'

'And don't be using all of Esme's hot water. A bath at five?'

'Sorry.'

'Don't apologise to me. It's Esme's water.'

There was a long pause in which Cynthia Brown would be dredging up what the counsellor had told them about how they could try and communicate better with each other.

'How's school this week?' she said after a while.

'It's great.'

'And you're enjoying your classes?'

'Yes.' Now Maggie paused – she had to keep this vaguely believable. 'Except maths. And I hate French. But otherwise, it's OK.'

'And you're getting good marks?'

'Yeah, pretty good.' It could wait till the end of term for her mum to find out the truth.

'And you've got friends? It's hard joining a new school in the second year, especially a few weeks into term.' She must be reading from notes.

'Everyone's really nice,' Maggie parroted in response.

'Well, that's certainly lucky for you.' A little of the real Cynthia Brown, the one Maggie was currently more familiar with, had crept back in, but she was soon back on track. 'You would tell me if anything was wrong, wouldn't you? You know you can always talk to me.'

Maggie sighed inwardly. Why did adults ever even say that? OK then: *I hate it here. I miss home. I miss the sea. I hate school. I don't have a single friend, and you know what? I don't want one. I'm here in this drab suburban place with my crazy aunt, the one Dad always told me everyone in the family hated, in her tiny flat because you can't cope with the simplest things like getting out of bed and going to the supermarket.*

Or what if she just said she was finding things hard? What would she get? *I don't think that's a very good attitude. You won't make friends like that. You're very lucky that Esme could take you in. You never think of me, etc, etc.*

So she just said, 'I know, Mum. Thanks.'

There was another long pause. 'And has your father been in touch?' Cynthia's voice instantly got tighter just mentioning him.

'No.'

'You're sure?'

Maggie sighed. 'I'm sure.'

'He said he was going to visit you, and I made one thing clear to him: he is not to bring that woman with him.'

'He hasn't visited. He hasn't even phoned me.'

'But just to be clear, *that woman* is not to take a step inside your aunt's house.'

After the call, Maggie sat on the edge of the sofa and let the darkness in the cluttered room grow around her. Esme was something of a hoarder and the huge old sofa Maggie slept on was covered in sheet music, books and old newspapers by day. She had to move it all off before she went to

8

sleep. The room smelt of corners not dusted and old books rotting quietly.

For some unexplained reason, Esme also kept a huge stuffed owl in a case on top of her upright piano. It stared at you wherever you were in the room. Those huge yellow eyes, like marbles, made Maggie feel sad. The owl's expression was fierce, but it was dead and stuffed and living in a dusty case in West Minchen. Surely not what it had imagined when it had flown out hunting on moonlit nights.

Beyond its frozen pointed ears, the garden was huge and overgrown, a relic from when Milton Lodge had been the home of a wealthy family, and there'd been nothing around it but fields. Esme said that before it all got cut down to build the suburbs, Everfall Woods had grown right up to the edge of the crumbling wall that still stood, just about, at the end of the communal garden.

The wall had fallen down in a storm a few years ago and no one had bothered to fix it. The one-eyed cat sat on its ruins sometimes, forever winking, and the foxes that slept in the tall overgrown grass would scuttle over it if you disturbed them.

Maggie opened the back door and stepped out. It was completely dark at ground level but the huge oak and smaller trees around it were silhouetted against a dark blue sky. She inhaled the cold air.

There was something about this place that wasn't right. She could sense it lurking just behind the neatly-paved drives with the sleek black cars silently parked and the perfect soft-carpeted homes. Something, not wrong exactly, but which made her skin tingle, something strange.

A voice rang out into the darkness, 'Maggie?'

She went back inside and closed the door.

Esme had arrived home and was brewing tea in the narrow kitchen. Maggie watched her through the quaint hatch cut into the wall to connect the two rooms. Her aunt wore her hair in a solid beehive, and toxic levels of hairspray often hung in the air in the mornings before Maggie left for school. The front was dyed metallic reddish brown but the back was grey, as if she couldn't reach or see it properly in the mirror.

Esme brought the tea through on a tray with a jar of biscuits and placed them on the little round table where they shared the occasional meal. She sat down, tapped out a cigarette and began smoking in the efficient yet moviestar way she had: little puffs out of the side of her mouth, a precise tap-tap into an ashtray, her beehived head slightly tilted, as if she suspected a camera might be rolling and she wanted it to capture her best angles. Her mum would hate that Esme smoked, let alone smoked in the flat. But then, what could she do about it anyway?

Maggie didn't remember, but apparently she'd met Esme once when she was small. Her aunt had been the very early, and very unwanted, child of Grandma Muriel before she was married. Esme had a different father to Maggie's dad, was fifteen years older and had grown up abroad. Maggie's parents didn't like Esme, until they needed her, and then they still didn't actually like her.

But Maggie did. She was different to anyone else she'd met. She was odd and didn't seem to care what other people thought about her. Esme did just what she wanted. Or so it seemed to Maggie.

She wore blue horn-rimmed glasses, a white shirt, a navy jacket, matching knee-length skirt and black Mary Janes with an elasticated band. She carried a neat black handbag, and a large wicker shopping bag that, more often than not, was empty. But then she had lots of weird hippie stuff too, like crystals and incense.

She looked at Maggie and smiled. 'You seem slightly glum, my dear.'

'I just spoke to my mum.'

'Ah, well. That would explain it.'

On the fourth finger of her right hand Esme always wore a beautiful ring that fascinated Maggie. She watched it sparkle there now. It was a snake eating its own tail, gold decorated with emeralds. It had a special name Maggie could never remember.

'What's your ring called again? An uru-buru?'

'*Ouroboros*.' Esme stubbed out her slim-line cigarette. 'Your dinner is in the fridge.'

'I'm not hungry.'

Esme consulted her tiny watch with the cobalt blue

strap. 'It's still early. But it's there when you want it. Derek and Phyllis are coming round later to play some music.'

She was a violinist, or had been. Maggie had heard her parents say, in that way people have when they are enjoying someone else's misfortune, that Esme had suffered a nervous breakdown and couldn't play professionally any more.

'You're very welcome to sit and listen, Maggie.'

Maggie made a face. 'I don't want to.'

Esme smiled again, amused. 'Well, there's a box of earplugs in the bathroom. I think it's Schubert tonight.'

Later, Maggie lay in the big pink plastic bath, a duvet wrapped around her, listening to the strains of a Schubert piano trio. The music didn't sound too bad when she'd finally got warm – Esme was a firm believer in not over-using the heating and the air in the bathroom was freezing.

Finally, at about ten-thirty, the music stopped and she heard the low murmur of voices. Maggie could only go to bed when they'd stopped gossiping. She might get to her sofa by midnight if she was lucky. Then again, the bath was pretty comfortable and she often fell asleep there until Esme came and woke her up.

It wasn't that Esme was unfriendly. In fact, she was very kind – the flat was small and she'd never even really met her before. It was more that Maggie was like another bit of furniture to her, another stack of old newspapers Esme could work around. She didn't care where Maggie went or what she did. At first it was a brilliant change after her mum's endless worrying and nagging, but Maggie had realised it actually made you feel lonely.

Maggie reached down over the side of the bath and picked her laptop off the mat. She was the only person in the whole world who didn't have a mobile phone – aside from Esme, Derek and Phyllis, of course, but they didn't count. However, in an unprecedented attack of guilt for messing up her life, her dad had given her his old laptop because she needed it for school.

School. Maggie let out a sigh and closed her eyes. The voices next door still murmured on in their comforting lilt. She was very cosy now, the old duvet wrapped tightly around her, her head at a comfortable angle against the cushion. If she could just press pause and stay here for ever. But no, the earth would move round, the sun would come up and she'd have to go to Fortlake Secondary. Fortlake – it sounded like a prison to her.

There was a sharp tap at the window that made Maggie jump. She froze and listened, but there was only the faint sound of traffic rushing past the end of the drive and the voices still murmuring next door. She must have imagined it, or maybe it was just a branch tapping against the glass.

She settled back down, but the tapping came again, louder. Maggie clambered out of the bath, still wrapped in the duvet. But she couldn't see anything behind the small frosted side window. She looked around for a weapon, but could only find a canister of Esme's super-strength hairspray. It would have to do.

She edged over to the window clutching it. Three raps came again – *tap-tap-tap* – very precise.

Maggie whispered, 'Who's there?' but there was no reply. Impossibly curious now, she undid the latch and opened the window.

From the cold rainy darkness a brown lump catapulted itself inside, flying just past her ear. Maggie let out a tiny scream, or the start of a big one that she managed to suppress when she realised who it was.

The fat one-eyed cat was shivering with cold and wet. He shook himself out and started to curl around her legs, purring loudly, and amidst the heady thrumming of the rain she thought she could hear him humming a little tune: *bee bop bi doo da, de da da. . .*

Maggie smiled and closed the window. 'Come on then.'

She climbed back into the bath and the cat immediately jumped in after her. It took her a few minutes to get warm again, and get the pillow in just the right place, but she had to admit, the cat was a wonderful foot warmer once he'd dried off. His purrs rippled into her feet and she soon fell asleep.

It was long after one o'clock when Esme woke her. The cat had gone, but as Esme led her to her sofa bed, she was too dopey to wonder where he might be hiding.

2

SCHOOL

Aunt Esme brought in two steaming cups of tea. She was rather different first thing in the morning. The beehive was yet to be assembled and her half-copper, half-grey hair was brushed out into a fuzzy pyramid that appeared to have some of the properties of a solid. Her face without make-up was pale and set back from itself.

Esme was already on her way back to bed with the paper and her tea. She shuffled off in her old slippers. 'Have a wonderful day at school.'

Maggie grimaced. The chances were slim.

She was late as usual, and by the time she made it to her classroom, registration was over and everyone had gone. She got to the hall just as the last seniors were taking their seats for assembly. Maggie sat on the floor at the back beside a random year ten, who glanced at her irritably, but otherwise didn't object.

Even from here, many rows away from the rest of year eight, Maggie immediately sensed Ida Beechwood's presence. And in just the same way, Ida knew exactly where Maggie was too. She turned round a few seconds after Maggie had sat down and they locked eyes.

Whenever Ida looked at her, no matter how much she tried to prepare for it, Maggie's heart started to beat faster and her cheeks flushed. It was seriously embarrassing and she just prayed that no one else noticed. But she knew that Ida had.

Ida never seemed to get nervous or angry; she never seemed to feel uncomfortable. She was always just confident. She was tall and slender, with curly black hair and perfect spot-free brown skin. She was very clever, very popular and good at sport – basically everything Maggie was not. Plus she had an amazing phone.

Maggie looked away, her cheeks red, and concentrated on Mr Minnow, the nervy head of music, who was playing something impressively rapid on the piano. Meanwhile the entire school, including the teachers, looked at their phones. But on the dot of eight-thirty, right in the middle of a fistful of notes, Minnow broke off abruptly – a sonic indicator of fear – and stood up. Reluctantly, the rest of the school followed suit. Amidst the rumble of hundreds of people getting to their feet, Miss McCrab, the headmistress, stalked in.

Le Crab, as everyone called her, favoured bizarre

Victorian-style dresses with high collars that were mostly black, though occasionally she splurged on an alarmingly bright print. Today it was big red poppies on a dark-blue background. She stood centre-stage, high above her helpless subjects, and assessed them in silence for a few moments, during which it always seemed like she was about to pick out one trembling student and accuse them of high treason. Then something far more terrifying happened – she smiled – but the effect was like someone suffering from trapped wind. As usual, her tangerine lipstick was slightly smudged around her mouth and had got onto her teeth. Presumably no one was brave enough to mention this to her.

She gestured for them to sit down. 'Good morning, Fortlake. I'm sure you're ready for another productive and hardworking week . . .'

Maggie automatically switched off and pushed a fragment of leaf around aimlessly on the shiny floor in front of her. When she came to some minutes later, she found that Le Crab had finished the usual boring morality tale about doing your best and treating everyone as you'd like to be treated yourself, and was going on about Everfall Woods again.

The ancient woods that bordered the school playing field were the remnants of the same forest that had once grown right up to the back of Milton Lodge. And Le Crab seemed convinced that it was the most dangerous place in the world.

'As you know, Fortlake pupils must *never* take the shortcut through the woods alone, and now, as the winter nights are drawing in, pupils of this school must avoid the woods altogether. Believe me, it is for your own safety. There have been a number of unpleasant incidents there over the years, and any pupil caught walking there will be given detention immediately.'

She was oddly obsessed with Everfall, Maggie thought, not for the first time. But even Le Crab couldn't control what her pupils did outside of school hours. And no one took any notice of her constant pleas. The teachers never gave anyone detention, and come four p.m. Everfall was full of kids smoking, kissing or just walking home together.

Finally Le Crab read out the rest of the day's announcements. There were the usual sports match results and dull notices about societies and upcoming events. But then there was something new. She held out one arm stiffly in the direction of where the teachers were sitting.

'We are delighted to welcome Miss Beverley Cane to Fortlake. She will be starting as our new school guidance counsellor next week.' A tall young woman with long almost white blonde hair reaching to her waist stood up and looked meekly around, stooping her shoulders slightly as if trying to make herself smaller.

A whisper went around the assembly but Le Crab held up a commanding hand and everyone fell silent again.

'Miss Cane will establish herself in room C12 next to the Nurse's office, and will be available during school hours for anyone needing to confide about stress or problems, whether at school or at home, and all in strictest confidence. Your form teachers will provide details of how to make an appointment.'

Miss Cane smiled shyly and gave a modest little wave. She was wearing a fluffy pink jumper and a velvet Alice band in her gorgeous hair. But Maggie noticed her eyes – they were an amazing emerald green and ice cold, as if they were looking out from somewhere much darker and steelier than the fluffy outer self.

As the whole school tailed out of assembly, Ida caught up with Maggie and shoved her hard in the back so that she tripped forward. 'Morning, Bruise.' She and her groupies, Helena and Daisy, sniggered then quickly walked away before the teachers noticed.

On Maggie's first day, when the teacher introduced her to the class in the usual way – 'This is Maggie Blue Brown. I'm sure you'll all make her feel very welcome' – Ida and her friends had all laughed.

Later on Ida came up to Maggie in the corridor and said, 'Maggie Blue Brown? What kind of a name is that?'

Maggie had felt the usual blush spread over her cheeks. It happened a lot and there didn't seem to be any way of stopping it, or at least she hadn't found a way yet.

Helena pointed. 'She's going bright red!'

Just then Mr Yates, their corduroy-clad bespectacled geography teacher, had ambled over. 'Everything OK here, girls?'

Ida changed in an instant, her face became sweet and friendly. 'Oh yes, Mr Yates. Just making Maggie feel welcome.'

'I see.' But he didn't walk on and looked searchingly at Maggie. So she smiled at him through her blush. Mr Yates smiled back uncertainly and shuffled off.

Maggie was not a snitch. Besides, if this was bullying Fortlake-style, she could handle it. Her old school had been much rougher. The boys didn't even fight here; they didn't seem to want to.

As soon as Mr Yates had disappeared round the corner, Ida looked back at Maggie, and her eyes became spiteful once more.

'Blue Brown – it reminds me of something. We'll call you the Bruise.'

On cue, Daisy and Helena broke into peals of hysterical laughter.

Ida smiled at Maggie, the same phony smile she'd just given Mr Yates. 'See you later, *Bruise*.'

Ida was the only person who picked on Maggie (or really took much notice of her at all). But from the moment Ida started hassling her, Maggie sensed they had a special connection – that underneath the meanness, Ida was somehow interested in her. She spent a lot of time in class staring at Ida. And when Maggie looked on the class calendar where everyone had written their birthdays and realised that Ida's was the same day as hers – the 21st June – it only added to Maggie's feeling that they were destined to become best friends. Though she'd never even had a best friend.

But apart from occasional run-ins with the most popular girl in the year, Maggie kept her head down. She sat at the back of every class and as long as she was quiet and looked thoughtful everyone seemed more than happy to leave her alone. Normally she just doodled or day-dreamed, half-wondering if long division existed in real life or if you'd ever actually need to know what happens when you put sulphur into water.

The last class of that day was geography, or colouring-in as Maggie called it. But she fully committed to colouring her drawing of a mountain with a cloud over it in various stages of precipitation because a boy called William Snowden with white-blond hair in a severe bowl cut always let her share his colouring pencils and it was the only kind thing anyone did for her, so she didn't want to waste it.

After class, Maggie took ages packing up her ruck-sack so that by the time she left only Mr Yates remained, anxiously combing his thinning hair and adjusting his tie. To her surprise, Miss Cane, the new school counsellor, was waiting patiently outside the classroom. She smiled her shy smile at Maggie and brushed her curtain of hair back from her shoulder.

Maggie walked off but paused by the water fountain to observe her. A few moments later Mr Yates rushed out, all flustered and apologetic. Then the two of them walked down the corridor towards the staff room, Mr Yates all bashful and embarrassed, Miss Cane all smiles and simpering laughter.

Maggie frowned. Either Mr Yates was more of a player than anyone could have imagined, or Miss Cane had a penchant for awkward corduroy-wearing men with slightly receding hair. Maggie didn't know much about relationships, but it seemed a little odd. She soon forgot about it though because the day was finally over.

3

DAN THE TREE

Despite Le Crab's warnings, for Maggie the only good thing about school was that she walked through Everfall Woods to get there and back. She always made sure she set off across the big playing field a good distance from any groups so she could enjoy the huge open space on her own, though even here the dense hum of traffic from some nearby road never ceased.

The edge of the playing fields gave way to overgrown grass that merged into a muddy slope down into the woods. As the day set, the thick bank of trees looked magnificent: the bronze leaves and evergreens clustered together in a rustling wall thrust this way and that by the breeze. Maggie went right in, down the bank, her loafers picking up thick wedges of dirt. She never took the paths on either side like everyone else did. Then she was alone, in the middle of the trees.

Maggie knew instinctively that this was a magical

23

place. The ground was currently a sea of pale orange and brown leaves out of which the dark sinewy trunks of the ancient trees emerged. Here, it was possible to imagine you were entirely alone and Maggie liked the sound of her feet pushing through the dead leaves. There were weird things too. Strange circles made of stones with carefully arranged branches in the middle, as if someone had crafted a shelter for the night.

She'd heard some of the Fortlake kids say that weirdos lurked here, waiting to snatch you away, and that a satanic cult met here some nights and went to the enormous Victorian graveyard that adjoined the woods. It was true that someone had spray-painted turquoise evil eyes on a few tree trunks, but Maggie wasn't sure that equalled devil worship.

The only weird person she'd ever actually seen there was Dan the Tree. She didn't know his real name, but that was what people at school called him. He was always in the woods, standing or sitting on a tree stump by a small copse in which saplings grew amongst long pale grass and brambles, all partitioned by a low woven fence.

Dan the Tree was a huge man with a solid protruding belly and thick glasses held together with masking tape. He always wore a faded bronze Puffa jacket, saggy tracksuit pants and a blue woolly hat. Maggie felt mean thinking it, but he was ugly, with thick untidy lips and grey straggly hair. He sat motionless, staring at a gnarled tree whose

24

branches curved so far over that they almost touched the ground, like an archway.

After Dan the Tree's mystic circle, it was a steady upward slope to the main path that led out of the woods. Here Maggie often paused for a while waiting for the endless groups of students to trudge past so that she could rejoin the path unnoticed.

That day it was busy and she had to wait a while behind a large tree as the lazy smokers and older kids laughed and talked their way slowly back to the road. But just as she thought it was clear, she saw a lone figure coming up through the gathering dusk. As she darted back between the trees, Ida Beechwood wandered slowly past her, apparently lost in thought. Maggie was taken aback – she didn't think she'd ever seen Ida alone before.

She let her get a good few paces ahead and then slipped out from her cover and walked behind her. Ida didn't hurry; in fact she dragged her feet. She drifted up to the gate and absentmindedly left it open.

Maggie followed her out and watched for a few seconds as Ida walked away. There was nowhere to hide on the broad residential street with the streetlights just coming on. But luckily, Ida was looking at her phone. It was the latest model, super sleek and thin with a huge screen, and a really expensive pink mother-of-pearl case that Ida had strictly forbidden anyone else to get. The bright blue light illuminated her face in the gloom.

After a few minutes, Ida stopped and looked back down the street. Maggie dived behind a big black car to avoid being seen. Peering round she watched as Ida crossed the road and stopped outside a huge gated property, a new-build that looked too big for the space, like it was pressing its face too close to the street. Ida put in a code and the metal gate slowly opened.

Maggie hurried along until she was level with the house. Behind the gate she saw a sweeping drive where a black sports car and another huge family car were parked. She watched Ida saunter up the curving flight of stone steps and let herself in. Through one window she could see a big plasma screen showing a frenetic cartoon and as Ida disappeared she glimpsed a creamy hallway full of light. Then slowly, slowly the gate eased back into place and the scene disappeared. All she could see then were the four upper windows, their blinds drawn, dark and lifeless. Maggie turned and walked slowly back to Milton Lodge.

She felt a surge of anger as she let herself into Esme's freezing flat. Why did some people have everything? It made her want to be sick. As usual the flat was in darkness when she got in. Maggie sat down on the sofa without bothering to turn on the lights. As her eyes got used to the near-darkness, she saw a white shape on the table. It was a note from Esme. Wearily she went over and squinted at it in the dark: 'Be back late. Dinner's in the fridge'.

4

THE QUEEN OF WEST MINCHEN

It was Saturday afternoon and Maggie lay back on the sofa feeling bored. Despite how much she longed for them at school, the weekends often stretched out emptily in front of her.

Esme appeared in the doorway. 'Any plans for this afternoon?'

She shook her head.

'Not seeing any friends?'

'Everyone's busy,' she lied.

'Perhaps you'd like to meet a friend of mine then? She's a very interesting person. Some say she's a witch.'

Maggie sat up, interested despite herself. 'A witch?'

Esme laughed. 'Well, she's very eccentric anyway. She never leaves her flat. But she knows all about herbs and healing. People go to her instead of the doctor; they call her the Queen of West Minchen.'

Maggie shrugged. Somehow she could never be gracious

when Aunt Esme tried to be nice to her. She didn't really know why. But Esme was not to be put off.

'Come on. You'll enjoy it. It's gloomy round here today.'

Dorothea Dot, known simply as Dot, lived on the other side of West Minchen across the High Street. Maggie trailed after Aunt Esme's quick steps past streets of terraced houses until they came to a house on a corner with a tiled turret pointing up into the grey sky. As they approached, a balding man in a smart blazer scuttled out clutching a small paper bag.

'One of her patients,' Esme whispered.

Dot lived on the ground floor and it took a long time for her to answer the bell. When she finally opened up, Maggie saw a tiny bird-like woman with cropped white hair and huge glasses, with the sunglasses attachment clipped on, that filled up half her face. She wore a headscarf and was in a wheelchair piled up with cushions to give her more height.

She peered into the street as if looking for someone before turning to them. 'And who is this?' she asked Esme.

'My niece, Maggie Blue. I told you about her, remember?'

Esme spoke to the old woman in a slow loud voice, as if she was slightly batty. But when Dot flicked up her sunglasses, Maggie only saw sharp intelligence in the intense black eyes.

She smiled at Maggie. 'Hello, my dear. I'm very old,' she said, by way of introduction.

'Hello, I'm twelve,' Maggie replied.

This seemed to tickle Dot enormously and she laughed as she wheeled back into her flat. There was a dark hallway with some doors on the left leading off it, but Dot led them into a huge room on the right that even on this grey day was suffused with light.

On one side was a large desk covered with serious-looking leather-bound books. Shelves rose up around it packed with more old books and glass jars containing various powders and dried leaves. There was a comfort-able-looking armchair by an electric fire and a table, also covered in books and notebooks. Most bizarrely, however, an enormous snooker table filled the other half of the room. Maggie looked at it with some astonishment.

'I could have been a top pro,' Dot said, following her gaze. 'If they'd let me play against the men . . . Even now, I'd wipe the floor with them. Mark my words. Hence why the Snooker Association never reply to my letters, I dare say.'

Esme rolled her eyes, but Maggie was so fascinated by the idea of this tiny old lady playing snooker that she forgot her awkwardness. 'Can we see you play?'

Dot grinned. 'Absolutely.'

She wheeled herself over to the table, picked up a short custom-made cue and rubbed some chalk on its tip, then pressed a button on her wheelchair. With a loud whining noise, the arms of her wheelchair flipped down. A further button raised Dot up a few more inches. The balls were already set up and she proceeded to break.

Maggie had watched snooker a few times with her dad on boring Sunday afternoons when it was raining and there was literally nothing else to do. But there was something mesmerising about watching this tiny old lady play such a perfect game, even with the laborious manoeuvring between each shot – the old peppermint green carpet surrounding the table was threadbare.

When she potted the final ball it was impossible not to break out into spontaneous applause at the performance. Dot bowed very solemnly from her chair, clearly delighted by the appreciation. She re-elevated her armrests.

'And now for tea.'

She returned a few minute later with a huge chocolate cake, three cups, a pot of tea and a jug of milk all on a huge tray balanced precariously on her tiny legs tucked under the tartan blanket.

Soon they were sitting round the electric fire gorging themselves. Or at least Maggie was. When she reached for her third slice of chocolate cake, Aunt Esme shot her a look, but Dot was delighted. And when Maggie looked up between mouthfuls she was a little disconcerted to note that Dot was staring at her with an intense curiosity from behind her large spectacles, but then the cake was so good, she just ploughed on.

Once her eating performance had been fully taken in, the ladies settled into conversation about various healings and herbal remedies Dot administered to the faithful of West Minchen, and classical music – their shared passion. Maggie barely listened; she was used to drifting off while adults talked.

Eventually, after what seemed like hours, Esme stood up and began to put the tea things back onto the large tray Dot had so precariously entered with.

'I'll wash up.'

'Oh, would you?'

Esme disappeared into the kitchen and the appropriate sounds of running water and clinking dishes soon followed.

Dot looked intently at Maggie. 'What do you think of West Minchen?'

She was so unbelievably old and her shock of white hair made her look both impish and ghostly. But it was less risky confiding in old people: they didn't care if you said something odd, because they were normally slightly odd too.

So Maggie decided to risk saying something truthful. 'I think there's something weird about it.'

Dot nodded, 'What kind of something?'

'I'm not sure. But behind all the nicely-paved drives and the perfect gardens and the boring streets, something's not quite right.'

'I see.'

'You don't think that's a strange thing to say?' said Maggie.

'I'm sure you're right.'

Maggie was so unused to people taking her seriously she found herself saying, 'I often get a strong feeling about people or places. Like I can read them. I don't know how. It just happens sometimes.'

Dot seemed entirely unfazed by this too. She simply nodded. 'You're good at understanding how people are feeling. Most people aren't. And perhaps you see strange things because you don't or can't close your mind. So you see more of the world. Not all of it, mind you.' And she winked at her.

Now it was Maggie's turn to look at her with intense curiosity.

'And there is something strange about this place, Maggie,' Dot went on, still eyeballing her as if she was trying to see inside her brain. 'But no one talks about it.' She drew her wheelchair nearer to Maggie. 'People disappear from here. They vanish without a trace.'

Beyond them in the kitchen, Maggie could hear Aunt Esme humming a meandering tune as the dishes clanked in the sink. Maggie felt uneasy.

'What do you mean, they disappear?'

'Just what I say.' And her black eyes shone with excitement.

Esme suddenly appeared beside them. 'I think we should get going, Maggie. I have to get to Elizabeth's for a poetry reading.' It was already getting dark outside and through the window Maggie could see the ghostly outline of the moon pale against the sky.

Dot was smiling at Maggie, but her eyes were strangely hard and serious, and so was her voice. 'You'll come back and see me, won't you?'

5

THE CAT

That night, Maggie was alone in the flat watching videos on her laptop when she heard a noise. Someone nearby was humming a meandering jazz tune: '. . . *de da dah dah, doo be bop baaaa . . .*'

Maggie flicked on the light and saw the substantial silhouette of the one-eyed cat pressed up against the rain-flecked window. As soon as he saw her, the humming stopped. He raised an indignant paw to the glass and scratched there pathetically.

Maggie opened the back door and he plopped down from the ledge and stalked in. He peered around the gloomy room whilst his tail swished with irritation. Maggie suddenly felt afraid that he'd leave. The evening seemed more bearable with his company, so she closed the door, sat down on the sofa and patted it.

'Come on, puss. Come up.' The more she patted, the more the old cat looked at her with a certain scorn. She tried again, 'Come on, puss-puss. Come up here where it's warm.'

He relented and began to purr, softly at first but then growing into a deep satisfied rumble, though his tail still twitched and he still didn't move. Maggie kept patting the sofa and saying 'come up here, puss-puss' like a mad woman until the cat opened his mouth and said in a clear low voice, 'My name is not *puss-puss*. It's Hoagy.'

Maggie froze. Several seconds ticked by then she let out a gasp and leapt up onto the sofa. Everything was silent except for the cat's purr and the *thump-thump* of her own heart that seemed like it might explode out of her chest.

The cat, on the other hand, was completely calm. After assessing her for a little while, looming above him like a pale statue, he started to lick his front paw, occasionally mixing it up with an ear sweep. After some minutes of this obsessive routine he paused and looked at her once again. Maggie still hadn't moved and continued to stare at him like she'd seen a ghost.

'I didn't think you'd be one of those,' he purred, and he began the same cleaning routine but on the other front paw. When the cat spoke, there was the rumble of his purr behind it, softer than usual, but there, so that his low warm voice vibrated in the otherwise silent room.

Hearing the cat speak again snapped Maggie out of her daze and she took the opportunity to leap right over the back of the sofa. Then she peered over it at the cat. Her voice was shaky when she finally managed to speak. 'Can you really talk? Or is it in my head?'

Hoagy shook his rotund head with disappointment. 'I'm not going to dignify *that* with an answer.'

Maggie tried to think. This was not . . . this could not be real. OK, sometimes she imagined things so vividly they felt real to her: like one time when she thought she could see little white demons riding the crests of waves in the sea back home or when she had sworn to her parents that she saw an old man flying home carrying his shopping bags every Tuesday evening. And yes, it was true that sometimes she could feel what other people were feeling. But this was something else.

Her mum always told her, went on and on at her, to be normal . . . D*on't stand out* . . . *don't be odd* . . . *don't say strange things* . . . But she couldn't un-hear this cat, could she? Maybe Dot had spiked that chocolate cake and she was hallucinating?

'Oh for goodness sake,' the cat muttered. He prowled to the back door, elegantly balanced on his hind paws to push down the door handle and then stalked out into the night.

As soon as he was gone, Maggie plopped heavily down onto the floor and looked up at the owl in its glass case for some sort of guidance. 'Was that real?'

But the old stuffed bird had nothing to say on the matter.

*

It was a few days before she saw him again. She'd bunked off double games and walked home through the woods, the trees thick against the colourless sky. When she got back to the flat, although there was already a tiny hint of the darkness to come, the night was some way off and a winter sun was still casting its dull white light.

Esme was out and Maggie opened the back door and went into the garden. She walked over to the great oak at the back that stood near a part of the old wall that hadn't yet fallen down. She ran her hand over its ancient rough bark and said, 'Hello.' And in her head, she imagined that the tree said 'Hello' back.

She glanced round to make sure no one else was in the garden or watching from a window then she slipped her arms around the old trunk and laid her head against the bark. Being close to a tree always made her feel better.

She used to do this at home and her dad, Lion (short for Lionel), would laugh at her and call her a tree-hugger. She didn't understand why hugging a tree was considered silly. Trees knew more than people did, you could feel it, all that time and energy collected up in them for hundreds of years. It made you feel good to touch them. Suddenly you faded away, or not so much faded, more all this other stuff started to run through you and made you forget about all the things you were worried about.

OK, so you were rubbish at school and you had no friends, but the earth was moving round at a thousand miles an hour in a big black universe that no one could understand, no matter what they said, and there were stars glittering in the sky. Even when it was the daytime they were there, you just couldn't see them. And this oak had seen all this thousands of times, was maybe connected to the stars, Maggie thought, though she couldn't have explained how. She smiled as her skin rubbed against the gnarl of the tree's bark.

'Quite an embrace.'

She spun round. On the broken-down wall Hoagy was observing her, his one eye gleaming with amusement. Maggie frowned. Somehow she didn't feel so afraid hearing the old cat talk now. Maybe it was being outside in the garden and in daylight, or maybe her brain had had time to get used to it? She let go of the tree.

'Would you like one too?'

She moved with surprising speed over to the old cat, and before he could protect himself, she picked him up off the wall and gave him a big squeeze. Instantly his sturdy round body became a mass of furry ripples, squirms and claws, and he fell heavily out of her arms onto the mossy paving stones.

He ruffled himself, outraged. 'Don't grab me like that.'

'It was a joke. Hug a tree . . . hug a cat . . .'

'I don't see a connection.'

'No, I suppose not.'

He shook himself again and observed drily, 'So you've come round to the fact I can talk then?'

Maggie shrugged. 'Do I have a choice?'

That cat's tail flicked with irritation but he said nothing.

'Can Esme hear you?'

'She can hear me purr and meow, and other cat things. But not like you can.'

'How come I can hear you then?'

'Search me.'

'Why doesn't Esme like you?'

Hoagy's tail flicked violently now. 'Because she's an idiot.' He wrinkled his nose as if smelling something unpleasant. 'Though, I must say, for a miserable old bag, she has a stupendous social life.'

Maggie giggled. 'It's true. She's got more friends than me.'

'That's not hard,' said the cat and began to clean himself yet again. Clearly he already knew a little about her.

Maggie sat on the crumbling wall and Hoagy, after another violent shake, re-ascended to his perch. They sat in silence for a little while looking back at the house through the unkempt garden.

'Do you ever get lonely, Hoagy?'

'Lonely? Pah! That's human stuff.'

'So you never want friends or anything?'

'Cats want things all the time – I mean maybe not friends exactly – but the key is that we don't have any self-pity. We want, we need, but we don't regret or worry.'

The concrete garages behind the flats next door were

covered in a dense tangle of ivy and other weeds, and from out of the thick covering a little russet fox poked his head. But when he saw Hoagy he changed his mind and disappeared again, or maybe it was because of Maggie. The trees and buildings were starting to fade against the pale sky and a faint moon was just becoming visible above the garages.

'Thanks for having me in the bath the other night. I may call on you again. It was surprisingly cosy.'

'Oh, no problem.'

They sat together, letting the dark and cold grow around them. Then after a while Maggie began to feel a freezing wind at her back, as if someone had turned on a powerful fan just behind her. She turned around and looked into the neighbour's garden. She felt very relaxed and calm just then, and her mind felt very clear.

That was when she saw them for the first time: six balls of light hanging in the air. They were like swirly yellow-white marbles, except they were the size of footballs. And they glowed like lanterns, hovering low over the perfectly ordered lawn that led to her neighbour's perfectly ordered house beyond. Maggie frowned because it seemed much darker over there, like it was somehow night already. Without thinking, she slipped over the wall and moved slowly towards the lights.

As she approached, she had the strangest feeling that they could see her, or at least sense her. Now that she

40

was closer she saw that their surface was like skin, lots of tiny cells that moved and fluctuated as if these strange balls of light had a pulse – as if they were alive. There was no obvious place where their light was emanating from – no bulb or flame or anything. And they just hung there in the air with no strings or supports. What were they?

Maggie was so curious she forgot to be afraid. She wanted to reach out and touch one, but when she tried something stopped her. Her outstretched hand hit some sort of invisible barrier. It wasn't a block or a wall exactly. It was more like a pulsing feeling that pushed her away when she tried to get close. Suddenly the balls of light clustered together, as if in conference. Then they rose up rapidly and zoomed away into the darkness.

Maggie tried to follow them but she tripped on something. She fell down onto the damp grass beside a child's red plastic car. Suddenly the chill had gone and the sky had got lighter too. She heard the cat purring loudly with amusement from his perch on the wall.

After a moment she realised that a family, nicely ensconced in the warm glow of their open-plan kitchen-diner, was staring at her from around their kitchen table: a mum, a dad, a girl of about ten and a little boy of maybe seven or eight who was scowling furiously at her.

The dad was pushing back his chair to open the door and come out and see what was going on. So Maggie jumped to her feet, made a small embarrassed wave, and scrambled back over the crumbling wall where the cat had been watching her, a rotund silhouette against the dark-blue sky.

As she hit the ground on the familiar overgrown side, a voice was calling out into the garden, 'Maggie?'

Hoagy's ears pricked up. He walked along the top of the wall, leapt onto the fence, looked back at her for a moment, winked and then disappeared over the other side with a heavy thump.

She could see Aunt Esme at the back door, illuminated with light from inside the flat, her beehive making her look like a chess-piece queen. She ran back to the house through the muddy dusk.

'Maggie?!' Then Esme saw her, waved cheerfully. 'Come in, dearie. I've made some tea.'

Maggie trudged inside. She thought, *I knew this place was weird.*

Later, she lay in a boiling deep bath thinking about the things that had happened. First of all, the one-eyed cat could talk. It wasn't just food poisoning. He really could. And now there were these strange glowing marbles in the back garden, made of skin and hanging in the sky. But some other sky, Maggie thought. Not the one that hung over West Minchen. Somehow they had been somewhere else. But how was that even possible?

She sighed and sank under the lovely warm water for

42

a moment, then burst out gasping and smoothed her hair back from her face. She was starting to understand why her mum was so obsessed with being normal. What if she turned out like Cynthia? What if she couldn't cope with the world at all? She shook her head to try and get rid of the bad thoughts, but they wouldn't go away.

She got out of the bath, her pale skin all red from the heat, and wrapped one of Esme's scratchy salmon-pink towels around her. Then she smeared away the thick condensation until her face appeared in the mirror. She hadn't bothered to tie her hair up and it hung in dark damp ropes around her face. She thought she looked stupid and boring; plain . . . uninteresting . . . not like Ida.

Ida always looked amazing and wore cool clothes and had her nails painted. She put loads of photos of herself online and she'd add a funny comment or hashtag too to make it seem like she didn't take herself too seriously. And she'd be in great places like in a nice restaurant with her family, or horse riding, or with her cousins, or on holiday beside a turquoise pool with big sunglasses on and a comment: 'My new sunglasses got me like . . .' and then the heart-eyes emoji.

It was pretty lame how much time Maggie had spent looking at these photos since she'd discovered Ida's online account. Now she knew what her parents looked like too. Her mother had the same curly hair. She always looked really fashionable and polished and smiled broadly in any photo she was in. Her dad looked more like a boring business sort. There was tightness etched round his mouth even when he was smiling. And he wore a big gold watch on his pale hairy wrist.

Almost everyone in her class had a page too; she found them all. Carl, the lonely boy, didn't, and a few other outcasts, but everyone else. She couldn't help but smile at herself in the mirror. Maybe it was just as well she didn't have a phone. It gave her an excuse not to post photos. I mean, what would she put online?

Her wrapped up in a duvet in the pink bathtub freezing to death, #pleaseturntheheatingon #lolnotlol; her rummaging through the latest fashions at Help the Aged on the high street, 'Second-hand shopping got me like . . .' then the big stack of dollar bills emoji; or maybe her sitting in the dark with a talking cat, #imnotweird #dinnersinthefridge.

Suddenly she burst out laughing.

6

HOAGY KEEPS AN EYE

It was a few days later that Hoagy leapt over the side gate and trotted along the side of the house, a light rain tapping pleasantly on his fur. Beyond him, the overgrown garden stretched away towards the broken-down wall, and he smelt a mouse somewhere nearby – that fetid, unclean smell that he so loved. His noise twitched. It was tempting. But no, he must stay on track. He was here to keep his eye on the girl.

The old lady was suspicious of anyone new and he had watched many people for her before. But this girl was a little different. She could hear him talk, for a start; so far he'd only met one or two humans that could do that. And she could see into the other world. When he'd told Dot about that, Maggie Blue Brown had suddenly become of great interest to her.

He crept along the back wall and peered in at the window, but there was no sign of life. So he returned over the gate and jumped up onto the crumbling window ledge at the front. There was a gap in the opaque white curtains and he could see someone moving about inside. He smiled and his one eye disappeared into a self-satisfied slit.

Esme's room was full of curious items: a crystal collection, a huge block of rose quartz, amethyst, onyx and tiger stone all arranged on the mantelpiece; there were star charts jumbled up with postcards of Beethoven, string quartet parts and unopened mail. On the low bed was a crushed-velvet throw in a kind of ochre colour with brightly embroidered cushions spread over it. Incense holders sat either side of the bed, and piled up everywhere were violin cases, books, music stands and interior design magazines.

Amidst it all, the girl was searching for something. She looked on a little plate on the dressing table, under the bed and then she opened the wardrobe and hurriedly checked the pockets of all Esme's coats and dresses. Finally, with a furtive look around, as if sensing she was being watched, she slid open the bedside table drawer. Hoagy saw her eyes widen. Her hand dove in and returned holding a five-pound note. Then she slammed the drawer shut and ran out of the room.

He made his way round the back again and snuck a look in at the window. The girl was checking down the back of the sofa now and had found a few more coins. Then she sat on the floor and counted up her ill-gotten gains. When

Hoagy knocked on the glass, Maggie Blue jumped a mile. But seeing it was only him, she relaxed and opened the door.

'What are you going to do with the loot?' he asked at once.

Maggie started. 'What are you talking about?'

'I watched you rifling through Esme's things. There's a gap in the curtains.'

Her cheeks flushed with shame. 'My parents forgot about pocket money . . . So I . . .'

Hoagy waved a paw. 'I don't care. Take as much as you want from the old bag.' And he jumped up and stretched out on the sofa.

But the whole thing seemed to inexplicably depress her. She sighed heavily and sat down beside him. 'I want to go to the cinema, that's all.'

The cat's tail twitched. 'You don't have to pay for that.'

Maggie looked confused. '*You* go to the cinema?'

Hoagy's hackles were up immediately. 'Is there a problem?'

'No, I just . . .'

'Are felines not allowed to enjoy films?'

'Sorry. I didn't know cats. . .'

'Clearly.' His tail flicked. 'It's Sunday so there's an old movie on. Today is *North by Northwest*, an undisputed classic. Have you seen it?'

Maggie shook her head.

'Well, then.'

*

They walked down the road, keeping a metre apart at all times, then snuck in the fire door of the old cinema down the road, which was often left ajar. It was boiling in there as usual, and the place was half-full of old people muttering to themselves or one other, it was hard to tell which.

Hoagy led Maggie to the far side near the front, and they sat beside each other on the worn velvet seats just in time for the trailers. Really these were the humans' best inventions: central heating and the cinema. The two combined was bliss, as far as Hoagy was concerned. Though it was so hot the old dears often dropped off and loud snoring interfered with the cat's enjoyment.

Sadly the girl was not very refined. Her review that day: 'I don't get it? This really old rich guy gets mistaken for someone else. He falls for a woman on a train who is so obviously lying to him it's stupid, and then he goes to the middle of nowhere and gets attacked by a plane. It was weird.'

Hoagy could only roll his eye. She might be able to see other worlds, but she was hardly a culture vulture. But after that day, they often snuck into the cinema together. And although the old cat wouldn't have cared to admit it, he really didn't find the girl's company so bad.

7

BRUISED

Things were getting better. OK, her only friend might be an overweight talking cat, but Maggie reckoned Hoagy was far more entertaining than most people she'd met. And after a few weeks, school was less scary and more a case of extreme but manageable boredom. But then one Monday morning, everything went wrong again.

Maggie couldn't find her red notebook, the one she always doodled in when she was pretending to take notes in class. And she didn't want anyone looking inside it.

During lunch break she went down to her locker to look for it. No one was about, so she sat on the floor, took everything out and spread it all around herself. But the notebook was still nowhere to be found.

She was just starting to think it must be back at Esme's flat after all when she heard a familiar voice, 'Hey, Bruise.' Out of the gloom at the back of the locker hall, Ida appeared and came over. She crouched down close beside her and smiled. Her voice was unusually soft. 'I've been meaning to ask you. What do you think of your nickname?'

Maggie couldn't think what to say. Instead she went red and looked down at the floor.

But Ida's voice was oddly friendly. 'No, seriously, what do you think of it? Do you like it?'

'Whatever. I really don't care,' Maggie managed to mutter under her breath.

'A nickname's a sign of affection. You shouldn't take it badly.'

'I don't.' Maggie started to hurriedly throw everything back into her locker so that it was even more of a shambles than when she'd started.

Ida stood and watched her for a few moments, as if fascinated by the whole chaotic operation. Then she said, 'Oh, by the way, is this what you're looking for?'

Maggie looked up and saw that Ida was holding her red notebook. She tried to grab it but Ida whipped it away.

'I hope you don't mind, but I took a look inside.'

Maggie could tell her face had gone pillar-box red now and her heart was thudding. She stared resolutely at the floor.

'You made a note of my birthday on the first page, which is cute.'

'It's my birthday,' Maggie said dully.

'Your birthday is the twenty-first of June?' Ida actually sounded interested for a moment.

'Yeah.'

Maggie heard the sound of pages being turned.

'Then I found these drawings.'

Maggie dared a tiny glance over. Ida was holding up a page on which Maggie had attempted to draw Ida's profile three times, before finally getting the angles right.

'And that's just one page,' said Ida, still smiling in her new weird friendly way that was starting to freak Maggie out. 'I especially like this one.' Ida held up the notebook.

It was one of Ida bent over her phone, her hair falling over one side of her face. Maggie looked down again. Why couldn't she have drawn some other people? She heard the sound of more pages being turned. Oh God, now Ida was holding up the page where she'd counted the letters of their names and found out their compatibility. It was low: twenty-three per cent.

'By the way, my middle name's Margot – if that improves our percentage?'

Maggie had never been so completely humiliated in her life. She started to feel anger pulsing through her, anger she had no idea what to do with. But when she looked at Ida, her face was clear of its usual sneer. The red faded a little – what was going on?

'There's something different about you,' Ida continued. 'You're not like everyone else. And, you know, that's cool.'

Maggie was suddenly hopeful. She started to feel a weight lifting, a lightening in her body.

'How are you finding Fortlake?'

'It's OK.'

'So why did your parents move here?'

'They didn't.'

Ida frowned. 'How come?'

Maggie took a breath in, wondering what to say. She couldn't think of a good lie so, unusually, she went for the truth. 'I live with my aunt. Um, my dad's not around and my mum's not very well.'

'Is she sick?'

'Kind of. She's depressed.'

Maggie thought she saw the flicker of a smirk run over Ida's face.

'Oh, sorry.' But then she twisted a piece of dark curly hair round her finger. 'So, I was thinking, Bruise,' and here she smiled, not her teacher's pet smile, her real smile, or so Maggie thought. 'Maybe we should be friends. What do you reckon?'

Maggie's mouth opened slightly – she couldn't believe it. Ida felt their strange connection too. She wasn't just making it up.

But then Maggie heard a stifled giggle and Ida shot an irritated look in its direction. But the owner of the laugh couldn't contain themselves any longer. And soon it was joined by another more high-pitched giggle. Finally Ida's face cracked and she too burst into hysterics.

Helena and Daisy jumped out from behind some lockers at the end of Maggie's row.

'Oh my god! Your actual face!' Helena burbled.

'You fell for it!' Daisy squealed.

Ida was the first to recover and all the humour left her face quite suddenly. 'You actually think I'd be friends with a total weirdo like you? You're more of a stalker. Stop drawing me all the time. It's creepy as hell.' And she walked off.

'What, are you in love with her or something?' Helena sniggered, as she and Daisy obediently followed their lord and master and disappeared down the corridor.

Maggie stayed on the floor for a while, gathering her thoughts and trying to let the shame and upset burn off her. And beneath it was the red anger churning dangerously inside her, but she pushed that away too – just let it go. She breathed in and out slowly.

Suddenly she became aware of someone watching her. She looked up and saw Miss Cane standing by the door that led back into the main corridor, a smile on her smooth alabaster face.

'Hi, Maggie. Is everything OK?'

How did she even know her name?

'Fine,' said Maggie.

But Miss Cane persisted. 'I'm not sure that's true, is it?'

Maggie normally hated people like this, people who pretended to be kind but were really just nosy and patronising. But there was something about Miss Cane's smile. It was almost irresistible.

Maggie got up, threw the rest of her stuff angrily into her locker and then slammed its door shut. She glanced at the huge clock on the wall behind Miss Cane.

'Don't worry about the time. I'll give you a note if you're late for class,' Miss Cane continued, her voice all sinewy and sweet. She moved closer. 'What's wrong? Tell me.'

Against her will Maggie felt the tears coming. She shifted from foot to foot and pressed her nails into the palms of her hands as hard as she could to stop them. 'Nothing much.'

'I just want to help you, Maggie.'

'Right.'

'Is everything OK at home?'

Miss Cane smiled at her again, an amazing glowing smile, and it was like a key turning.

Maggie heard herself say, 'My mum's not very well. She's in hospital; she's so depressed she never gets out of bed. And I don't know if she's going to get better.' She realised it was a relief to say it all out loud.

The school counsellor was close to her now, and her voice was very soft. 'It sounds like your mum is really unwell. You must be having a tough time right now. But that's OK. Everyone has tough times.'

Maggie looked down at the floor. She found herself saying, 'I don't want to be like her.' And she instantly felt ashamed and sorry.

Just then the bell rang its hysterical call to class. They

both jumped and their eyes locked for a moment and Maggie remembered how cold Miss Cane's green eyes were.

Maggie grabbed her bag. 'I'd better go.' And she ran out.

On the upper corridors, the smell of the science labs filled her nostrils as Maggie marched angrily along – why had she said so much? She never did that. It was something about that woman's smile. She'd just made that mistake with Ida, like, ten seconds earlier. It never paid to talk; it was always, always a mistake.

She came to a halt outside the chemistry lab's door, deeply reluctant to go inside. Through the graph-paper window she could see her class sitting there at the long wooden desks, and the back of Mr Philips' balding head.

Calm down, Maggie, she said to herself. *Just calm down.* Ida was an idiot. But maybe Miss Cane was all right? Maggie took a deep breath and pushed open the door to the lab.

As soon as she walked in, Ida, Helena and Daisy burst out laughing. The rest of the class looked mildly bemused and some even started laughing too, as if worried they'd missed a joke.

'Sorry I'm late,' Maggie mumbled.

Maybe he felt sorry for her, because the usually strict Mr Philips just nodded, prepared to let her tardiness slide for once.

Red-faced, Maggie wandered into the room and took up her usual spot beside William Snowden. It wasn't that they were friends, more he didn't seem to mind her, or expect anything of her. She always felt comfort when he moved his exercise book along a bit, just to make her feel that he was making room for her, and gave her a brief smile; then they could sit together in silence during class with no need for any chat.

A few rows ahead, Ida turned round, grinning, and gave her a little sarcastic wave. Maggie felt William Snowden glance at her to see if she'd respond, but she kept looking straight ahead.

After about fifteen minutes, another teacher knocked on the door and whispered something to Mr Philips. He told the class to get on quietly with their work and went out.

After a while Maggie noticed people whispering and looking at her. Something was being passed round. Her heart starting beating with dread. Finally it came to William Snowden beside her. Maggie snatched her notebook out of his hands. On it a note read: 'Maggie Brown loves Ida Beechwood.' And the page was open on where she'd tried to work out their compatibility using their names.

Maggie looked up and locked eyes with Ida.

Then Ida shouted so everyone could hear, 'What's your problem, Bruise?'

A few people giggled.

Maggie looked hard at Ida, the girl with the perfect life, and suddenly she didn't feel shy. Instead she got that brilliant feeling where she really didn't care any more. She stood up and walked over to her. 'No. What's *your* problem?' Her voice was loud and aggressive and she heard the class gasp around her.

Ida was astonished, but she quickly recovered. She stood up and sneered at Maggie. 'I hate people who are weird. It doesn't make you special, it just makes you weird.'

In a flash of instinct Maggie moved towards her and pushed her. It wasn't very hard, just a little shove to get her to back off. But with a shrill cry, Ida fell dramatically to the floor.

Maggie watched in disbelief as Ida rolled around on the ground, and Helena and Daisy rushed over to her. Then to Maggie's astonishment, Ida started to cry. How could anyone cry over something like that? She couldn't believe it. It was so embarrassing.

Then she noticed that Ida was looking over at the classroom door as tears streamed down her face. 'She pushed me,' she was saying, 'she pushed me!'

Mr Philips surveyed the scene with a disinterested expression. He rolled his eyes, wrote something on a piece of paper, folded it up and said, 'Maggie, go to Ms McCrab's office at once.'

Maggie could not believe it. She snatched it out of his

hand, went to her seat, grabbed her bag and walked out without looking back.

As she walked slowly along the deserted corridors and down to the staff area, she wondered what to do. Could she just make a run for it? What would they do if she ran to Esme's and refused to ever go back? Would they force her? Would they put her in care? That's what her mum had said would happen if she didn't go and live with Esme. Cynthia had no family and Lion's two other sisters lived abroad and had about eight children between them as it was. No one else would take her.

There was a row of chairs outside Le Crab's office and Maggie sat down in one glumly: she hadn't had Ida down for being a snitch.

'Did you hear about Alan Yates?'

The staffroom door in front of her had opened and a teacher was standing in the doorway, on her way out.

'I know. Poor man.'

'Apparently he's too upset to teach,' the woman in the doorway continued. 'I mean they only went out for a couple of weeks.'

Someone chuckled. 'It was pretty obvious that Miss Cane was way out of his league.'

'But Alan's normally so dedicated to the job.'

'Well, he doesn't seem to care any more.'

Another voice spoke up, 'There's something in the air.

This woman I know who's a therapist says she's never been so busy.'

'At least someone's happy.'

There was an eddy of laughter then the woman in the door spoke again, 'Urgh, I've got 10C next. That's enough to make anyone depressed.'

She turned and suddenly noticed Maggie sitting there. Her face froze up and she gave Maggie an angry look as she walked quickly away.

The door swung shut behind her and the voices faded away. It was true, Maggie thought, Mr Yates the geography teacher hadn't been in school for a while. They'd been told he had a virus.

'Miss Brown!' Le Crab loomed up beside her. 'In my office, *now*.'

Maggie hurried in and heard the door close ominously behind her. Then Le Crab walked round and sat at her desk. She was almost taller seated than Maggie was standing up, like a long black pole.

The room was so different it was as if Maggie had stepped into another world. While the rest of the school was bathed in standard-issue fluorescent tube lighting, here there was a thick green carpet and a glass desk lamp that shone bottle-green light onto a dark wooden desk. The wall shelves were filled with books, except for a few gaps where curiosities were displayed: there was a highly-polished white shell, the slightly pink opening turned to the ceiling as if calling for help; the skull of a creature with a small snout; a fossil of some centipede-like creature; a jar with something that looked like a jellyfish inside. Thick green curtains blocked out the light and there was a long green velvet couch that carried the imprint of a tall thin body, though Maggie could not imagine Le Crab napping.

'Why have you been sent to me?' Le Crab spoke in a low almost soft voice, very different to her tone in assembly, and it frightened Maggie far more.

'I don't really know.'

'Give me your detention note.' Maggie handed it to her. 'And don't stare at me.'

Maggie flicked her eyes away and looked at her hands that clutched desperately onto one other.

Le Crab looked up. 'Why did you push Ida Beechwood?'

'I hardly pushed her.'

'So why did she end up on the floor crying?'

Maggie smiled to herself. It was funny the way you were told to always tell the truth, but telling it always seemed to get you nowhere. The only truth she'd learnt today was that Ida was a snitch. 'I'm not sure.'

'You're not sure why pushing someone makes them fall over?'

'Yes, but I—'

Le Crab held up her spindly hand. 'I don't want to hear it.' She opened a drawer in her desk, pulled out a file and flipped it open. A frown formed over her pale stern face. She looked up.

'You're hardly excelling, are you, Miss Brown? Not only that, your record of attendance is appalling.' She let that hang in the air for a bit. 'I also note that you were temporarily suspended from your last school for breaking someone's collarbone, which I believe was an accident, but still. You appear to be accumulating a history of violence. Wouldn't you agree?'

Maggie thought it best not to say anything.

'I let you into the school, *after* term started, as a personal favour. I don't do many favours. Did you know that?'

Maggie looked at her with genuine surprise. Who could possibly have asked for a favour for her from this woman?

'Well, I'm not getting much back for being generous, am I?'

Again she let the silence sit for a while. But this time Maggie felt angry. She thought, *I didn't ask for anything from you.*

'Detention until the end of the week. You may call your guardian Ms Esme Durand now to explain why you will be home later than usual.' She picked up the phone receiver and handed it to Maggie.

Maggie took it, but then had to ask for the number. The headmistress glanced at her curiously but read it out to her from the file. Maggie knew that her aunt wouldn't be in and wouldn't care anyway, but she thought it best not to mention this.

After several rings there was a crackly pause and then Esme's funny old-fashioned answerphone message: 'Hello there. I fear that Esme Durand is unable to take your call just now. But please do leave a friendly message, if you so wish, after the high-pitched tone . . .' *Beeeeeeep.*

Maggie was suddenly nervous. Le Crab's eyes were upon her. 'Um, Esme? It's me . . . Maggie. I, um, I have to go to detention today so, it's like, I will probably be back at your flat a bit late. Sorry about that. Um . . .' She shot a glance at Le Crab who was glaring at her. 'Anyway, sorry. OK, bye.' She hung up with the feeling she'd failed a test.

Le Crab surveyed her as if convinced she'd left a fake message, but she suddenly seemed bored of the whole thing. Her poker-straight body slumped a little and she waved her hand at Maggie dismissively, 'Come back here at three-thirty. I'll find something for you to do.' Maggie went gratefully to the door. 'And don't be late.'

8

NOW YOU SEE HER

For detention, Le Crab instructed her to write an essay about why violence never achieves anything, and then tore it up in front of her. The usual pointless teacher stuff, Maggie thought. Why did they even bother?

Afterwards, she stomped defiantly over the water-logged playing field towards Everfall Woods. Night was falling, but she really didn't care. Teachers were stupid and boring; everyone knew that. But she'd thought Ida was the best and it turned out she was just a teacher's pet. Why had she ever wanted to be friends with someone so lame?

She plunged into the trees now and puffs of her breath rose up towards their spooky silhouettes high above her in the cold blue air. Apart from these woods, she hated everything about this stupid place. She didn't want to go back to Esme's miserable cold flat and be on her own, and she didn't want to see Fortlake School ever again. She wanted to go home, to her village and to her house whose windows overlooked the endless grey sea.

She stopped walking and the air in her lungs felt cold. The truth was she didn't have a home to go back to any more. Her dad Lion had gone off with a much younger woman from a nearby town, and her mum was in hospital in Norwich and wasn't getting any better. Everything had changed.

She sighed and let the chill seep in, her anger fading away. She had reached the copse and in front of her the trees looked blurry. She shook her head but they remained somehow out of focus. She felt a current of very cold air flow over her face and ruffle her hair. Where was it coming from?

It was then that she saw there was an opening, like a window hovering in mid-air, as if cut into the normal world. Its edges shimmered slightly with white light. Inside were the same dark trees, but somehow she knew it was another place.

'You can see it?' said a voice very close to her.

Maggie screamed and the window disappeared. She found Dan the Tree's huge form standing right beside her.

'You can see it,' he said again, and this time it wasn't a question. 'The dark world.'

Maggie had to crane her neck upwards to speak to him; he was like a giant oak. 'I don't know what you're talking about.'

He was holding a torch in his huge grimy hands and

stray light from its beam illuminated his sad watery brown eyes.

'She took me there,' he said.

'Who?'

'The wolf,' he said.

Maggie shivered. The kids at school were right – he was weird. Maybe he did kidnap people and deliver them to satanic cults. Maggie's heart started thumping.

'I've got to go.' She walked the first few steps but then she started running, tripping and scrambling over the tree roots.

'Wait!'

His voice pursued her through the trees but she didn't look back and her breath was ragged by the time she reached the safely lamp-lit streets.

Then she trudged slowly back to the flat. It was dark and empty. But when she heard Hoagy's familiar tap-tapping on the window she put her headphones on and pretended not to hear. She no longer wanted to be a person who could hear cats talk and see other worlds. She wished it would all go away.

She spent the rest of the week in detention. Then after that she had to attend every lesson because Le Crab was on her case about her attendance record. And although she didn't ignore Hoagy, she tried to avoid him. It was probably better that way.

After her dramatic fake fall, Ida also seemed strangely subdued. She didn't call Maggie the Bruise any more, and ignored her. For her part Maggie tried not to look at her or think about her, but somehow she always found her eyes drifting back to Ida from her place at the back of class. But she was determined not to be interested. She only hoped Ida would bully her again so she could push her properly the next time.

The weird thing was that she kept seeing Ida and Miss Cane together – chatting in the corridor, smiling at each other as they walked past, and once, she saw Ida going into Miss Cane's office. Though Maggie couldn't imagine what Miss Perfect would need to talk to the school counsellor about.

There was also a rumour flying round the school that Mr Yates didn't have the flu, but had been dumped by Miss Cane. And that he was so upset he'd disappeared and no one knew where he was. But otherwise the days dragged past. Maggie just kept her head down and waited for all the minutes in the day to tick by, her only comfort being that they definitely would.

Finally it was the Friday before half term. The last lesson was geography and Maggie decided to treat herself and bunk it off, hoping that Le Crab would take her eye off the register for once, or just forget about it over the break.

So after seventh period's particularly brutal dose of

nineteenth-century history from Mrs Niblet, Maggie drifted slowly down the corridor, falling behind the rest of her class, and mingling with other years rushing about in all directions. She trudged slowly up to the first floor, looking as if she quite fully intended to climb on to the second for a guaranteed forty-five minutes of geographic ennui, but at the last moment, she darted into the toilets by the stairs and made for the furthest cubicle.

Two older girls were in there doing their make-up in the mirror and generally wasting time. But they didn't even glance at her.

'I just can't face Mr Norton.'

'He's such an idiot. He can't even spell properly.'

They giggled evilly.

'Here, let me use some of that mascara.'

'Oh-kaay.'

'Why does it always go clumpy on me? It never does on you.'

'Because you don't know how to put it on right. Here.'

'Give it back.'

'No. You're rubbish at it.'

Someone else came in and Maggie recognised the flat nasal tones of Mrs Bridges, the squirrel-like deputy head who was surprisingly scary despite being five foot nothing and so thin it looked like she might blow over in a strong wind.

'Girls, don't you have class to get to?'

The seniors sighed and left, the door swinging shut behind them. Maggie lifted her feet up and held her breath.

'Anyone else hiding in here?'

The Squirrel patrolled the cubicles to the end, but didn't push open any of the doors. She trotted out and Maggie sighed with relief – that had been close. A few more minutes hiding here, and she'd slip away.

One of the toilet's high opaque windows was propped open despite the chill and Maggie climbed onto the old-fashioned radiator and peered out. The metal ridges were lovely and hot under her scuffed shoes.

From up here she could see the car park and the art building, and one of the caretakers trudging slowly across the yard. And, to her astonishment, she realised she could see Ida.

She was sitting on one of the benches by the netball cage staring straight ahead. She looked odd. Not obviously: her hair was perfect, as always, her school clothes and shoes and her pink phone, which just now hung vacantly from her hand, were all in place. It was her expression that was strange: she looked very far away.

Without trying, Maggie felt something click in her brain. Then she felt a weird energy pulsating between them, even at this odd angle – and then it started. Waves of feeling flowed up to Maggie, so strongly that she felt like she was going to burst into tears: Ida was full of pulsing self-hatred, and a melancholy that glowed like lights in a dark storm.

Abruptly Ida stood up and walked purposefully across the car park and towards the playing fields. The link between them was broken and the feelings faded away.

Maggie watched her walk away in a kind of shock. How could Ida Beechwood feel like she wasn't good enough? How could she hate herself? Wasn't it the same Ida Beechwood who aced every class, who had loads of friends, who was amazing at sport, who lived in a castle, had the best clothes and the best hair and the best dusky pink mother-of-pearl phone case? Who had everything that everyone else wanted? Maggie could not believe it. She felt she had to talk to her.

She opened the cubicle door and walked quickly past the long wall of mirrors without a glance. In the corridor, the eerie quiet of lesson time had descended upon the school like an enchantment. There was not a soul in sight.

Maggie slipped out and ran down the stairs to the side entrance. The route through the car park and to the playing fields was very visible from several classrooms. She'd have to hope no one was glancing out. She counted down from five. On zero she started running and didn't look back.

She made it to the playing field and in the distance saw Ida, a small figure now against the dark woods. But Maggie's breath was hurting her lungs and she had to slow down to a trot.

When she made it to the trees, their bare branches reaching up into the white wintery sky, Maggie took the designated path, the one she never took. But there was no sign of Ida, only an old lady in a purple woolly hat walking her two beautiful Dalmatians, who sniffed at Maggie but found nothing of interest and sauntered on.

She didn't see anyone else and when she reached the gates on the other side, there was still no Ida. Nor could she see her walking home along the street beyond. So she must still be somewhere in the woods.

Maggie leant against the railings and breathed in the sharp air. As she did she saw a movement much deeper amidst the trees, where she herself normally walked. A flash of green: the distinctive and hideous Fortlake blazer. She set off towards it, her footsteps muffled by the yellow and bronze leaves.

Soon she realised she was heading straight for the copse. Large plump crows bounced alongside her and greedily pecked at the earth, entirely unafraid and only flapping away when she was almost upon them.

High above her at the very top of a dead tree reaching up to the sky like a sombre totem, a single crow burst into squawks. Maggie observed the bird's dense black silhouette against the sky. It seemed like a warning, but of what?

She'd almost reached the copse when she caught sight of Ida again. She was standing near the old gnarled tree where Dan the Tree normally sat. Maggie wanted to call out to her but she hesitated, afraid of the harsh look Ida would throw her if she turned and saw her there; how she'd tell everyone that the Bruise had followed her like the weirdo stalker she was. So she stayed where she was, hiding behind a tree.

Then Maggie heard the rustle of leaves; another person was walking towards them. Of course! Ida was waiting for someone. She'd never come here on her own. And after a few moments, someone did appear. But never in her life could Maggie have predicted who it would be.

Miss Cane, the school guidance counsellor, moved over the leaves towards Ida. But she was dressed a little differently, in a long black coat and killer heels that mercilessly speared the damp muddy ground. Her white-blonde hair hung perfectly down her back. When Ida saw her, she smiled gratefully.

Maggie's brain raced. Was Ida getting counselling from Miss Cane out here? But why would they meet in the woods? Especially when Ida should have been in geography class. It was all too weird.

In the distance from across the field, Maggie heard the shouts and screams of kids leaving school. And Miss Cane heard them too: she turned her head sharply in their direction, more like a wild animal than a human. Then she leant close into Ida, whispered in her ear and took her hand. The two of them stepped over the low woven fence, until they were right in the middle of the copse. Maggie edged a little closer towards them through the trees.

Miss Cane still held Ida's hand and smiled at her, encouraging, kind. With her free hand, she reached out into mid-air, and it was as if she was holding onto something invisible, peeling it back. Then she yanked Ida's arm with such violence that Ida cried out in pain and surprise. As she did, Miss Cane disappeared and there was a wolf, a huge white wolf with a torn ear and terrifying green eyes that locked onto Maggie through the trees. Ida screamed in terror, the wolf grabbed her in its jaws, and they were gone.

Maggie rushed forwards through the trees, a wave of panic sweeping over her. She kept saying, 'I don't understand, I don't understand. . .' She blinked. Her eyes must be deceiving her. Maggie looked past the copse, at the silent trees all around her. But they had disappeared into thin air.

A few crows landed nearby and hopped about, their sleek bodies, their alert beady eyes seemed to know things. Her mum told her once that Dickens kept a pet crow because they were amazingly intelligent. Around her, the birds' dull sabre-like beaks methodically attacked the ground.

Maggie whispered to them, 'What happened? Can you tell me what happened? Did you see?'

One of them looked at her very intently when she spoke and hopped a few paces across, and she followed. It was almost hidden beneath the leaves, the gorgeous dusky pink case she had coveted ever since she'd seen it. Maggie knelt down and picked up Ida's phone. It was deliciously cool and heavy in her hand. She slipped it into her pocket and ran.

When Maggie got home, she felt nerves in the pit of her stomach. She sat on the sofa and tried to think. The weird man in the woods had mentioned a wolf. But could Miss Cane really be a wolf? She couldn't forget the way that Miss Cane had pulled Ida's arm, so hard, so violently, and how Ida had cried out in fear.

She looked at the phone then pressed the centre button so the screen asked her for the passcode. Maggie thought for a moment then on a whim she put in their shared birthday: 210607. To her astonishment the security screen was sucked into its own vortex and suddenly she was there, in Ida's world. The screensaver was a close-up of a large fluffy cat, a grey puffball with beautiful blue eyes – even her cat was ridiculously good looking. She clicked on 'Photos'.

There were hundreds of images: most of them of Ida herself. She clicked on one. It was a photo she recognised from Ida's online posts: a close-up of her in a yellow jumper, her head tilted slightly to one side, her eyes wide, looking up at the camera, pouting and her cheeks slightly sucked in.

Maggie scrolled quickly past anything that looked like a selfie until she found pictures from a family holiday somewhere very exotic: perfect blue sea and white sand, the pasty tight-jawed father and the boy playing in the sea, the mother on a beach towel, more selfies and dinners and bad over-exposed photos of the place they were staying in.

She looked in 'Notes'. Most of them were just boring reminders. But then she found something. All it said was: 'I wish I could be someone else'. A few days later Ida had written: 'I hate my dad. I hate Mr Philip Beechwood and his stupid briefcase and his stupid car. He's an idiot'. Maggie laughed.

Suddenly the phone started ringing. Maggie dropped it in horror and it landed with an onerous thump on Esme's dusty old carpet.

One thing she knew was that she couldn't pick up. She couldn't explain how she had the phone or why she'd taken it.

The phone stopped ringing, but a few minutes later it started again. Maggie curled up beside it feeling sick. She put it on silent and watched as the screen lit up again and again with the word, 'HOME'.

9

SATURDAY

The next morning she went out into the garden clutching the phone and sat on the broken-down wall. She stared into the neighbour's garden thinking she might see the strange orbs again. But there was nothing, just the dull perfect garden with its long neat rectangle of grass. After a while, the little boy appeared and stared at her so angrily she had to turn away.

Then she heard a low humming: *bee bop di doo be doo daaa.* She spun round and sure enough the old fat cat was swaggering towards her, his one eye squinting with pleasure in the unexpectedly warm sun. She jumped off the wall and ran towards him.

When he saw her, Hoagy held up a paw, possibly expecting another hug. 'Humph, humph. What's all this?'

'Ida disappeared in the woods.'

'Isn't that the one that got you detention and bullies you?'

'Yeah.'

'So? Problem solved,' he purred.

He began to move away, his tail arching and twisting behind him: *bee bop di doo bee doo bee du daa.*

Maggie went after him again. 'You don't understand, even if I hated her, I'd still have to tell someone that I saw her disappear.'

'You don't hate her?'

'No,' said Maggie, and to her annoyance she blushed.

Hoagy let out a long sigh and shook his old furry head. 'Humans.'

'Hoagy! Listen to me! Ida vanished into thin air. Miss Cane grabbed her arm and she screamed. She was terrified. And then there was this wolf, this huge white wolf . . .'

'A wolf?' The cat's eyes narrowed; he was suddenly a little more interested.

'Yes.'

'Hmmmm.' The cat's tail flicked from side to side. 'Well, she's probably been taken to another world.' His whiskers twitched. '*C'est la vie.*'

'What do you mean "another world"?'

'Did you think this is the only one? Aah, bless.'

'What are you talking about?'

'You've seen the one at the bottom of the garden, haven't you?'

'Those lights are from a different world?'

Hoagy was bored now. 'Obviously.'

'I don't . . . but that's crazy.' Maggie showed him the

phone. 'Look. I found this, in the woods. It's Ida's phone. She never goes anywhere without it.'

Hoagy squinted at the screen, preened and vibrated all over in an insane way Maggie had never witnessed. 'Who is that feline?'

'It's her cat, I guess.'

'You know where this cat lives?'

Maggie was suddenly resolved. 'Yes, and I'm going there now.'

'Marvellous. I feel like a stroll.'

'You're coming?'

'I've suddenly realised that I am very interested in your friend's disappearance.' And he started to purr very loudly.

Despite his ulterior motive, Maggie was grateful to walk to Ida's with Hoagy. Although because it was out of his usual territory he insisted on walking a little way behind so as not to attract any attention from, as he put it, 'suburban busybodies, angry felines and local witches.'

Maggie felt very nervous by the time they got to the imposing gates that protected Ida's house from the outside world. A box glowed with a blue light where you pressed a button to speak. Maybe she should just push the phone under the gate?

She was about to turn and run away, but then the gates started to open, and an oblong security camera watched her silently above the entry phone. Quick as a flash, Hoagy, who'd been waiting patiently at her feet, darted in and disappeared round the side of the house.

As the slick sweep of drive emerged, she saw a woman with dishevelled curly black hair in a thick white bathrobe coming down the front steps of the house towards her. From the photos she knew it was Ida's mum. She'd been crying.

'Are you a friend of Ida's?' And suddenly she was right beside her, her face riven with anxiety and lack of sleep. 'Do you know where she is?' She took Maggie's arm and gripped it hard.

'Cathy, let me deal with this.'

The dad, the one Ida thought was an idiot, had appeared. He was dressed in a smart jumper and trousers and didn't look like he'd been crying. He only seemed angry. He strode forward towards them and Maggie instinctively shrank away. There was something scary about him.

'Are you a friend of Ida's?'

'Not exactly.'

'What does that mean?'

She thrust the phone out at them and Ida's mum fell upon it, crying.

'I found her phone in the woods this morning.'

Her mum was holding the phone to her chest and saying, 'Oh my God, oh my God,' over and over again.

But Philip Beechwood was assessing Maggie coldly with

a look that wasn't entirely unlike his daughter's. 'How did you know it was hers if you're not friends with her?'

'Everyone knows it's hers. It's the nicest one in class.'

'You found it in the woods?'

Maggie nodded.

'What were you doing there?'

'I just went for a walk.'

He took the phone from his wife rather brusquely and looked at it, as if checking for damage, like he thought Maggie had stolen it. 'And you haven't seen Ida? You don't know where she might be?'

Maggie felt guilty playing dumb, but she said, 'Isn't she at home?'

'She didn't come home after school last night. We're supposed to be going to the Caribbean in two hours' time. None of her friends know anything about it. She wasn't planning a sleepover, as far as we know.' He stared hard at Maggie for a few long seconds. 'Tell me, does she have a boyfriend?' His voice was very harsh, metallic.

'I don't know. I don't think so.'

'You're not friends with her, you said?'

'No. She doesn't really like me.'

Philip looked her up and down as if quite approving of his daughter's taste in this matter. 'And you're in the same class?'

Maggie nodded.

He was about to say something else when the boy from

Ida's photos came onto the front porch. He paused for a moment, his sweatshirt and tracksuit bottoms very blue against the stern grey and white of their castle. Then he ran to his mum, and as she hugged him he burst into floods of tears.

Now his son was crying, Mr Beechwood seemed keen for her to go. 'If you hear anything from Ida, please let us know at once.'

He pressed a button and the gate slowly started to close on the scene of the sobbing mother and child. But just as it was about to click shut he remembered something. 'What's your name?'

But the gate closed, sealing Maggie off from their world, and she ran.

When Maggie got back to the flat, she heard Esme's voice on the phone. She sounded anxious and Maggie immediately thought of her mum. She found Esme standing by the phone like a statue.

'Is everything OK?'

Her aunt jumped at the sound of Maggie's voice. Her face was pale. 'That was the school. A girl from your class has gone missing. They want every pupil who is still in the area to attend an emergency meeting this afternoon.'

The hall was shrouded in a solemn hush. Parents stood around in groups talking in low whispers, gripping their children's hands as if to keep them safer. Maggie caught sight of Daisy and Helena standing with their parents and she could tell they'd both been crying.

Moments later Miss McCrab swept into the hall wearing a long black dress with a strange high ruffle around the neck. Maggie had never seen her look so imposing and her face was like white stone. She ascended to the stage and stood looking at them for a few moments. Silence fell.

'Most of you will know why I have called this emergency assembly and I would ask you all to listen extremely carefully to what I have to say.'

Le Crab glanced to her right and, following her gaze, Maggie saw Ida's parents sitting close to the side of the stage, holding hands. Even Philip Beechwood's eyes were rimmed with red now, though his face was still stern and angry looking.

'One of our pupils here at Fortlake, a much-loved and talented member of our community, Ida Beechwood from year eight, has gone missing. She was last seen yesterday afternoon just before we broke up for half term. She has never gone missing from home before, nor has she ever gone for so long without contacting her family. Ida's family, the school and the police are very concerned and eager to know anything about Ida's possible whereabouts and her movements on Friday.'

Here again Le Crab glanced at Ida's parents, as if seeking a word or signal of approval for what she was about to say. Then she continued, 'Ida did not attend geography class yesterday, her last lesson before the school broke up for half term. Anyone who knows Ida knows she is not a student who is likely to miss class.'

Maggie couldn't imagine what the headmistress would say about her if she went missing.

'Her closest friends have told us Ida said she was going to the toilet, but that she never showed up to the class, nor responded to their calls or the messages they sent in light of her unexplained absence. Ida's phone was found in Everfall Woods this morning.'

Maggie looked down, ashamed that her lie was now being told to the entire school.

When she looked up again, Le Crab seemed to be eyeballing every single person in the hall. She spoke very slowly. 'If any of you heard or saw ANYTHING relating to Ida's disappearance on Friday, however small, however insignificant it may seem to you, please come forward. Whatever you have to tell us, you won't get into any trouble. And if you are keeping a secret for Ida, please believe me when I tell you that now is not the time for secrets.'

Maggie shivered; she had a distinct feeling that someone was watching her. She looked across the hall and met the cold green eyes of Miss Cane. Very slowly the woman raised her top lip and bared her teeth, which were sharp and pointed like a wolf's.

'Representatives of the local police and all available teachers will be at the school, all day. Please let us know anything suspicious or unusual, if you saw any unknown individuals hanging around the school that day, anything unusual at all.

'Finally, if she is present, could Maggie Blue Brown please report to my office immediately after this assembly.'

At the sound of her name, Maggie turned back to the stage, a hot and terrible flush rising up her cheeks as everyone stared at her.

'Why do they want to see you, Maggie?' Aunt Esme whispered.

Maggie looked at Esme. 'I found her phone in the woods.'

Aunt Esme frowned at her, perplexed. 'Why didn't you say so?'

Maggie said, 'Will you come with me?'

By the time they managed to get to Le Crab's office there was already a line of pupils and parents outside waiting to tell all the things they'd noticed that had seemed insignificant, but which now, in light of events, had suddenly assumed great importance. Maggie couldn't imagine what they had to report.

They joined the back of the queue, but when Mrs Bridges, the Squirrel, saw Maggie she marshalled them to the front of the line. She knocked sharply on the door to Le Crab's office and, without waiting for a reply, swiftly opened it and pushed Maggie and Esme inside.

The statuesque figure of the headmistress leapt up behind her desk, though today the thick green curtains had been swept back in order to allow some daylight in. Seated beside the headmistress was a scruffy middle-aged man in a rumpled suit, straggly dark hair swept optimistically over his shiny bald head. He looked at Maggie with shrewd dark eyes.

Esme smiled at Le Crab. 'How are you, Muriel?'

Le Crab gave her a stiff little nod. 'Esme.' Then she introduced them to the scruffy man. 'This is Maggie. She's in the same class as Ida. Ms Esme Durand is her guardian.'

He smiled at Maggie in an over-friendly way that didn't suit him, and beckoned her and Esme to sit down.

'Hi there, Maggie. My name is Detective Hammond and it's my job to find out where Ida might have gone.'

Maggie grimaced inwardly. He was one of those adults who pretended to be your friend, like you were too stupid to figure out that they were faking it.

'Can I ask you where you found Ida's phone?'

'In the middle of the woods.'

'I see. And how did you know it was hers?'

'It's the best one in class. Everyone knows it's hers.'

'I see. Well you've already been an enormous help. So, because you've been so great, I want to pick your brains about a few other things.'

Detective Hammond asked her about finding the phone, where she found it, what time, about whether they were friends . . . on and on, and sometimes in circles, until Maggie started to wonder if they thought she'd abducted Ida.

After a while, Le Crab whispered something in Detective Hammond's ear. He frowned. 'OK, Maggie. Just a few more things . . .'

Just then, there was a discreet knock. The door opened and Miss Cane appeared. She smiled calmly at everyone, but kept her mouth firmly closed, hiding the pointed little incisors. Maggie felt a lurch of fear.

Annoyed to be interrupted mid-interrogation, Detective Hammond asked sharply, more like the real him, Maggie thought, 'Who is this, sorry?'

Le Crab answered firmly, 'Miss Cane is the school guidance counsellor. She thought she should be present in case any of our pupils became upset by the situation.'

Hammond's eyes narrowed. He didn't seem too pleased. 'I see.'

Miss Cane took a seat on the incongruous green chaise longue in the corner, crossed her long sleek legs and smiled meekly at the detective. Maggie felt the cold green eyes settle upon her.

'Now Maggie, the headmistress tells me that you also bunked eighth period on Friday. Is that right?'

'Yes.'

'Can you tell us why you bunked off?'

'You won't get into any trouble, Maggie,' cut in Le Crab sharply. 'Just tell us why you weren't in class.'

Maggie looked down at the thick green carpet, the colour of grass. 'I find geography boring.' It was the truth anyway.

Hammond laughed but with no real mirth. 'Not a crime, as far as I know. What did you do instead, Maggie?'

Maggie looked down. 'I went to hide in the toilets.'

'And did you see Ida at any point?'

'Yes.' A weird tension flowed through the room like electricity when she said that word, and immediately one side of Maggie's head began to ache.

Hammond continued, trying to hide his eagerness. 'You saw Ida? What was she doing?'

'I was just looking out of the bathroom window on the first floor waiting until I could escape.' Annoyance flickered across Le Crab's face, it was possibly the wrong choice of word, but Maggie ploughed on. 'And I saw her sitting on the bench by the netball cage.'

Hammond scribbled something down in his notebook. 'And what time was this?'

'Three-twenty, I guess. The bell had just gone.'

'Was Ida with anyone, Maggie?'

Maggie shook her head, 'No, but she seemed upset.'

The ache in Maggie's head increased until she winced in pain. She touched the side of her head. She never got headaches like this.

'How did you know she was upset, Maggie? Was she crying?' Detective Hammond was leaning forwards and even Le Crab leant slightly towards her.

Maggie didn't know how to explain. 'No, she wasn't crying. I just . . . I can just tell how people are feeling sometimes. She was feeling low, she . . .' The pain was almost unbearable. '. . . she seemed unhappy . . . like she was depressed or something . . .'

'Depressed?' Detective Hammond once more scribbled furiously in his notebook. He frowned. 'I don't understand how you could know that, Maggie.' He looked at her, 'Are you all right?'

Maggie was clutching her forehead. 'It's just a headache.' Another shooting pain went through her temples and she winced.

'Miss Cane, get Maggie some painkillers and some water,' Le Crab instructed.

The dark figure to her left got up swiftly, and the pain in Maggie's head miraculously vanished. She realised she didn't have much time and her words came out all in a hurry.

'Ida got up and walked to the playing fields, towards the woods, and then I saw Miss Cane walk that way too.' It wasn't quite true, but it was the closest she could get.

Detective Hammond frowned. He indicated the door that Miss Cane had just disappeared through. 'That Miss Cane?'

'Yes, yes. She was wearing a long black coat and high heels . . .'

The door opened and immediately the pain started to come back, throbbing in her temples. Miss Cane placed the water and two tablets on the desk in front of Maggie and said in her softest voice, whilst touching her gently on the arm, 'There you are, Maggie. These should make you feel a bit better.'

But Maggie could feel those awful wolf eyes boring into her, as if they would burn a hole in her. Then Miss Cane flinched. Her eyes had flickered over to Aunt Esme, and she lurched back slightly.

Behind the desk, the other adults were looking at each other in some confusion and embarrassment.

Aunt Esme touched Maggie's arm and smiled at her. 'I think Maggie needs to go home. She doesn't look well.'

Detective Hammond smiled, but his jaw was very tight. 'Perhaps we could have another chat with Maggie when she's feeling better? And we'll need her to show us exactly where she found the phone.'

Aunt Esme smiled in her usual kind way as she stood up. 'Of course, of course. That's no problem.'

The pills and water remained untouched on the desk and they left.

It was Esme who broke the silence as they walked up Church Lane. 'Did you really see Miss Cane following Ida?'

Maggie was surprised by the question. 'Yes. I mean I saw her walking towards the woods.'

Esme stopped, her face suddenly serious. She took her hand. 'Maggie, you have to tell the truth about this. It's not a game.'

'Why would I think it's a game?' She looked at her aunt's concerned face. For all her eccentricities, Esme suddenly seemed the same as all the other adults: when it really mattered, she didn't believe her.

'I've got to go somewhere,' Maggie said.

She snatched her hand away and started running. She heard her aunt calling her, but she kept going and didn't look back.

10

THE DECISION

It took her ages to find, but she finally saw it – the weird turret fit for a suburban princess or, rather, the Queen of West Minchen. She ran up the path and pressed the bell before she could change her mind. The old lady was in the hallway sorting through a huge pile of mail.

'There you are,' said Dot. She looked at the letters, shook her head and chucked it all back on the floor. 'I hate the mail. There's never anything good.'

Maggie followed her into the same huge light room and saw that this time, the snooker balls were already scattered around the table.

'Would you like some tea?'

Maggie nodded and Dot wheeled herself off humming a tune.

Maggie sat down on a battered armchair and looked at all the jars of herbs and the heavy bound books. She wished she could just curl up and go to sleep and forget it all. But soon Dot reappeared, a tray balanced on her legs with a pot of tea and a large lemon cake upon it. She smiled but her eyes were watchful beneath her shock of white hair.

Maggie ate a large slice then blurted out, 'You know you said people disappear . . . well, I think I saw someone disappear.'

'You did?' said Dot through her own mouthful of cake.

'This woman who works at my school turned into a wolf and snatched this girl away and . . . well, they disappeared. They vanished.'

Dot didn't flinch. Maggie noticed little bits of cake stuck in her faint moustache.

'Do you know where they went?'

Maggie twisted the ends of her hair around her fingers. 'It sounds stupid but I think they might have gone to another world.'

Dot's eyes glittered with interest. 'Really?'

'Yes. Wait, you believe me?'

'Of course, I do,' Dot replied.

Maggie was so surprised she just sat and stared at the tiny old lady until Dot spoke again, 'You care about this girl.'

It was a statement not a question and Maggie blushed. 'She doesn't like me though. But I want to try and get her back.'

The old lady's face was grim, 'I'm sorry, Maggie. I don't know how you can see this other world. You're certainly unusual. But you can't find your friend now.'

'What do you mean?'

'You're better off forgetting her.'

Maggie was stunned. 'I don't understand . . .'

'She's gone. And no one from this world can help her.'

Maggie hadn't expected this. 'But . . . but I thought you would help me.'

Dot shrugged. 'I would if I could.'

'But I can't just leave her there, wherever she is.'

Dot looked at her intently then smiled and shrugged. She wheeled herself over to one of the huge bookshelves and picked up a sort of apple pick – a long pole with a basket attached at the top. She started prodding at a book on the very top shelf.

Eventually it fell down with a crash into her lap and she started leafing through it. Finally she stopped on a page. She passed the book to Maggie. 'This is the only place the laws of passage between worlds have ever been written down. But no one has ever done it. No one from this world, at least.'

The ancient brown page was decorated with beautiful ink drawings of trees and strange birds and flowers Maggie did not even recognise. Its centre was covered in a block of dense ornate calligraphy that was almost impossible to read. Maggie could just about make out that it was a list.

'Is this how you cross to the other world?'

Dot nodded, 'But you won't be able to do it.'

'Can I rip this page out?'

Dot laughed. 'Are you out of your mind, girlie? Here.' She thrust a pen and paper at Maggie. 'Copy them down if you really want to. But I warn you: it won't help you.'

So Maggie sat at Dot's desk and laboriously copied out what she managed to make out as the six laws of crossing. It was very hard to read, but finally she thought she had them. Beside her, the old lady had fallen into a doze in front of the electric fire. She was tiny, like a little bird. Maggie had never really noticed before how vulnerable and old she looked. Instead of waking her, she crept out and walked slowly back to the flat.

Maggie was relieved to see Hoagy sitting on the front mat back at Milton Lodge. Maybe he could help her? She sat down on the doorstep and told him all about what Dot had said and the instructions she'd copied down for crossing to the other world.

'So, I was wondering . . .'

The cat held a paw up to his white chest in horror. 'No, no, no. *I'm* not going there.'

'I can't go alone,' pleaded Maggie.

'Well, I'm busy.' The cat rolled luxuriantly onto his side and proceeded to rasp-lick his belly.

'How long for?'

'Oh, the foreseeable,' he explained between licks. 'I'm courting Barbara, and believe me, it's a full-time job.'

'Who's Barbara?'

'The humans call her Fluffy,' he scoffed, 'but her real name is Barbara.'

Maggie couldn't believe it. 'Ida's cat?'

'A magnificent beauty,' purred Hoagy and his eye went to a slit. 'She appreciates my street-tough qualities. Honestly, the number of pampered tomcats who've tried it on with her. Pah! They couldn't wrestle a kitten where I come from.'

'And where do you come from?' Maggie asked irritably.

Hoagy ignored the question. 'The point is, I can't leave her now with all those fur-balled idiots sniffing around. There's one especially persistent black cat; makes a frightful mewling sound in the garden every morning. He thinks it's charming. All black cats are in the pay of witches and sorcerers. Did you know that? I really can't allow it.'

'But doesn't Fluffy, Barbara, whatever, want to find Ida?'

Hoagy's whiskers twitched. 'Of course she does. She misses the extra treats and tummy rubs, but frankly the girl wasn't bringing much more to the table than that.'

Maggie was suddenly curious. 'You've been in Ida's house?'

'Ooh yes,' he purred. 'It's very luxurious, lovely soft carpets and furnishings. Everything smells good too – very clean.' He jerked his head back towards the Lodge. 'Unlike this slovenly hovel.'

'Do you live there now?'

Hoagy's tail swatted the ground. 'No. It's got bad vibes.'

'How come?' asked Maggie.

'The adults fight all the time. The thing that really bothers them is that the school say their little darling was unhappy just before she disappeared, and the man absolutely won't believe it. He's convinced there's a boy involved because she wasn't getting straight A's any more.' The cat's fur bristled a little. 'Barb says he's never done it, but I'm a good judge of character and I can quite see him kicking a cat at some point, possibly down the stairs. Such persons are to be avoided.'

'I didn't like him either,' Maggie agreed.

'Not that he's ever noticed me in his house.' He went back to licking his front paw. 'Humans are so shockingly unobservant. It never ceases to amaze me.'

Maggie knelt down and touched Hoagy's shoulder, though cats don't really have shoulders. 'Hoagy, you're my only friend. You've got to help me find Ida.'

The old cat's tail twitched more vigorously. He trained his one eye upon her. 'Cats don't have to do *anything*. They certainly don't have to do dangerous things because human girls ask them nicely. Pah! That whole nine lives thing is a disgraceful urban myth.'

Maggie stood up. She was shocked by how upset she felt. Obviously the cat didn't care for her at all – they weren't really friends. Anger flickered through her like a red-hot spark. 'I hope Barb realises how old and selfish you are, and dumps you.'

Hoagy's tail flicked malevolently and he half-hissed, half-purred, 'And I hope Ida hates you even more when you find her.'

Maggie got her front door key out and started rattling it in the lock, but it wouldn't open. Turning round she snapped, 'And I hope you get run over on the way to Fluffy's!'

Hoagy's purr was a violent vibration beneath his voice, 'And I hope you get stuck in another world and never come back!'

Maggie took a deep breath, though she hadn't quite decided what insult to hurl at him next. 'And I hope—'

But the cat cut her off with a violent explosion of hissing before he skittered away across the road, ingeniously avoiding the stream of traffic.

Maggie looked at the front door. On second thoughts, she couldn't face going back into the flat just yet. So she turned and drifted aimlessly back into West Minchen feeling that anyway no one cared where she was or what she was doing. She could be out all night and no one would even notice she was gone.

She walked slowly along the streets peering in at people's houses until she came to the high street and looked vacantly into shop windows, seeing herself half-reflected there. She could see her face, but it was blurred. That was how she felt sometimes – like she didn't really exist, or at least not in a definite, clear way.

She wandered on and suddenly caught sight of herself in a real mirror. It was an old gilt thing, propped up in the window of yet another charity shop – the Cats Defence League. Though she was no longer convinced cats needed much defending.

She stopped and examined herself. She looked how she'd always looked since she was about five: no better, no worse. Her eyes were too big and her hair was too thin and straight. She'd always been herself, Maggie Blue Brown, and to be honest, although she wasn't very pretty or striking or anything, she'd always liked herself.

It was other people who didn't seem to get her. They were always telling her who she was. And it occurred to her for the first time that maybe they had no idea at all. Her mum said she needed to be normal. Other kids always said she was weird. The teachers told her she was lazy and some of them thought she was stupid. No one believed her when she told the truth. But maybe none of them had a clue? The pale face in the glass smiled faintly: the thought appealed to her.

The sky had been darkening for some time, and suddenly with a dramatic roll of thunder, the heavens opened. Light from speeding cars flickered over her and the rain quickly soaked through her clothes. But Maggie didn't move.

She thought about Ida. Where was she? Was she afraid? Was she hoping someone would rescue her? The police, teachers, parents – they'd look in all the wrong places and they'd never listen to Maggie even if she told them what she'd seen.

Maybe she *was* weird. After all she could hear cats talk and see strange lights in other worlds. But she couldn't change that.

The old lady behind the counter inside was starting to give her a few funny looks but, despite that and the rain, Maggie still didn't move. Her eyes looked huge and dark in the glass, and in them she saw the flicker of something new, something she barely recognised. Maggie understood then: it was up to her. She was the only one who could rescue Ida, and she would do it alone. She smiled: then Ida would have to be her friend, whether she liked it or not.

PART TWO

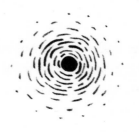

11

THE DARK WORLD

Maggie stood by the copse very early the next morning. The sky was white and a thick mist hung low on the ground. She couldn't believe she was really trying this. She was wearing her too-small duffel coat and a long cobalt blue scarf she'd found hanging by the door as she crept out of the flat. All she'd brought was a bottle of water and the instructions she'd copied from Dot's book.

The birds twittered manically above, encouraging or warning her, she couldn't tell. Most likely they didn't care. Like Hoagy, she thought with a surge of self-pity; like everyone.

The first problem was that she could no longer see the portal hovering in the air. She shifted a little one way and then the other, and tried to relax, but nothing happened. Was she forgetting something? She got out the crumpled piece of paper. Instruction number one was kind of vague. 'Don't look and you will see.'

But Maggie understood. If you tried too hard, it

wouldn't work; she had to relax her focus, let her vision go panoramic, like before. But after a couple of minutes she still only saw the desolate misty copse. She rubbed her eyes and sat down on Dan the Tree's stump. *Don't look*, she thought again. Maybe it was literal?

She closed her eyes and listened to the sounds of the wood around her: the rustle of the crows rooting in the undergrowth, squirrels scuttling across dead leaves and chattering angrily overhead, and the rumble of early morning traffic. She pictured the opening as she'd seen it before, how it looked like a big TV cut into the air. She told herself it would be there.

Sure enough, gradually she began to feel a foreign cold air flowing over her. She smiled, opened her eyes and the paper slipped from her hand. There it was: the window to another world. Through it Maggie could see more trees, but it was darker and there were black leaves on the ground. She stayed very still.

She took a deep breath. 'Don't be scared,' she said to herself. But she was; she was very scared. Her heart was pounding as she made herself recite instruction two under her breath, 'Draw close to the portal.'

Maggie walked slowly towards the shimmering window until she reached the edge of the other world, or was it the edge of her world? The air got colder still and she felt a breeze start to blow over her, as if a storm was brewing in this other place.

The next instruction played in her head – she had memorised them all on the sofa last night. Number three: 'Touch one edge of the portal. There will be power there. Allow it to flow.'

Maggie reached out and touched the left-hand side of the window. Its texture was unexpected, like soft rubber, and a sharp prang of electricity jolted through her. It was painful, it hurt her teeth and rumbled in her ears, but after a few seconds it calmed to a pleasant hum that ran warmly through her entire body.

Number four: 'Rub your fingers together, gently, without haste – the edges between worlds will part.'

She obeyed and sure enough, she felt the two edges separate. There was something warm and sticky between them, something like jam, as if the substance between the worlds had melted.

Number five: 'Release your world. The power will increase. Do not let go.'

Slowly, and using both hands now, Maggie managed to prize her fingers from the layer closest to her. Immediately, the current surged, far worse this time. Her nostrils quivered and her hair stood on end, painfully and from the roots.

She felt aware of another presence suddenly. She looked up and saw an enormous heron on an overhanging branch, its huge grey body as still as a statue. She'd never seen a heron in the woods before; was she hallucinating? But she couldn't think about that now.

She closed her eyes. The last instruction was the easiest to remember but the hardest to actually do. Number six simply said: 'JUMP!'

It felt like her brain was shaking inside her skull, but still she didn't let go. Tears came into her eyes. She gritted her singing teeth and counted down in her head, 'Five . . . four . . . three . . .' Around her the birds began to chatter hysterically, as if warning her. 'Two . . . one . . .' There was nothing else for it. 'JUMP!' Maggie closed her eyes and flung herself into the space in front of her.

Her fingers peeled away from the edge and she fell for a long time through misty cold air. Finally she landed with a bump on soft spongy ground and lay there for some time letting the current shiver off her. Tentatively, she prodded at her aching teeth, but they all still seemed to be in place, which was a relief.

The air here was cold and dense, and it took a few moments for her eyes to adjust to the gloom. But when they did she saw treetops above her, black against a sky of deepest blue. It was that time just before night falls. She sat up, but all she could see was the forest stretching away on all sides.

After a moment or two she realised there was no sound. No birds or creatures rustled the leaves, no cars or lorries poured down distant roads, no voices or shouts rang out. The silence frightened her.

She looked around. But the window wasn't behind her any more and there was no obvious way back to West

Minchen. The gap through which she had come to this world had disappeared. Though the same old gnarly tree was there – that was something. She scrambled to her feet. She hadn't really thought about finding her way back. There weren't any instructions for that.

She took off the blue scarf and tied it to the tree so she wouldn't lose her bearings. Then she walked a short distance from it in all directions. But there was no window, either to her world or any other. In fact there were no distinguishing features at all: no clearings, copses or playing fields, no buildings, just an endless flow of trees leading into more blackness.

12

NOT ENTIRELY HUMAN

Something strange was happening, something he didn't understand. And the old lady was in quite a state.

It had all started that morning. Very early he had been trotting along the deserted pavement having decided to make a quick trip to Mrs Hacker's in Long Lane. Some choice cuts of meat were always available there if you could stand being mollycoddled within an inch of your life. And frankly at that moment he could.

He glanced down at his protruding white belly, which rumbled loudly. A few slices of prosciutto and a succulent chicken breast from that dolt Mrs H and he'd be cooking on gas.

But something caught his eye just by the gate that led into the woods. He stopped on the opposite side of the road and squinted with interest: was that Maggie? But what was she doing there at this time? His tail flexed. Ah, he remembered now – she really was crazy enough to try it.

The girl looked pale and worried. She walked quickly into the woods leaving the gate open behind her. Hoagy sniff-sniffed at the air. Of course, *he* wasn't scared. No, no, no. He just wasn't an idiot. He wasn't going to get soft in his old age, not for some random girl who'd taken a liking to him. And yet . . .

Maggie was almost out of sight. Quick as a flash, Hoagy slipped through the railings and followed her through the trees. The chicken would have to wait – at least for a little while. It was very cold in the woods and the dampness seeped unpleasantly into his old bones. He hissed at a few squirrels as he went, just for the fun of it – idiots!

A few minutes later, he watched as Maggie, trembling all over with fear, raised her hands up into mid-air as if she was holding something. She stayed like that for several seconds, then she lurched forwards and suddenly she was gone. For all his blasé attitude, he'd never seen anything like it – the girl had disappeared without a trace. He didn't move for some time then, abruptly, he shook himself all over.

Not his problem, not his problem at all. If she wanted to cross to another world, that was her lookout. Frankly, he had no idea why she was so keen to get this nasty girl back. But one thing he did know, as sure as KitSnak was the number-one bestselling feline treat, Dorothea Dot would be very interested in this new development.

He went and prowled around the portal, sniffed it,

and even tried to paw at it, though it was invisible to him. Perhaps he should wait and see if Maggie came back again, just so he knew. He wasn't concerned, he didn't care; but still, it would be good to know how she got on, purely out of intellectual curiosity.

But then he heard heavy footsteps plodding through the leaves behind him. His bitten-up ears swivelled wildly in their sockets, and his eye became wide and unblinking. Someone was coming, someone very heavy who smelt very bad. Frankly he wasn't in the mood to be sociable, so he scrammed through the trees and out of sight.

Later, when Hoagy told Dot that Maggie had crossed over to the other world, she was speechless for a moment. In fact he thought she might have died. She didn't move for almost thirty seconds and he was about to go and nip at her ankles to make sure she was OK when she started wheeling herself round and round the room.

He could hear her muttering. Finally she stopped long enough for Hoagy to ask, 'What's wrong with you?'

She looked at him as if seeing him from very far away. Hoagy realised she was frightened.

'Don't you see? Anything that can cross between worlds alone is not human, or not entirely. Not even witches can do it. So who is she?'

'She's not a human?' Hoagy asked confused. 'She certainly smells like one.'

Dot shook her head and suddenly she looked about a thousand years old. 'All I know is that I have missed something very important about this girl.'

13

GIRL FROM ANOTHER PLACE

Maggie must have drifted off because she woke up to find something sniffing at her. At first she thought it was Hoagy, but then he didn't sniff like that, like a dog. And anyway, they weren't on speaking terms now, so it couldn't be him. Her eyelids felt unbearably heavy. When she finally managed to prize them open, she screamed.

Three little grey animals jumped back in fright as her cry pinged around the silent black trees. They made quietening gestures at her with their paws then moved closer again. They put down their small grey sacks, held three flickering lanterns right up to her face and stared at her with dark worried eyes.

Maggie had never seen animals like them before. They stood on their hind legs to just over a metre tall, and were covered in thick, rather unappealing pale grey fur that ended in a long thin tail. They had small snouts and looked a bit like racoons, or rats, except their ears grew on the side of their heads, and there was something human about their faces, which were furless, pink and wrinkled.

Maggie tried to get up but the creatures leapt away again in fright and held up their wrinkled paws, which she now saw ended in extremely long and agile clawed fingers with some sort of webbing or extra skin in between. So Maggie held her hands up too and slowly they all lowered their hands/paws in a truce.

It was the younger creature who spoke. He had a sweeter more sensitive face than the others. 'You don't belong here,' he whispered. He didn't say it in an unkind way, more as a statement of fact.

'I know,' Maggie whispered back, 'but I'm trying to find someone, someone else who doesn't belong here.'

'That's not our business, girl from another place,' the strange thing replied.

Above them, weak light started to flicker down through the trees. The three creatures looked up anxiously. Maggie saw that two orbs, just like the ones she'd seen in her neighbour's garden, were hovering above the forest canopy.

'We mustn't be found with you,' the younger creature said, and without further consultation the three of them grabbed their small grey sacks and ran.

Maggie leapt to her feet in a panic. But they were already scuttling away as fast as they could.

'Don't leave me!'

The creatures swerved and darted between the trees

with great agility, occasionally pushing off from a trunk with their odd webbed paws. When he realised she was following them, the younger one made a shooing gesture like she was an enormous cat.

'Go away!' He was so intent on telling her, he didn't see the tree until he smacked right into it. He dropped his sack and fell to the ground with a yelp of pain.

The older creatures stopped in their tracks, but when they saw what had happened they only hissed and barked at Maggie then turned and kept running. Maggie watched them go in disbelief. Were they really leaving him?

Maggie bent down and shook the creature, but though he writhed around in pain, he didn't open his eyes. There was nothing else for it: she picked him up. He was amazingly light and she could feel his ribs. Sweating, even in the dark chill of this world, Maggie hurried on looking for somewhere to hide.

When she glanced behind her the balls of light had disappeared from the sky and instead she saw two small boys running through the trees, whooping and shrieking. They only seemed to be playing. She wasn't even sure if they'd seen them, but for some reason they scared her more than the orbs and she ran faster.

She found the older creatures a few hundred yards on, stamping on a patch of earth not obviously distinct from any other. One sniffed at the ground whilst the other held a long sinewy paw out as if it was a metal detector. It nodded and they both moved slightly to the side and began stamping again.

In Maggie's arms, the little grey creature began to groan. Maggie looked over her shoulder. The boys were getting closer. One of the older creatures gave a final stamp and suddenly the earth beneath them gave way like a trapdoor and they both disappeared into the ground.

Maggie ran over and saw beneath her a perfectly constructed chute disappearing into the earth. She couldn't see the bottom, it was just blackness. She had no desire to go down there. But behind her, the strange boys were closing in, giggling and shrieking wildly. And so, for the second time that day or night, or whatever it was, and this time holding a weird grey creature in her aching arms, Maggie closed her eyes and jumped.

She landed in a pile of warm dirt and coughed and spluttered to get the bits of earth out of her mouth. For a few moments, she could still hear the shouts of the boys, but then they faded away into the woods and all was silent again.

There was a rustling close beside her. Then two bright lights ripped open the darkness and Maggie saw that she was lying on a pile of earth mixed up with rotted bark and leaves. The two older creatures were on their haunches in an adjoining tunnel that wound deeper into the earth, holding up their lanterns to inspect her. One of them hissed and barked at her then disappeared down the tunnel.

The other remained a moment, observing her. Its voice was very shaky when it spoke, 'Shifters fear the deep earth.' Then it barked into the tunnel, threw the sack over its shoulder and, on all fours now, disappeared swiftly down it.

Maggie looked up at the sky far above her head. She'd actually thought she could do this on her own? How unbelievably stupid was she? Now she was trapped underground. She'd never get out. The soil would collapse on top of her. She'd just die here and no one would ever know.

Beside her on the pile of dirt, the creature began to stir. Then he suddenly sat bolt upright and his lantern sparked into life.

'Who were those boys?' Maggie asked.

The creature looked at her and his already wrinkled brow wrinkled a little more. 'The Children; the most feared shifters on the Island.'

'Shifters?' Maggie asked. But he was now too busy grooming himself to answer. She tried again, 'What kind of creature are you?'

'An umon, of course,' he replied, looking rather offended. And he continued to eye her with great suspicion whilst licking his paw. After a while he said, 'Why are you here, girl from another place?'

'My name's Maggie. I'm looking for a friend.'

The creature wrinkled its snout. 'What is a friend?'

Maggie didn't quite know where to start. She tried a

different tack. 'Has anyone like me come here recently? She's a bit taller than me but—'

'Everyone knows the shifters bring your bodies across and take you to the city,' the creature interrupted. He looked at her quizzically. 'But it seems to be younger ones now.'

'Which city?'

'Sun City – where I serve.'

'Can you take me there?'

He shook his head vigorously. 'I will be ended if they know I helped you. Besides, if you go to Sun City, you will not return.'

'Just show me where it is.'

At that moment a drop of very dark blood ran from the wound on the umon's head, trickled down his snout and dripped onto the earth. He put a wrinkled paw to his forehead.

'Bloodiness! Bloodiness!' He looked at Maggie desperately.

Maggie noticed another deep gash on his flank. She got out her water bottle and tried to clean him up. But the creature was so fascinated by the plastic bottle he seemed to forget his pain.

'What is that?'

Maggie let him take it and he squeezed it in and out, observing the crunchy popping noise it made.

'Most useful. A water carrier.'

'So, Sun City?' prompted Maggie, trying to get him back to the point.

The creature sat and thought for a moment then said very solemnly. 'I will take you to the city walls, but no further,' he nodded at the plastic bottle, 'if you will give me this water carrier.'

Maggie nearly laughed with surprise, but managed to restrain herself. 'OK.'

'Let us go.' And the creature nimbly began to climb up the walls of the earth tunnel back to the forest floor.

'I can't climb up there,' Maggie called up to him.

The umon looked down at her, his claws tight around a root. 'You cannot climb?'

Maggie shook her head.

The creature's huge eyes contemplated her for a moment or two. 'I will get the things we need.' He scrambled up to the top then poked his head back down. 'Don't move!' he hissed and disappeared from sight.

If only I could, thought Maggie. She looked around. Perhaps she might be able to squeeze through the tunnel the other umons had disappeared down? But what if she got stuck? What if the earth tumbled down on top of her before he got back? *Just don't think*, she told herself – *don't think, don't think, don't think* . . . She had no option but to sit still and hope that the strange grey creature was as good as his word.

14

SUN CITY

Maggie didn't know how much time had passed when a coarse yellow rope suddenly appeared in front of her. She looked up and saw the little umon peering over the edge. His lantern cast deep shadows so that his eyes looked like empty hollows.

'Climb up,' he whispered.

When Maggie stood up her limbs reminded her that she hadn't eaten and had barely slept. And she had no idea how she was supposed to use a single bit of rope to get out of a deep hole.

'I can't!' she whispered back.

'You must stay down there for ever then,' the creature said.

It clearly wasn't a joke. Maggie took hold of the rope again.

'Use your hind legs,' the creature called down.

OK. Her legs. Gripping the rope she levered her legs

up the side a little way. But her arms gave out almost at once. And after a few seconds she dropped down again to the dirt at the bottom. She kept picking herself up and trying again, but she could never lever herself up any further.

Maggie crouched down for a moment to get her breath back and tried to think. She stood and ran her hand over the walls of the tunnel. They were sturdy but kind of soft. Maybe if she could dig her feet into the wall, she could pull herself out that way?

She looked up at the creature. He was like a worried owl peering down at her. She smiled and gave him the thumbs up, trying to act as if she felt confident. Though she immediately doubted thumbs up were all that big in this world.

But by kicking her feet hard into the earthen walls she could slowly and very painfully drag herself a bit further up the rope. Then she used her other leg and dug once again into the damp walls and dragged her body up a little more. And so on.

Her legs and arms ached, her stomach muscles hurt, but finally, oh finally, sweating in the cold air she managed to reach the top. In one final effort, she dragged herself out of the hole and slumped onto the soft forest floor. Blood stung her palms from rope burn, and she wiped them on the warm damp earth beside her.

Meanwhile, the umon had already untied the rope from

around the trunk of a nearby tree and was meticulously winding it up whilst giving her a curious look.

'Can't bodies climb in your world?'

Maggie started to laugh, but her stomach hurt too much and she stopped. The creature shook his head, mystified. But clearly not one to dwell on irrelevant curiosities, he put the rope away in his sack that he must have retrieved on his travels. Inside, Maggie saw strange pinkish-white mushrooms that glowed like little neon lights in the gloom.

Just then, Maggie's stomach rumbled, or more like it cried out in desperation. She looked at the creature, wondering how to explain. 'I'm sorry . . . I didn't really plan to be here so long . . .' The creature looked at her blankly. So she pointed at her stomach. 'Hungry.'

Irritation flickered over his pink face. But he reached again into his sack and removed a block of a brownish solid substance. With a tiny knife that he extracted from somewhere else on his person, he cut off a neat slice and handed it to her.

Maggie nibbled one corner very cautiously. But to her surprise, it tasted good, malty and rich. And she ate the rest in a matter of seconds.

The creature watched her with a mixture of horror and admiration. Then it nodded slowly, as if understanding something, and motioned for her to follow.

They retraced their steps through the forest, until they found her scarf, still tied round the gnarled tree where she'd left it. Maggie felt an overwhelming desire to get out of this world, but instead she pointed at the scarf, 'This is where I came through.'

The umon went over and sniffed it, as if setting his GPS, then came back. His eyes narrowed. 'And in return you will give me the water carrier?' he asked again.

'I promise.'

They walked for a long time through the forest and saw nothing in the beams of the umon's lantern – no people, no animals, no birds – only an endless procession of trees whose black leaves now blended with the sky. There weren't any pathways or landmarks, or anything to differentiate one part of the forest from another. Maggie realised she'd have no chance of finding her way alone. She needed the umon to survive.

After a long time he spoke, 'We were lucky to escape Eldrow's Children. Of all the shifters, they can read the deepest darkest thoughts. And they can end you in a heartbeat. Do you see?'

Maggie nodded, not really seeing at all. But just then she saw a faint shimmering light that dappled the black canopy above them. After a few more minutes, the mysterious light was starting to get bright and they could see each other easily. The umon put out his lantern, got down onto his belly and indicated that Maggie should do the same. They wriggled forwards through the soil and dead leaves until they finally made it to the last line of trees and Maggie gasped in amazement.

Below them in the valley, a beautiful city glittered in the darkness. Maggie had never seen anything quite like it. It wasn't like the cities she knew from home with congested roads, tower blocks, suburbs and aeroplanes flying through grey skies. Instead it glowed like a jewel in a dark velvet box.

Every street was ablaze. A huge buttressed wall enclosed a vast area packed full of pale stone buildings that sat higgledy-piggledy on top of each other in a complex maze. And clustered around the city walls, like a fungus at the base of a magnificent tree, was a sprawl of tiny shacks, hovels that looked like matchboxes.

The umon pointed at them. 'We live here.'

In the very centre of the city, at the highest point, a great palace stood watching over everything. Maggie could make out figures dancing at its windows and music drifted out into the still air.

The umon cocked his head and listened to the strange music. 'Eldrow holds his revels in the dark-time,' he whispered, 'for the great and good of the city. And it must always be light. There is never darkness in Sun City. But Eldrow is the most cruel of all the Islanders.'

'So there's really no sunlight here?' asked Maggie.

The creature shook its head sadly. 'Only a little at white-time. The sun has fled.' He got up and slung the sack over his shoulder. 'Girl from another place, do not move or the shifters will find you. I will see if there is word of your *friend*.'

Maggie began to protest, but the umon had already scampered away from her. So she pushed herself into the leaves as far as she could and watched him walk down into the valley until his lantern looked like a little star moving along the ground.

Now she was alone, Maggie tried pinching her arm as hard as she could: it hurt. She didn't know if that was a real test to see if you were dreaming – she'd just seen it on the TV. And anyway, what if you could dream you were pinching your arm really hard?

But then looking down at the strange and beautiful place, Maggie felt certain Ida was there. She could sense her. But where exactly? In one of the stone houses? Or was she in the huge palace with its music and flashing lights? When the umon got back, she would persuade him to take her inside.

Around her, the air had grown even colder and the sky lighter. She huddled down into her old duffel coat as far as she could go. Then she heard a strange cracking noise above her. Maggie shivered and looked up. Suddenly a sharp piece of ice speared the ground in front of her. She screamed. Almost at once more pieces began to fall from the sky in a jagged blizzard.

In a panic, Maggie got up and ran deeper into the woods trying to avoid the sharp daggers of ice, but the leaves did little to protect her. Eventually she found shelter under a thick overhanging branch, and watched in terror as the giant ice shards came streaming down.

Then just as suddenly, the ice stopped falling and the ground was a carpet of glinting diamond shards. The air temperature began to rise and it rose so fast that in no time the ground was soaking wet and all the ice had melted.

Maggie emerged and was leaning back against the black sodden branch wondering what on earth had just happened when she spotted the small solitary figure of the umon walking towards her through the trees, a little further along from where he'd left her. She watched as his light went some way into the trees behind her and he disappeared from sight. But then suddenly he was right beside her.

'Why did you move?'

'Didn't you see the storm?' cried Maggie. 'What was that?'

But the little creature only shrugged. 'Ice rain. Listen, girl from another place, the Children are searching for you. Everyone knows a body has crossed without permission and they're splitting up to find you. We must hurry.' And with that he set off into the forest again. He set a much brisker pace than before, running through the trees.

'Wait!' Maggie loud-whispered after him, but he either

didn't hear or didn't want to. Maggie scrambled up and ran after him. 'Wait! I have to get into the city.'

He stopped and shook his head vigorously. 'Impossible.'

'But what about my friend? I have to find her else I'll have come here for nothing.'

'Then you came for nothing. If you want to know the way back to the blue cloth, you must follow me now.' He dashed off again and Maggie had no choice but to follow as his diminutive narrow shoulders dipped effortlessly through the trees.

As she scrambled over the wet ground she thought about how the other umons had abandoned him, left him unconscious and alone. They hadn't even bothered to make sure that he was alive. They'd just grabbed their sacks and run off. Was that how it was here?

She called out to him as she struggled to keep up, 'Do you not have friends in this world?'

'I don't understand,' said the creature as it danced through the trees.

Maggie was huffing and puffing so badly that he stopped and looked at her with the same silent reproach as when she'd asked for food. Maggie gratefully leant against one of the slender trees to get her breath back.

She took a long drink from her bottle and then offered it to him. He accepted and once he had drunk, examined the bottle again with the same interest before reluctantly handing it back. Then his face wrinkled into a deep frown.

'Is it good to have a friend?'

Maggie smiled. 'Very good.'

'This other girl you seek is your friend?'

Maggie felt red rising to her cheeks. 'Not exactly.'

The creature looked confused. 'Why not?'

Maggie's blush deepened in the darkness. 'Well, it's kind of got to be a mutual thing. The other person has to want to be your friend too. I'm a bit different to other people in my world. They don't like that.'

The creature nodded gravely. 'Difference is not rewarded here either.'

On an impulse, Maggie held out her hand. 'We never said hello properly. Like I said, I'm Maggie.'

The creature looked completely perplexed by her outstretched hand, which he did not take.

'What's your name?' asked Maggie. 'You know, what are you called?'

The creature shook his head and furrows wrinkled his tiny pink brow. 'I am not *called* anything.'

'You don't have a name?'

The creature just stared at her.

'Maybe we should choose one for you?' Maggie thought for a moment. 'How about Frank?'

Frank was a boy who'd been in her class at primary school. He was tiny and very good at climbing trees. She'd always liked him and he hadn't hated her.

'Frank . . . ?' the creature repeated, unconvinced.

Maggie took this as a positive, grabbed his small wrinkled grey paw and shook it vigorously. 'Great. Hi there, Frank.' The paw was cool and slightly damp to the touch. The umon looked terrified, so she added, 'This is something we do in my world. It's fine.'

An unreadable look passed over the little creature's thin face. He snatched his paw away and began to move briskly through the trees away from her.

'It doesn't have to be Frank,' she called after him. But she had to start running before he disappeared.

Maggie was utterly exhausted by the time they reached the tree with her soggy blue scarf still tied around it. There had been a short but violent rainstorm – thankfully without ice – as they'd neared the end of their journey, and they were both soaked.

Now the sodden creature lit only by his lantern and shivering, held out his pink wrinkled paw, patient but expectant. It was true – he'd kept his side of the bargain. So she took out the empty plastic bottle. His eyes lit up and he snatched it from her.

'Wait!' she cried, but Frank had already disappeared without a glance back. Without his little lantern everything went black. Maggie sighed. She felt lonely. She was cold and she had no idea if she'd find the portal again. She groped her way back to the gnarled tree and sat down, too tired and hopeless to care about the wet ground beneath her.

But she'd barely had time to catch her breath when a small figure emerged silently from the trees. As her eyes adjusted she could just make out one of the little boys, his golden almond-shaped eyes glowing in the darkness. He started to giggle, a soft childish cackle that left Maggie cold with fear.

Then right in front of her, in a way that Maggie could barely process, the boy morphed into one of the glowing orbs and hung in the air. Maggie was transfixed and after a while she started to feel something, like gossamer threads were winding into her body, going into and under her skin. She tried to recoil but then, with just as little warning, all the invisible threads retracted and she felt very calm. The orb moved closer to her, shimmering now, and she had the strongest urge to reach out and touch it.

But just as she was about to do so, the orb reared up and slammed into her neck. An electric shock pulsed through her and she screamed in pain. It pushed her to the ground and a white haze surrounded her as it pressed painfully into her mind. She could feel this thing invading her mind, going through every memory as if rifling through a filing cabinet. She wanted to scream and shake it off, but she couldn't move.

It felt like the probe had reached somewhere very tender, very painful, and she cried out again and begged it to stop. But it kept prodding relentlessly, pushing at it so that Maggie thought she might pass out with the pain. But then the orb hesitated, as if it was confused. And gradually she realised that the hazy cocoon of light around her had begun to clear a little.

She became aware of her surroundings again and she noticed that something hard was falling from the sky – was it more ice-rain? She squinted through the hazy light cast by the orb into the canopy above. Was she dreaming or were bits of twig falling down onto them?

The orb too was curious and rose slowly up into the canopy. And as it did, Maggie woke up from her trance. She could hear the noise of the leaves shivering above her and she felt her mind stretching out to the sides.

A voice from somewhere above her whispered fiercely, 'Go!'

She looked up and saw Frank staring down at her. Then he tore away down a tree trunk and ran for dear life with the orb in pursuit. Maggie watched, feeling very calm and detached from the whole thing. And when she turned to look behind her, she was not surprised to see a glowing white rectangle levitating in the darkness – the portal.

She moved over to it and peeled the layers of the worlds apart as before. Her whole body started to shake, her brain hammered and rattled in her skull. She was just about to jump when she heard a horrible shriek.

The orb slammed into her back so hard that Maggie was winded. She started to feel more pain go through her and her will began to drain away. But somehow she hung on to the edge of her world and a tiny determined voice kept shouting from some unknown place right in the centre of her, 'Jump . . . Jump . . . JUMP!!!'

With her very last scrap of energy Maggie flung herself at the white window. The painful electricity shivered off her and it felt like she was being plunged underwater. Her ears popped, her lungs hurt and she blacked out.

15

THE SCHOOL GUIDANCE COUNSELLOR

It was freezing cold and raindrops were hitting her. She could hear birds singing and in the distance she heard the persistent hum of traffic. Her eyes flew open and she sat bolt upright. Traffic? She got up and kicked the rain-slicked leaves joyfully, flinging her arms about. But then she felt weak and had to lean against a tree to recover. She became aware of the serious ache in her stomach, and how her upper and lower lips were stuck to each other like velcro. But she was back in West Minchen and that was all that mattered.

The sky seemed to suggest it was early morning sometime, and as she trudged back along the grey streets, men and women in smart sportswear came briskly out of their front doors and glanced at her coldly before jogging away. A heavyset man with a tanned boulder-like head topped by a shock of white hair stared at her with two piercing blue eyes as he chugged heavily past, his be-lycraed body bulging unhappily at the seams.

Had the orb done something to her? She touched her face – it felt normal. She tried to see herself in the windows of the parked cars, but they were dark and distorting. So she put her head down and hurried back to Milton Lodge.

She crept into the flat, cold and exhausted, but instead of the hoped-for silence, she heard a voice; Esme was talking to someone. She closed the front door as silently as she could and edged into the living room.

'She's very slight, about a metre and a half tall. She has long light brown hair and noticeably large grey eyes. Well, actually sometimes they look green, or maybe hazel. But no, I'd say they're grey. What was she wearing? A duffel coat and my blue scarf is missing. . .'

'Esme?'

Her aunt spun round, startled. A small noise came out of her open mouth and she dropped the phone. Maggie could hear the voice on the other end of the line saying, 'Hello?' but Esme seemed unable to speak. So Maggie broke the silence with the only question that seemed to matter to her just then.

'What day is it?'

It turned out that it was Monday morning. She'd been away for nearly twenty-four hours and Esme was just reporting her as a missing person.

After the initial shock, Esme smothered her in embraces and kisses until her hair pyramid had lost all structure. Maggie felt embarrassed by such a show of emotion – it wasn't something she was used to – but secretly, it felt nice to have been missed.

Afterwards, when Maggie finally got a look at herself in the mirror, she realised why the respectable folk of West Minchen had been slightly perturbed to see her on their nice clean streets. Her face was covered in mud and she had a deep cut across one cheek she couldn't remember getting. It was dark with congealed blood, as were the cuts on her hands from the rope burn. Her long hair was greasy, tangled and full of leaves, and her clothes were caked in mud.

When she finally emerged from the bath, warm and clean, she found her aunt waiting for her with toast and hot chocolate. Maggie sat on the sofa and stuffed down a few slices before her aunt could ask the question she'd been dreading: 'For God's sake, Maggie, where on earth have you been?'

'I went to the woods to see if I could find Ida.'

'For a whole day and night? Where did you sleep?'

'I don't really know.'

'You don't know? Maggie, what are you talking about?'

'I mean, I slept in the woods.'

'Why would you do that? I've been so worried.' Esme shook her head, irritable suddenly. She stood up abruptly.

'You must be exhausted. Finish your hot chocolate and go straight to bed. We can talk about it tomorrow.'

Maggie didn't have to be asked twice. After she'd eaten some more toast, Esme helped her make up her bed on the sofa and she fell back into its old familiar sags into the deepest of sleeps.

When she woke it was the middle of the night, though which night she had no idea. She felt like she might have been asleep for a week. A cold breeze flowed over her and she shivered as she padded barefoot to the kitchen to get a glass of water.

The flat was silent and the digits on the old microwave read 03:04. Beyond, somewhere in the night, she heard a strange bird screeching. She shivered again. She felt a pain in her head, a throbbing. Cool air was coming through the back door, which was open for some reason. She turned. Through the kitchen hatch she saw a figure standing by the stuffed owl on the piano. And something pale glinted in the darkness: long white hair. Maggie froze with fear.

Miss Cane switched on the lamp on top of the piano and looked at Maggie with her wolf eyes. They glowed angrily for a moment and then went out, and the cold that remained was even more frightening.

Maggie looked around the little kitchen for something she could hit her with. But the pain in her head only got worse and, anyway, she knew it was pointless. An egg pan wasn't going to take out this woman or thing, or whatever she was. Without wanting or meaning to, Maggie found herself moving into the living room and sitting on the sofa.

'You were lucky. You confused one of the Children,' Miss Cane said in a dead empty voice, so different from the warm kindly simper she used at school. 'He got to a part of you he couldn't understand. That's the only reason you made it back here.'

Miss Cane drifted over to her and it was as if her feet barely touched the ground. She stood in front of her. 'Tell me,' and suddenly she lunged forward and dug her claws so hard into Maggie's shoulder that she cried out in pain. 'How did you cross over? Who helped you?'

'No one,' wailed Maggie. But the claws only went deeper. She started crying.

'Who helped you?'

Maggie felt little threads start to delve into her head like before, with the orb. 'Stop it! Stop it!' she screamed. 'I don't know, I don't know, honestly. I don't know how I did it. I just did it.'

To her surprise the threads retracted and suddenly Miss Cane was leaning right in her face. She could feel her hot meaty breath on her cheek. 'No one crosses to the Island without permission. You will never go back. You will promise me.'

Maggie managed a nod, but the claws dug in still deeper. 'If you dare to re-cross, the Children will know; they will find you. We will punish whomsoever helped you, and I will personally make sure you never get home again.'

Maggie's voice was tiny. 'Please let go,' she begged.

But the wolf-woman only smiled. 'And you won't find Ida there, either. She's gone for ever. Forget about her.'

Through the haze of pain, an abstract part of Maggie's brain noticed the cat. He was sitting in the open doorway observing Miss Cane like cats observe dogs from high fences – with an indistinguishable mixture of fear and contempt. But the mellifluous tongue of Miss Cane began again and mixed with the pain, Maggie forgot him. Her voice wasn't cold any more. It was sinewy and soft, a poison seeping into her veins.

'Fortlake School is a very good place for me. There is a lot of excellent material there. I'm not ready to leave. So if you dare mention me to the detective or that ridiculous headmistress again, I will end you in your own bed at night. Don't think I won't.'

Maggie was getting faint and she could feel the hot seep of her own blood staining her T-shirt. Her brain had almost accepted that this mad wolf-woman was never going to let go of her shoulder, when behind them, a door opened and there was the sound of footsteps shuffling along in old slippers. The terrible wolf eyes tore away from Maggie as Aunt Esme's fuzzy pyramid shuffled into view.

As it did, an odd look came over Miss Cane's face – a look almost like fear. She snarled at Maggie, showing her horrible pointed teeth. But she let go and Maggie slumped back. As Miss Cane ran out, she fell to all fours and Maggie glimpsed the thick white fur of the wolf disappearing into the darkness.

The main living room light was switched on and Esme appeared, squinting and confused.

'What on earth are you doing? Why is the back door open?'

Maggie didn't know where to start, so she just mumbled, 'I had a bad dream.'

Esme shook her head, still half-asleep. 'Well, close it, will you? And get that mog out of here.'

She shut the light off again and shuffled back to her room. Maggie put her hand to her shoulder and felt the hot seep of blood. She slumped down onto the floor and clutched her shoulder.

A low purring came from the side of the sofa. 'What *was* that thing?' The purring grew in intensity. 'It's like nothing I've ever smelt.'

Maggie wanted to burst into tears, but she gritted her teeth. Hoagy was no longer her friend. 'I'm glad it was interesting for you. Why are you here anyway? Has Fluffy kicked you out?'

'She *is* a little demanding,' the cat hissed.

'Poor you.'

'So you crossed to the other world?'

'What do you care?'

The cat seemed unperturbed. 'Did you notice how that thing was afraid of Esme?'

What was he talking about? Maggie suddenly felt overwhelmed. She wanted him to go away. 'No, I didn't and I don't care,' she replied angrily. 'Just go away. Go on, shoo! Shoo!'

Hoagy didn't move, but his eye had become an angry slit. 'You're shooing me? *Really*?' And he stalked out.

Wearily Maggie locked the back door and peered out into the darkness, but the wolf had gone. She went to the bathroom and cleaned up the blood that Miss Cane's claws had drawn from her shoulder then took a couple of painkillers. In the mirror she looked pale and unhappy. And she looked afraid.

Miss Cane had said that Ida was gone for ever, that she'd never find her. Just like Dot, she'd told her to forget her. But why would she go to such an effort if that was really true? Despite everything, this thought gave Maggie a little bit of hope.

She trailed back into the living room. If she did nothing, Ida would be lost for ever; if she went back, well, Miss Cane had told her exactly what she'd do. Maggie shivered. From his permanent perch, the stuffed owl looked at her mournfully. He'd seen everything, but he couldn't say a word – he was trapped. Maggie thought she knew just how he felt.

16

THE BETRAYAL

Maggie woke to the comforting sound of something sizzling in a pan. Esme was in the kitchen humming along cheerfully to some classical music on the radio. She poked her head through the hatch. 'Ah, you're up!'

Moments later she appeared, a pencil stuck into her restored beehive and a blue gingham apron Maggie had never seen before tied over her usual navy uniform. She carried two plates of sausage, eggs, beans and toast. She put them on the table and went back for the mugs of tea.

Maggie went sleepily to the table. 'Thanks.'

'Don't mention it, dear. You're getting too skinny.'

Last night's disturbance seemed to have been forgotten. And with the bright winter sunshine streaming in, Maggie wondered if it had all just been an awful dream. But then she felt the searing pain in her shoulder and the cold eyes of the wolf-woman flashed into her mind. The feeling of fear lurched back: she wasn't even safe here, in Esme's flat.

Esme let her eat most of her breakfast before saying, 'That detective is coming round in a little while.' She was trying to sound casual. 'What was his name again?'

Although it felt like a million years ago that she'd been interrogated in Le Crab's office, his name came to Maggie's lips at once, 'Hammond.'

'Ah, that's right, yes, Detective Hammond. I said you weren't feeling well, but he says he doesn't mind germs.' Esme coughed.

Maggie was filled with dread, 'What does he want?'

'He probably has some questions about Ida.' She gave Maggie a strange look, then noticed the marks on her T-shirt. 'Is that blood?'

Maggie clamped her hand over the large stain. 'I picked a spot.'

Esme nodded, unconvinced but maintaining her cheery air, which seemed somehow false. Her aunt was being kind of weird, Maggie thought.

After breakfast Esme brought in the local paper and then went out, promising to be back in time for Detective Hammond's arrival. To Maggie's horror the front page of the *West Minchen Bugle* featured a large photograph of Ida under the heading, 'LOCAL GIRL STILL MISSING'.

Ida was in her favourite pose – chin tucked in, looking out from under her eyelashes. But they'd managed to find a photo where she was smiling instead of pouting. No one looking at this photograph would believe how much she didn't like herself, thought Maggie. It didn't even seem possible to her any more. Maybe she'd got it wrong? Maybe she'd imagined it all.

Her mind wandered to the strange sunless land and the magnificent glittering city, crazier than any vision she'd ever had, and the little grey creature, and the jagged ice storm. None of that seemed real either. But something had to be.

Detective Hammond still sported the same rumpled suit and weary jowly face, but today his eyes were sharper, more hawkish. He smiled at her when he came in, but it was a cold smile.

'You don't look too poorly to me.'

The woman police officer with him smiled at Maggie too, but with bland cheeriness, and got out a notebook and pen. Hammond nodded at the paper on the sofa beside Maggie. Ida's face still stared up at them from it.

'I'll be honest with you, Maggie. Things aren't going well. Normally with a case like this, we'd have a lead – a sighting, something on CCTV, reports of a strange individual hanging around – but since Ida went missing, four days ago, *four days ago*,' he carefully enunciated these three words, 'we've heard nothing. That's a very long time, don't you think?'

Esme bustled in with the coffee and a plate of biscuits. She crashed the tray down on the table and all the cups rattled together.

'Look, Maggie,' said Hammond irritably waving away Esme's offer of refreshments, 'I don't think we should waste any more time. A couple of things have come up since I spoke to you.'

The woman officer slurped her coffee and, with a loud crack, made significant headway into a ginger snap. Hammond shot her a look of profound irritation, but pressed on.

'Miss Cane, whom you said you saw walking towards the woods at around the same time Ida disappeared, was with a pupil that day. The student had a prearranged counselling session and was there, with Miss Cane, at exactly three-twenty p.m. So we'd like to know why you said you saw her crossing the fields after Ida?'

Maggie felt the wound in her shoulder throb. Miss Cane had no doubt hypnotised some poor Fortlake kid into coming out with this rubbish, or maybe given them some similar marks on their shoulder.

'I did see her,' Maggie insisted. 'I don't know what she was doing. Maybe she just went out for some air. Maybe it had nothing to do with Ida. I never said it did. But I saw her out there and she was walking towards Everfall Woods.'

The officer scribbled down some notes.

'You're absolutely certain it was her?' asked Hammond.

'She's pretty distinctive.'

Hammond was studying her face. 'We also tracked Ida's phone signals. They're not always one hundred per cent accurate, but it seems the phone may have left the woods on Friday evening. Do you know anything about that?'

Maggie shook her head.

'So you're going to keep saying you found it in the woods on Saturday morning where you just happened to be going for a walk?'

'But I did.'

The scratch of the officer's pen on her notepad was the only sound as Hammond let the silence hang. Maggie felt hot and sticky from the lying.

The detective said nothing for a few more excruciating moments, then he changed tack. His face softened, though he couldn't get rid of his intense exhausted stare. He hiked up his crumpled trousers and sat forward in his seat, leaning a little towards Maggie. 'Look, Maggie. One thing we can be sure of is that people don't just vanish into thin air. Somebody always knows something. In fact they often know a lot. But they don't say anything. They're trying to protect somebody. Trust me, though, it's never a good idea.'

Maggie stared at his hairy legs visible above the worn-out socks.

'And I know there's something you're not telling me. Is there a boy involved? Someone older? Has Ida run away with him? Was something going on in her family that was upsetting her? Whatever it is, you have to tell me, Maggie. Because, listen up, I don't want to scare you, but these cases often don't end well, you understand me? By staying quiet you are putting Ida at risk. If anything happens to her, it could be your fault because you didn't speak to me today.'

The woman officer spoke for the first time, slightly pleadingly and under her breath, 'Boss,' and shook her head. But Hammond dismissed her brusquely with his hand.

Maggie looked at Ida's face staring up at her from the local paper. She felt sick. It was true – if anything happened to Ida, it would be her fault. But not in the way this man imagined.

Hammond interrupted her thoughts, 'Have you anything else to say to me, Maggie?'

Maggie shook her head. His eyes got harder and he stood up.

'Well, if anything comes back to you, call me here.' He dropped his card onto the table. The officer got up too and they both left. Maggie heard doors slam and a car revving and swiftly driving away.

After a moment she became aware of Esme hovering about in front of her. She was smoking in her usual fastidious way, but something was up. She sat down where the detective had been only a few minutes before and stubbed out her cigarette with a sigh. Maggie's eyes were suddenly drawn to the ouroboros ring: it glowed on Esme's finger, as if lit from its own private source. Maggie felt drawn to it. She wanted to reach out and touch it . . .

But then Esme coughed nervously. Maggie looked up

and saw that her eyes were troubled behind her glasses and she looked tired. It was the same expression Maggie had seen on her parents' faces before, a kind of resigned disappointed look when she was in trouble at school.

'You know, Miss Cane called me while you were away.'

Maggie's blood ran cold. Her mouth opened, but no sound came out.

'She's worried about you, Maggie. She told me a few things I didn't know.' Aunt Esme looked down and fiddled with her skirt hem. Then she looked up with a false brightness. 'None of it matters, my dear. You're going through a lot at the moment. I'm sure it's all quite natural.'

Maggie must have looked shocked because she went on, 'There's no need to look so worried. Really, she was very kind. She just told me she'd been helping you. That you're being bullied at school and that, well, there's an awful lot going on in your head.'

She coughed and put out her cigarette. 'Miss Cane thinks you might know where Ida's gone. And she warned me that when you came back you would spin some crazy tale that only someone with as good an imagination as yours could make up. Not that you've done that, but . . .'

Maggie wanted to be sick. And Aunt Esme kept talking in this new voice that didn't suit her; a responsible concerned voice, like adults put on sometimes, when basically what they're saying is: I don't believe you; I think you're a liar.

'What with the police and Ida and all of this, I have to wonder where you really went the other day. Did you really spend all that time in the woods? Can you tell me, Maggie? Because I think I should probably know, don't you? And Detective Hammond needs to know. This is serious.'

Maggie's voice trembled. 'You wouldn't believe me if I told you the truth. Just like Miss Cane said.'

'Try me, dearie. You never know.'

'I *do* know. That's why she called you. Can't you see that? She called you so you wouldn't believe me even if I told you.'

'Told me what?'

Maggie leapt to her feet in exasperation. 'I thought you were different, but you're just like all adults. You'll believe some creepy school counsellor over me though you don't even know her.'

'No, dearie, she was just concerned . . .'

'She's not concerned about anyone. She's pure evil.'

Esme sat back in surprise, close to laughter. 'I'm not sure I'm getting "pure evil" from Miss Cane, my dear.'

'Would you believe me if I told you she's taken Ida to another world? And that she's a wolf? And that she's threatened to kill me?'

'Maggie, come on—'

Maggie stood up. She was burning with anger. 'So that's why I can't tell you. Leave me alone!'

'Maggie! I'm sorry, I just—'

Maggie ran to the bathroom and slammed the door. She got into the pink bath, pulled the duvet she kept in there over her and lay back looking at the flaky paint on the ceiling and the suspicious damp brown stain in one corner. She'd never felt more alone in her life.

17

BACK TO SCHOOL CLUB

Maggie spent the next few days recuperating and trying not to speak to Esme whose efforts to be extra nice to her made her even more annoyed. Her mind was full of umons and orbs and ice rain and the wolf-woman, but she was too tired to figure it all out and she slept most of the time.

On Thursday afternoon she was woken at five p.m. by the shrill ring of Esme's ancient telephone. Her mum. She'd forgotten all about it.

She rolled off the sofa and ran to the phone, getting to it just before the machine picked up.

'Hi,' she said, rather breathlessly.

'Maggie?'

'Hi, Mum. How are you?'

'I'm not well, Maggie. You know that.'

'I'm sorry, I just meant are you feeling any better?'

'Why would I be?'

Maggie's heart sank. 'I don't know.'

There was one of their usual long silences until her mum dragged up the energy to ask her usual question, 'How is school?'

'It's half term.'

'Ah, so you've been having fun with your friends, I suppose.'

'Yes.'

Her mum knew she'd never really had any friends. She honestly didn't know why she did this every week. But then Cynthia Brown said something different that made Maggie long for their normal stilted conversation.

'I'm glad you're so self-sufficient, Maggie, that you're able to get along so well without me. Because if anything were to happen to me, I know—'

'What do you mean?'

'I mean, I know you would be OK.'

Maggie felt like screaming, 'I wouldn't be OK, I'm not OK.' But she said nothing.

'And that is a comfort to me.'

'But Mum, nothing's going to happen to you.'

'I hope you're being polite to Esme.'

'Yes.'

'And if you hear from your father—'

'I haven't heard from him.'

'Make sure he doesn't bring that woman to see you. Do you hear?'

*

When Monday came round again, Maggie didn't have much choice but to go back to school and act as if things were normal, at least until she came up with a new plan. She'd never imagined that her hatred for Fortlake could get any stronger. But that Monday morning her dread seemed almost insurmountable.

She walked so slowly she hoped she might be going backwards. And she felt very odd. Perhaps you couldn't just pop into other worlds without feeling changed, without leaving a bit of yourself behind? Because it felt like all the houses she passed, all the cars rushing by, the people in buses and those walking along the street were less real. It wasn't that she doubted their existence. It was just that this world didn't have the last word on things any more. Or maybe she felt more at home in the other world with its darkness, its strangeness? But she didn't like that idea too much.

The first person Maggie saw as she trudged into the concrete forecourt was Helena. She was sitting by the bike shed, alone, her headphones clamped over her ears. When she saw Maggie she stared at her hard. Not in the teasing, snide way like before. All that had gone. She looked at Maggie like she really hated her.

Maggie put her head down, rushed into the main school building and up to her classroom. Despite her best efforts, she was somehow on time for registration, so she pretended to be finishing work in her exercise books. She felt like everyone was staring at her, but was too nervous to look around and see if it was true.

All day no one said a word to her. Not her classmates, none of the teachers who merely nodded or dismissed her when she explained that she'd been ill and hadn't been able to do any of the homework they'd set for the half term. Even the dinner ladies seemed to be avoiding her. Only William Snowden was nice. He lent her a pen in maths and smiled at her.

It was such a relief when the last bell finally went. Maggie shoved all her books into her rucksack and ran out of the classroom. She didn't want to go back through the woods, so she left Fortlake by the main entrance and turned down the wide residential street instead. At first nothing seemed wrong. But after a while, Maggie became aware of a group of four or five kids on the opposite side of the road. She dared a quick glance and saw the nasty green of Fortlake blazers.

But it was only when the traffic quietened that she heard their chant:

'Maggie Blue Brown isn't well in the head,
She's weird and she's creepy, and she's better off dead!'

They sang so perfectly in unison: their hatred of her had really brought them together, which was nice. Maggie tried to smile, but she couldn't persuade the muscles in her face to move.

Still, if she kept her head down, she'd be OK. People lived on this street and cars kept coming past, obliterating patches of the song: *she's weird. . . she's creepy. . . dead. . . in the head. . .*

Keep walking, Maggie told herself. *Keep walking. They won't do anything. It's just a stupid song.*

It was quieter on the road now. But all she needed to do was cut up Church Lane, go round the crescent, and walk along the main road back to Milton Lodge. It was still ten minutes away, but if she picked up her pace she could cross over a little way ahead of them and run.

After another flow of cars went past, Maggie suddenly dashed across the road, and using her slight advantage, ran up Church Lane. But the group was determined, and her running gave them licence to pursue. Still chanting the song, albeit more raggedly, they managed to surround her halfway up the street. Maggie started walking again, but they blocked her way until she had to stop.

Helena stood right in front of her. Daisy was there too, not giggling for once. There was a girl called Thea that Maggie hardly knew, and two infamously mean girls from the opposite form called Rachel and Sita who, so far, Maggie had managed to avoid.

Around them the street was peaceful. Yellow lights glowed from the cosy safe homes and somewhere close by a would-be clarinettist stumbled up and down a minor scale.

'We were hoping to catch up with you, Bruise,' said Helena.

Behind her someone pulled at Maggie's battered rucksack. She recognised Rachel's smirking voice, 'Ninja Turtles? Really?'

Everyone sniggered and someone gave Maggie a shove from behind so that she nearly fell over.

Don't react, don't react, don't react.

'Why did you have Ida's phone, Bruise?' asked Helena, and her face looked very cold.

'I found it,' said Maggie in a very quiet voice she barely recognised.

'Don't lie, Bruise.'

'Did you do something to Ida? Something weird cos you're so in love with her?' Maggie turned. It was Rachel and her face was contorted by a sneer. 'Seriously, what did you do?'

'I didn't do anything.'

They weren't like the kids from her old school. They were nasty, but they'd probably never even been in a fight. They wouldn't touch her. They were soft. All she had to do was keep moving.

So Maggie waited a moment then nimbly sidestepped Helena and started walking really fast. They were quickly around her again, but she was right – they didn't actually get in her way. Instead they started whispering nasty stuff about her. Then Thea got her phone out and walked ahead taking photos.

'Why are you so weird, Bruise?'

'Why are you stupid?'

'Why are you so ugly?'

'What have you done with Ida?'

'What did you do to Ida?'

They danced around her like a Greek chorus, but she was almost at Church Crescent. A man walking a black and tan terrier went past and pretended not to see anything. Only the dog looked at Maggie and its face was very kind.

Finally they were coming round the corner and Maggie felt a surge of relief as she saw the main road ahead with all the lights from the cars rushing past. She was aware of a couple of people on the other side of the street looking – but maybe they thought it was just a game.

Thea still walked backwards, the flash on, videoing the whole thing Maggie now assumed. They would probably share it later on messages and laugh at her.

So let them, thought Maggie, and the first dangerous flash of red burst in her chest like a firework. *Don't react, don't react, don't react* . . . She was almost at the main road.

They were still whispering their lame insults at her and she was breathless from walking along so fast when she heard Helena's voice cut through, suddenly louder than the others, 'You're going to be a mental patient, too.'

Blood pounded in Maggie's ears and almost crushed the

breath out of her lungs. She span round and saw Helena's stupid mean expression, her leering enjoyment of the fact she'd finally hit a nerve. 'You're going to be a mental patient, just like your mum.'

Without another thought in her brain, Maggie punched Helena in the face as hard as she possibly could.

At least she was missing double physics, Maggie thought. There was always a silver lining. It was 9.30 a.m. and Maggie was sitting in Le Crab's office, Esme beside her. Le Crab, at her desk, was monumental in indigo. Whilst on the other side of the room sat Helena with one very large black eye and two very concerned parents.

They had all just watched a video of Maggie punching Helena in the face, though naturally the minutes of footage leading up to this moment had been thoughtfully edited out. As had the sound, which Thea claimed had failed. So although it was clear Helena had said something to upset Maggie, no one could hear what it was, and for some reason she couldn't explain, Maggie refused to tell anyone.

All in all, it was a succinct short film featuring Maggie Blue Brown, unwanted ward of Ms Esme Durand, punching Helena Grace Thompson, beloved only child of Debbie and Chris Thompson, squarely in the face.

It was hard for Maggie not to extract a tiny bit of pleasure from seeing the shock on Helena's face when she realised she was actually being hit. But it was a hollow void-like pleasure, a feeling of total emptiness behind a millisecond of triumph.

In truth, Maggie felt like crying, but she'd managed to set her face into a mask. With a little help from digging her fingernails into her palms, which were still raw from when she'd climbed out of the hole in the dark world, and so hurt more. The pain helped keep the mask on.

Now it was time for the summing up. Le Crab turned her haughty attention to Helena first. 'Helena, it's quite clear to me that you and the others are far from blameless—'

Here Mr Chris Thompson raised his hand and made a slight high sound like a cat mewing, but one stern look from Le Crab and he was instantly silenced.

The headmistress continued, 'For now, please go back to class. I'll speak with you and the others later this week. As the nurse has already indicated, if you have any headaches or feel at all unwell, please go and see her immediately. You may return to class.'

The Thompsons got up and filed out silently, though not before Helena had shot Maggie a strange look. It wasn't triumphant nor was it full of the same hatred as before. But Maggie didn't have time to wonder what was going on in Helena Thompson's head or anyone else's, because Le Crab now turned her terrifying attention onto her.

'Miss Brown, I can see you were provoked. And quite frankly, no one has yet been able to give me a satisfactory explanation as to why five girls were dancing around you, videoing you on the street. Girls whom, I happen to know, are not your friends.' She paused to assess Maggie. 'But all this pales in comparison to the horrible violence you used against a fellow pupil of this school. Have you any idea how serious that is? Let me tell you. It is deadly serious. Do you understand?'

Maggie nodded and looked down.

'Not only that, it has come to my attention that you lied about seeing a member of my staff going to the woods on the day of Ida Beechwood's disappearance. It is a lie that has wasted police time in what is a very terrible matter for the school and the community.'

'I didn't—'

But Le Crab cut her off. 'I'm not saying you understood the seriousness of your lie, Maggie, but it was still a lie. You are a grave disappointment to everyone here at Fortlake School.'

After her monologue, the headmistress let silence hang in the air during which Maggie continued to dig her nails into her sore hands even harder until the pain was excruciating. Esme wasn't looking at her and hadn't for a long time.

Le Crab continued, 'I have no choice but to suspend you from school. During this time, you will catch up on *all* the work that you have failed to complete. You will hand this in directly to me in two weeks' time, when you will also hear the decision on your future at Fortlake.'

She coughed and vaguely shuffled some papers round on her desk. 'Ms Durand has informed me that your mother is perhaps not in a fit state to receive a call from me. However, I will be calling your father later today to inform him of what's going on.' She looked at Maggie coldly. 'That's it. You can go.'

Maggie and Esme stood up. But for some reason Maggie felt compelled to speak. Or more it felt like the words tumbled out of her mouth against every scrap of common sense she possessed. But she'd been thinking of it since this woman had called her a liar.

'I don't care what you think about all the other things, but I'm telling the truth about Miss Cane. You need to watch her, she—'

Le Crab looked utterly shocked. She shot out of her chair so that she towered above them both, a dark menace. 'You're lucky I haven't expelled you without review. Please remove yourself immediately.'

'Come on, Maggie,' Esme said softly, and she took Maggie's hand and dragged her out.

Maggie trudged along with a heavy bag full of assignments. She'd promised to do it all, of course, but secretly she'd decided that she wouldn't be doing a thing. The worst they could do was to expel her, and that was fine with her.

Esme smoked silently beside her. She didn't seem angry,

just fed up. She was probably wishing she'd never let her come to stay. Maggie could hardly blame her.

As they turned onto the weed-infested driveway they saw the one-eyed cat sitting on the doormat. He held something that looked a bit like a cigar between his jaws.

'That wretched cat,' sighed Esme. 'You'd think he'd have got the message by now.'

Maggie said nothing. She missed Hoagy a lot. But she would never say sorry – wild horses couldn't drag an apology out of her because it wasn't her fault. He'd proved he didn't care about her at all, and that was that. When she walked past, she didn't even look at him.

Before Esme went out that night, Maggie got some textbooks, spread them around herself in the living room and tried to look busy. But as soon as she heard the front door close, she pushed them all aside and sat staring at the wall. She wished she could disappear.

The phone ringing made her jump, but she ignored it and soon heard Esme's stupid answerphone message speaking into the empty hall. The caller didn't leave a message, but immediately the phone rang again, and then again. By the fourth time Maggie was on her feet, but she just missed it. It rang yet again and this time she snatched it up. '*What?!*'

'Maggie?' said a familiar voice. 'Is that you?'

'Who's that?' Maggie asked, but she already knew.

'Dot.'

'Esme's gone out.'

'But it's you I want to speak to.'

Maggie didn't feel like talking to anyone. 'What is it?'

'You never told me how you got on.'

'With what?'

'If you crossed to the other world or not.'

'You said it was impossible, didn't you?'

'You couldn't do it?' Dot sounded disappointed. 'For some reason I thought you were . . . Well, sorry to bother you . . .'

'But I did cross,' Maggie blurted out.

There was a long pause then, 'Can you come over to see me, Maggie?'

'Now?'

'Yes. *Now.*'

Maggie walked through the empty West Minchen back streets. She wasn't entirely sure why she was going there, except that Dot had said that she must. And she was the only person who had ever taken her seriously and had listened when she'd said there was something off about this stupid place.

She rang the bell and the door opened immediately, as if Dot had been waiting in the hall for her to arrive.

'Come in, my dear.'

Maggie followed her into the large room with the snooker table now lit only by two low lamps. She sat down in the same battered armchair and told the old lady everything.

There was no one else after all. Dot didn't interrupt once and when she had finished there was a silence so long that Maggie wondered if she still believed her. But then Dot spoke and her voice was trembling with excitement.

'I knew you were special, Maggie, from the moment I met you. I just didn't realise how special.'

Maggie had often fantasised about someone saying this to her. But now it was happening she wasn't sure that she liked it.

'I know people who can help you find her, people in the other world. They're called moon witches. They will help you rescue Ida.'

'Witches?' Maggie exclaimed. 'Really?'

'They won't be sitting on broomsticks and cackling, if that's what you're worried about.' Dot shook her head and muttered, 'How they ever came up with all that rubbish I'll never know.'

'Why would they help me?'

'Because I'll ask them to.'

Maggie frowned. 'But how do you even know them?'

Dot ignored her and instead clapped her hands together with glee. 'Normal people cannot cross between worlds. Don't you understand?'

No, Maggie did not understand at all; she didn't want to. 'But I am normal.'

Dot was almost dancing in her chair. 'Are you sure?'

'Of course, I'm sure.'

'Maybe you don't really know yourself, Maggie. Maybe you don't know who you are at all.'

'That's not true!' Maggie said angrily. But what Dot was saying frightened her. Secretly she'd always felt like something about her life didn't quite add up; that she and her mum were more than just a bit different.

'You want to rescue your friend, don't you?' said Dot, interrupting her thoughts. 'You're the only person who can do it. Without you, Ida is lost.'

'Really?'

'*Really.*'

'But how do you know all this?' Maggie persisted.

'It doesn't matter. I know a lot of things,' Dot hissed. 'Just listen. There is one very important thing. When you cross, you must take the ouroboros with you.'

'Esme's ring?' asked Maggie, astonished.

'Yes.'

'But she won't even let me try it on.'

Dot's voice hardened, 'Then you must take it.'

Maggie was shocked. 'I can't steal it.' Finding a bit of change from behind the sofa cushions was one thing, but taking Esme's beloved ring?

'It's an amulet,' Dot said.

'A what?'

'It protects you from evil things.'

'But why would I need that?' asked Maggie, feeling a quiver of fear go through her.

'The serpent eating its own tail is an ancient symbol of wholeness, infinity, and power through balance. Evil things don't like to go near it and it will give you strength.' Dot's voice trembled with emotion suddenly. 'It is the most precious object in the universe. Once you have put it on, you must promise to never take it off.'

'What is this all about?'

But Dot ignored her again. 'Do you promise me? If you want the strength to rescue Ida you must wear it.'

'I don't know if I'm going back yet.'

'Yes, you do. Do you promise?'

There wasn't exactly much for her in this world, but she still hated being bossed around. 'Fine,' Maggie snapped, 'I promise.'

'Good. Now help me into my bed. I'm exhausted.'

And it was true: Dot had become very haggard-looking over the course of their *tête-à-tête*, as if the conversation had drained her of energy.

Maggie pushed the old lady into the back room and helped her onto a low bed covered in tartan rugs. She was tiny, like a little bird, and Maggie found she could easily pick her up in her arms. She noticed how thin Dot's skin was – it was almost translucent.

As she laid her gently on top of the bed, Dot mumbled, 'The one-eyed cat will accompany you. I will tell him how to find the witches – you can't do it alone.'

Maggie was surprised. 'You can hear him talking too?'

'Lord, yes. I only wish I could switch him off.'

Maggie laughed despite herself, but she said, 'He won't come with me.'

'The one-eyed one is devoted to you,' Dot insisted.

Maggie shook her head. 'Hoagy doesn't care about anyone but himself.'

The old lady smiled sleepily. 'He was very agitated when you went to the other world. He even went and hung around the woods waiting for you to come back.'

Maggie frowned. 'Are you sure?'

But Dot was already fast asleep and snoring lightly.

Maggie felt relieved to get out of there and walk back to Milton Lodge in the cool night air. She could not have imagined that as soon as she closed the door of the flat, Dot sat bolt upright in her bed as far from sleep as it was possible to be. She wrung her tiny wrinkled hands together and her face was riven with anxiety.

18

TOGETHER

Hoagy sat on the window ledge in the miserable drizzling cold clutching the small leather case between his jaws. How it had come to this, he'd never know. His tail flicked violently with irritation. Witches could ask cats favours and, for some reason, cats tended to obey them. It wasn't a spell, exactly, more that they were the only people in the known universe who could actually tell a cat what to do.

So against all his better judgement he had found himself promising Dot to go to another world with this girl. And now it was promised, he could not go back. He might as well get on with it.

He observed the girl as she sat at the small table eating toast. She was very different to other humans, though he couldn't say quite how. She was like a little sprite, hardy and self-contained, with her huge eyes that seemed to see beyond this world and her long tangled hair that she never brushed. She was so slight, so vulnerable-looking, that even an old campaigner like him felt the need to try and protect her. Still, he couldn't quite forget her wish that he be run over on the way to Barbara's. That truly was below the belt. So he would do what was asked of him and no more.

He tapped on the glass and the girl span round. Her face broke into a smile that she immediately repressed, as she remembered that she was supposed to hate him. She walked over and let him in without a word. As soon as the door was open a crack he whipped inside. Esme might be stingy with the heating, but anything was better than sitting in that freezing garden all night.

Hoagy jumped up onto the sofa and dropped the little leather case he'd been clutching between his jaws for hours.

Maggie grabbed it. 'What's this?'

'It's a message Dot wants me to take to the witches. She's forbidden me to look at it.'

'But she hasn't forbidden me,' Maggie said. And she began trying to prize it open, but it was sealed with a solid reddish wax. After a while she gave up and dropped it back on the sofa beside him.

'You're definitely going back?' he asked.

Maggie looked down and he could see that she was afraid. 'I don't know. I suppose so. Dot says I'm the only one who can rescue Ida.' She sat down beside him and allowed him to snuggle close to her. He could tell that she was trying not to cry. Eventually she said, 'How old are you, Hoagy?'

'Who me? Eleven.'

'And how old's that in cat years?'

'Oh pah! That's all rubbish. I'm eleven, that's all.' He began to clean his back furiously, licking away the thought.

'Did Dot tell you we have to take Esme's ring?'

The cat nodded. 'She mentioned it. Don't worry – it won't be a problem.'

An hour or so later they heard the heavy outer door of the Lodge slam and a few moments later Esme talking to herself in the corridor outside.

By the time she came through the front door, Maggie was on the sofa pretending to be asleep and he was hiding under her duvet. The fact that Esme's noisy shuffle around the kitchen suggested some sherry may have been consumed during her musical evening, only worked in their favour. Finally, after dropping the butter knife twice, stubbing her toe on the door and giving a small yelp, Esme wandered off to bed singing an uneven lyrical tune.

Immediately Hoagy emerged from his hiding place and purred loudly. 'The old bag is tipsy. Quite perfect. I'll give her a few minutes and then . . .' He jumped off the sofa without bothering to conclude and after a few moments he was in the corridor listening at Esme's door.

He sat there, stock still, for half an hour or so, until he

was sure she was asleep. Then slowly he pushed open the door. The bedside light was on and Esme was lying on top of the covers still fully dressed and snoring her head off. He drew closer.

She looked oddly frail at that moment, her sharp gaze hidden by slumber. Quite suddenly he regretted his betrayal. He shouldn't have sought revenge for being locked out by breaking in, peeing all over the flat *and* leaving a dead vole on Esme's pillow – that had been a bit much. Then again, there'd been no call for Esme to chase him with a broom and block up the cat flap.

The undisputed fact of the matter was that Mrs Hacker gave him chicken and gravy for every meal and Hoagy was convinced that no feline in North London could have resisted that lure.

He leapt noiselessly onto the bed and slunk close to her. Then using his pink rasping tongue he gently eased the ring from her finger. As he did he felt nostalgic – a very dangerous emotion for a cat. He was sorely tempted to stay there and snuggle by her side until morning rather than disappearing into another world with the girl. But it was too late now.

Silently he dropped back to the floor and padded into the living room, holding the ring delicately in his jaws, a hunter with the spoils.

Maggie was sitting up expectantly. 'Did you get it?'

He jumped up onto the sofa, unclenched his teeth and dropped it into her lap: the golden ring. Maggie picked it up and they examined it. The snake's body was made of gold, a very lustrous almost pink colour that glowed in her hand as if lit from its own private source. Encrusted on the serpent's head and body were tiny emeralds and diamonds that vanished along the very bottom, then reappeared again just as the tail disappeared into the snake's mouth.

'It's so beautiful,' said Maggie.

'And powerful,' he purred.

'How did you get it?' Maggie asked.

'Oh, it was easy. I just licked her fingers until it slid off. She's out for the count.' Suddenly Hoagy's fur bristled. 'Maggie, I never told you about the wolf-woman.'

'Miss Cane?'

'Urrgh. I have never encountered a beast like that. Anyway, you were so busy *shooing* me out, you missed something.'

'What?'

'When Esme came in and she disappeared? It had nothing to do with the old lady. It was the ring. Things that have bad intentions don't like amulets, especially not powerful ones.'

'Actually she was a bit like that in Le Crab's office, too,' said Maggie thoughtfully. 'She must be afraid of it. That's something then.'

She slipped the ring onto her middle finger. At first it was too big, but to their astonishment the ring tightened on her finger – the snake ate more of its tail – until it was a perfect fit.

'Did you see that?' she whispered to Hoagy and the old cat nodded thoughtfully. She stared at it in wonder. 'Maybe it will protect me?'

'I don't really know how it works,' Hoagy remarked, 'but as long as it deters that awful Cane creature, I shall be satisfied.' He shot Maggie a dark look. 'I've heard about shape-shifters before, but I've never met one . . . or smelt one. Quite revolting.'

'Shape-shifters? How do you know all this?'

'Cats know most things. It was quite right we were so worshipped by the Egyptians. I really think someone should bring that back. But that's another matter. Now, are we ready?'

They were not. He sat perfectly still as he watched Maggie creep round the kitchen putting whatever food she could find into her rucksack. She packed water and Hoagy's sealed leather case, then changed into jeans, T-shirt, trainers and a warm jumper.

Then she sat down and wrote a note to her aunt on the back of a Musicians' Union envelope, which he read over her shoulder:

Dear Esme,

I really appreciate you being so kind to me, and I'm sorry I'm in so much trouble at school. But it'll all be fine, so please don't worry.

Also, I'm really sorry, I had to borrow your ring. I will bring it back. I just really need it for now. Sorry again.

Love, Maggie x

Maggie sighed, folded the paper in two and wrote 'ESME' in big letters on the side. It was all a little pathetic, thought Hoagy. But that was humans for you.

Having reassured her that cats have an internal clock that is totally reliable, he promised to wake her at six a.m. So she shoved him up a bit, got under the duvet and they both fell asleep.

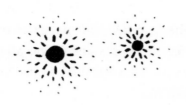

19

THE RETURN

When Maggie and Hoagy got to the copse the next morning, pale light rising around them, they found Dan the Tree sitting in his usual spot. He beckoned them over.

'We were in a forest just like this one,' he whispered conspiratorially, as if they were in the middle of a conversation, 'but I never saw any light there. We were in the dark world.' His watery eyes grew larger. 'She dragged me along the ground as if I weighed no more than a twig.'

Maggie and the cat looked at each other not knowing what to say.

'When I got back – and I don't know how I got back – I didn't have a scratch on me, except for this. Look.'

He lifted a clump of his lank greying hair up at the back of his neck. Just behind his left ear, Maggie saw a small hole, or at least it had been a hole. His flesh had grown over it again so that it was slightly raised. It made Maggie feel a bit sick.

He turned back to her and his awful melancholy eyes grew harder. He stood up and Maggie realised again how tall he was. He was like a wide oak tree. 'Do you know how to kill a shape-shifter?'

Maggie shook her head; she didn't want to know how to kill anything.

'By not caring what happens to you. They prey on fear and on hope. But if you have none, they can't control you any more. Then you just stab them, right through the heart.' He smiled and Maggie caught an unwelcome glimpse of jumbled brown teeth.

Maggie shivered. He was frightening her.

The huge man stepped closer to her so she could smell his unwashed scent. 'Why are you going back?'

'I have to find my friend. I mean, actually, we're not really friends—'

'Don't bother explaining,' Hoagy hissed irritably behind her.

Dan the Tree shook his head slowly. 'You won't find her.'

'I will,' Maggie said defiantly.

But he didn't seem to hear. 'If you need me, I will be there.'

'But you can't even cross,' Maggie reminded him.

But Dan the Tree only shook his head. 'I know it's my destiny to return, to go back to the dark world. I will be ready and this time I won't be afraid.'

Maggie nodded, certain she didn't want Dan the Tree

to be ready for anything. She gestured at the copse behind her. 'Well, you know, we'd better get going.'

Dan the Tree nodded and pushed his glasses up his nose again with his filthy fingers. Without another word he wandered off through the trees until he was lost from view.

Hoagy licked his lips as if trying to rid himself of a bad taste. 'That man has gone past the point of needing a bath. He requires a jet wash.'

Maggie turned back to the copse. To the place she had seen the portal last. Very easily this time the window appeared, its edges shivering in the cold air.

She glanced at the cat. He looked so old and worn out with the rips in his ears. 'Are you ready?'

Hoagy sniffed. 'What have I got to be ready for?'

'I mean, are you sure you want to come?'

'Do I have a choice? Besides, I've done a lot worse than visit "the dark world" or whatever that man calls it,' he boasted, puffing out his chest.

Maggie couldn't help but smile, but she still hesitated. Something inside was screaming at her not to go back. But the cat leapt up onto her shoulders and his radiator-like warmth gave her a little courage. And on her finger, she felt the ring: it was hot; it sort of glowed on her finger. As it did, she felt stronger and her mind became clearer.

Maggie moved over to the window, reached out and touched it. She let the shock pass through her for a moment then gently separated the two layers. Gritting her teeth, she let go of the West-Minchen layer so that the current surged through her. This time, to spare them both too much fur-raising electricity, she jumped straight through.

She felt Hoagy fly off her shoulders. For some time she fell alone through a dull white light until she landed with a heavy thud on the soft earth of the other-world forest. She lay there for a few moments, winded and sore.

It was the white-time and a pale unhappy light clung around the tops of the trees.

Hoagy sniffed the air, his whiskers twitching manically for a few seconds. 'Let's go. It doesn't smell right here.'

Maggie looked around – it was the same endless sea of dark trees disappearing to an invisible horizon. 'Are you sure you know where you're going?'

Hoagy's fur bristled. 'Do you think I'd allow myself to be led into an unknown world by a hapless human if my cat-nav wasn't in tip-top condition? I know where we're going.'

'Fine. I was just asking.'

The forest was silent apart from the crunch of their feet and paws on the leaves. The cat went ahead, his tail curling, constantly sniffing the air and sometimes the trees, as if that helped him find his way.

After a while the land rose up slightly. Hoagy raced on in front of her and Maggie saw he was sniffing at a low crumbling brick wall. The trees were sparser here and a little further on the land suddenly dropped away into a large hole. Hoagy sniffed at it urgently. Then he ran off into the trees.

'Where are you going?' Maggie cried and dashed after him.

But the old cat kept up a relentless pace. They raced past more overgrown holes of varying shapes and sizes, and occasionally dark rusty shards of steel that stuck out of the ground at strange angles. Then the trees began to thin out even more and the land kept rising.

'Ha!' Hoagy purred triumphantly, as they mounted the crest of a hill. 'This must be the Strange Plains. Dot told me about this. It's like the heath at home, except in more garish colours.'

Sure enough the ground was covered in heather that glowed in various shades of neon pink and purple. And amidst it grew slender mushrooms, their translucent caps balancing on gossamer stalks, tiny land-loving jellyfish like the ones she had seen in the little umon's sack.

Panting, Maggie stood beside the cat and looked over an entirely new terrain. Darkness was falling and ahead of them a huge full moon glimmered over the pinkish glowing plain that eventually rose up again into distant hills.

But even from here, you could see that the land had been ravaged. Wide horizontal steps had been cut into the hillside revealing a rich dark peat. And they could see lights in the distant hills glinting across the vast empty space.

The crossing through the portal and the walk in the thick cold air had made them tired, so they shared some water and lay back in the heather. It wasn't completely dark yet, but they could see the stars. There were thousands of them bunched into tight brilliant clusters, no patterns or constellations like there were in their world. Then again you hardly ever saw the stars in West Minchen – more often the night sky was tinged with a polluted orange haze that hid them all.

'This Ida creature,' purred Hoagy, after a while. 'She must be very special. I mean, she doesn't like you, she bullies you and yet here we are in a whole other world to find her.'

'You didn't have to come,' said Maggie, annoyed he'd brought it up.

'Pah!' said the cat. 'That's debatable. The question is, why did you?'

'No one saw what happened to Ida except me. And they wouldn't believe me if I told them. I mean, even if she was my worst enemy, I'd still try and help her.' But, the thought flashed involuntarily into her mind: if Helena or Daisy had disappeared, would she really have come back?

'Is that so?' retorted the cat, equally unconvinced.

'You'd rescue another cat if, I don't know, they were drowning in a pond or something. Even if you hated them.'

'Yeessss,' drawled Hoagy, 'but only if I happened to be walking past. I wouldn't take the trouble of going to another world to find the pond.'

'That's cats for you then,' said Maggie sharply, ready to change the subject. 'Anyway, I'll probably get expelled when I get back, so even if we do find Ida, I won't know her any more.'

Hoagy's ears pricked up with interest. 'Expelled?'

'I punched someone in the face.'

Hoagy's purring surged. '*You* punched someone?'

'This stupid girl Helena said some bad stuff about my mum.'

'*You* punched someone?' Hoagy repeated incredulously.

Maggie shrugged. 'I lose my temper sometimes. Everything's fine and then someone says something or does something unfair, and suddenly I feel this red surging through me, and I do something stupid.'

'I'm scandalised,' purred Hoagy, thoroughly enjoying himself. 'What else have you done?'

'Oh, I don't know.' Maggie thought about it. 'I got mad with this girl at my old school once so I shoved her and she just happened to fall over and break her collarbone, but that was an accident. And anyway, she'd been shoving me about too. And I hit this boy once because he bullied a girl in my old class, he kept telling her she was fat and ugly. But he didn't tell anyone I hit him because I was a girl, so I didn't get into trouble for that. I punched a couple of walls in my mum and dad's house once.' Maggie had never said it all out loud before. When you put it all together, it wasn't a great CV.

'Impressive,' purred the cat, and she could tell that he was smiling his funny cat smile.

He was lying on his back, one paw stretched out over his head, the other half-bent over his white belly. Maggie smiled too and rubbed his tum, and his purr turned into something akin to a loitering motorcycle.

'But you're a fighter,' she said. 'You must have done worse than that.'

'I could fight off several tomcats single-pawedly in my heyday,' Hoagy recounted, modestly. 'I'm quite legendary in the West Minchen area. But I've never lost my temper.'

'You've lost your temper at me,' Maggie reminded him.

'Tsssk. Not really. Cats get annoyed, irritated, irked, disgruntled, peeved, but never angry. That's human stuff. From my observations, it's an awful lot like when you cry. Just with different noises and facial expressions.'

'Don't cats cry?' asked Maggie.

'Pah! We don't even have the necessary glands.' Hoagy rolled back onto his belly and looked at her, his one eye glinting mischievously in the half-light. 'You know, I read the girl's diary.'

Maggie stared at him in amazement. 'You read Ida's diary?'

The cat's eye narrowed with pleasure. 'I was so bored

with Barbara one day that I wandered into Ida's bedroom and picked the lock. Another thing I'm rather good at. That's why Esme installed bolts on the back door.'

'Ida's diary has a lock on it?'

'Tragic, isn't it? Especially as it's such dull stuff. She hates her dad – no arguments there – but otherwise she just complains about everything. There's a boy she likes and there are lots that like her. There's a bit of stuff about her friends annoying her and homework and worrying about her hair. Hardly Pulitzer-Prize-winning.'

'Which boy does she like?'

'Someone called Snow.'

Maggie couldn't believe it. 'William Snowden?'

'That's it. She thinks he likes her too, but he's too shy.'

Maggie felt an unexpected pang. Without realising it, she'd let herself think William Snowden maybe liked her a little bit. But why would he? Anyway, she wasn't interested in boys. So she said, 'Does she mention me at all?'

'Quite a few times.'

'What does she say?'

The cat stretched out luxuriantly, enjoying himself. 'Hmmmm, let's see. That you're weird, that you don't have any friends, that your clothes are extremely lame.'

'Does she mention the fact she's always horrible to me?' she asked indignantly.

'Humans don't tend to mention their faults,' observed Hoagy.

'Not even in their diaries?'

'Especially not there.'

Maggie shook her head. 'Ridiculous.'

'She does say something else.'

'What?' asked Maggie, trying not to sound too eager.

'That even though she thinks you're sad and weird, she sometimes feels like she wants to talk to you. Typical human rubbish.'

Maggie smiled. Maybe it hadn't been a total lie when Ida had spoken to her by the lockers, when she'd suggested they be friends?

Hoagy sniff-sniffed the air and his eye narrowed. He looked from side to side.

Maggie was watching him carefully. 'Do you still know where we're going?'

'Of course,' he purred, but then his tail flicked beside him. 'The only thing is . . . It's confusing here. I'm not sure navigation is the same in this world. But I'll be fine. I'll figure it out.'

'You don't know where we are?' exclaimed Maggie.

'Not exxaaactly.'

'Hoagy?!'

'I've got us this far, haven't I? That's more than you could have done. I just need a nap.'

He got up and shook himself, and a tiny *eeoow* escaping his mouth as he did a big yawn. He padded round in a circle a few times and was about to resettle when his ears pricked up and his whole body went tense. He looked out into the darkness.

Maggie sat up, 'What is it?'

'Look!' hissed Hoagy.

In the distance, a line of bright flickering lights moved swiftly across the glowing plain. Maggie and Hoagy flattened themselves into the heath and watched as the procession came closer.

Maggie recognised the bright lanterns of the umons. It was a group of about twenty of them, all running rapidly, one or two racing along on all fours.

'Umons,' she whispered.

'U-whats?' asked Hoagy.

'They're these little creatures that live here,' Maggie explained. 'I met one when I was here before.'

'Don't you mean huge rats?'

'Are they going in the right direction?'

'I think that's the general direction,' he muttered.

Maggie jumped up. 'We should follow them. They can help us.'

Hoagy's tail flicked. 'But we've no idea where they're going.'

'Yes, but they're going *somewhere*,' said Maggie. 'Come on.' And she started to scramble down the side of the rock. Reluctantly, Hoagy followed and they slipped down together onto the pinkish soil.

20

THE GREAT O

The one saving grace was that the land was flat, but the umons moved rapidly and the soft ground made it hard going. Before long, Maggie was panting and Hoagy's thick pink tongue stuck out like a piece of velcro.

When they finally reached the base of one of the hills the ground began to slope upwards. And as it did, everything grew lighter. The terrain had changed to dry grassland where odd black flowers shaped like tiny cylindrical tubes grew amidst a few clusters of the little mushrooms.

Up ahead, the umons ran straight over the hill, but when Maggie and Hoagy reached the top, panting and exhausted, they stopped in their tracks. The biggest and most beautiful moon Maggie had ever seen hung low in the sky, bathing the land in bright, luminous light. Maggie was transfixed and the magical glow filled her brain so fully that she felt like staying there for ever.

But then, in the distance she heard the umons barking

and howling at each other. She snapped out of her reverie and looked round, but her eyes were too dazzled. Maggie blinked furiously and they cleared just in time for her to see the last yellow lantern disappear round a bend far below them on the other side of the hill.

'Hoagy!' she cried, but he was still in a trance. 'Hoagy!' He didn't move. So she yanked his tail and a terrific mewling sound came out of his mouth.

'Come on! We're losing them!' she shouted and started running down the slope. It was much steeper on the other side and loose earth slid away from under her feet. She landed at the bottom in a heap. Seconds later a pile of fur arrived beside her, jumped up nimbly and swiped at her with a vicious left hook.

Maggie clutched her arm. 'Owww! What did you do that for?'

'Don't ever touch my tail again,' Hoagy hissed, and in the sharp shadows of the moonlight he looked quite wild.

'You were fixated on the moon, you idiot. And now we've lost them.'

'To hell with those weird grey things,' spat Hoagy.

'So much for not losing your temper,' Maggie retorted.

'I told you. Spending too much time with humans has a terrible effect on felines.'

'So you keep saying. Come on.'

Maggie set off along a rough path that had been cleared through the grass. It curved in a wide sweep around a body of water whose ripples caught like stop-frame animation in the chilly moonlight.

As Maggie rounded the corner, she saw the enormous moon in front of her again, its luminous disc nearly touching the water. Silhouetted sharply against it was a wooden cabin around which a large crowd of umons had gathered, their lanterns flickering together like one huge spark. At the edge of the crowd, hooded figures only slightly taller than the umons stood, still and watchful.

The umons had organised themselves into regimented rows. Each held a small stick in their left paw and a lantern in their right. On the cries of the hooded figures they went through a series of manoeuvres before practising fighting against one another, shouting in time as they clashed sticks. On another shout, they all dropped their sticks, placed their lanterns more carefully on the turf and ran into the lake.

Maggie and the cat crouched down in the long grass and watched as the umons splashed about in the water chattering and barking happily, until, on more shrill cries from the hooded figures, they returned to shore and sat quietly on their haunches.

Now a low mellifluous voice came from somewhere. Maggie couldn't make out any words clearly as the soft chant flowed up and around the little valley. It was hypnotic and her eyes were drawn to an even tinier figure that hobbled out by the lakeside. The voice was so intoxicating that Maggie didn't notice when one then two umons stood up and sniffed the air. Nor did she notice when several more began to move stealthily through the long grass.

She only knew things had gone wrong when she felt something strike the small of her back. Maggie cried out, painfully winded, and tried to roll over but the little creatures were all over her. She heard Hoagy screech and hiss beside her, and saw a windmill of his flailing claws.

The chanting had stopped and barking umons now completely surrounded her, their paws pressing her to the ground, their snouts pushing into her eyes and ears, and the sound of their excited chattering filling her brain. After struggling a little, Maggie gave up and let herself be lifted by multiple tiny paws.

She was carried into the cabin. It was completely bare inside except for lanterns that burnt low and a small tapestry hanging on one wall that showed the moon against a deep blue sky. The umons laid her down gently on the floor and multiple pairs of big anxious eyes surrounded her.

Then Maggie heard a faint but familiar voice. 'Girl from another place?'

She looked around. 'Frank!'

His worried face loomed over her. 'You came back, friend.'

But then came the same mellifluous voice she'd heard by the lake: 'Leave them.' And Frank's face faded away with all the others.

Maggie sat up and saw a very wrinkled old man wearing a dark brown robe tied with a purple sash. He was as tiny as a small child, but looked about two hundred years old. A network of jade veins ran through his arms and his long white hair trailed along the ground. Maggie thought she could see the old man's pulse juddering beneath his tissue-paper skin and his bony fingers were covered in gold rings. He stared at Maggie intently.

Then, with unexpected agility, he sprang towards her and grabbed her right hand. His grip was very cold and strong, and Maggie cried out, afraid he would crush her fingers. The ancient man examined the ring on her finger then glared at her with his malevolent violet eyes.

'Who are you?'

The ring glowed on Maggie's finger – it was trying to tell her something. His grip tightened and she winced in pain.

'Why are you spying on us?'

Maggie glanced over and saw Hoagy pinned down by two of the hooded figures. His fur was strangely flat and he looked afraid.

'No, no. We're not spying. I'm looking for my friend.'

'And who is your friend?'

Maggie couldn't stop her voice from shaking. 'Ida, she's called Ida. She was brought here against her will and I want to take her home.'

'She is a sleeper?'

Maggie didn't understand. 'I don't know.'

'Where did you get this ring?' insisted the ancient man.

Instinctively Maggie knew she must tell the truth. 'I stole it.' He released her hand and she felt bold enough to say, 'Could you let go of my friend, too?'

He nodded to the hooded figures and Hoagy scuttled over to Maggie and jumped into her lap. She could feel his heart going ten to the dozen. Suddenly she remembered the leather tube Dot had made Hoagy bring with them and something occurred to her.

'Are you moon witches?'

Still glaring at her, the ancient man nodded.

Maggie managed to say, 'We have something for you.' She got up and found the tube in her rucksack and handed it to him.

The ancient broke the seal easily with his bony fingers and extracted a small piece of paper from within it. As he read it his eyes flared with a violent light and for a moment Maggie feared she'd made things worse. He beckoned the other witches around him and they all stared at Maggie as if trying to bore into her soul. Maggie wished more than anything that they would stop.

'You come from another world,' he said at last.

Trying to sound confident enough for both of them, Maggie said, 'Dot said you would help us. We want to go to Sun City. Do you know how to get there?'

The ancient witch's purple lips cracked into something

close to a smile. He nodded. 'First tell us why you wear the ring.' And he pointed at it again with a long bony finger.

Maggie looked down at the ouroboros: the snake's head was still glowing as if lit from its own private source. 'Dot said it would protect me. But I just want to get my friend. I want to get my friend back and go home. That's all.'

Maggie became aware of another presence in the shadows. It moved forwards and she saw it was a tall grey bird, a heron. Its grey, white and black feathers glowed in the low light as it stalked towards her on strange spindly legs. She'd seen one recently, somewhere very unexpected. But where? She couldn't remember.

She had seen herons before, flying low over the marshes back home, huge and angular, but she had never been near one. Up close it seemed like a creature from another time, a mythical beast. It was strange and beautiful.

Despite its big beady yellow eyes, the heron looked at Maggie in a very human way, as if there was a person hiding inside its body. It was a look she remembered seeing occasionally in her mum's eyes before she got sick – an intense benevolent interest that was almost too much to bear.

The heron was very tall and as it drew closer, Maggie felt a fine mist sinking over her, and within it a curling line of smoke that seemed to sink deeper and deeper into her mind, calming and soothing her, until suddenly it was gone, and she realised that the bird had moved away. She wished it would come closer again. The heron whispered something into the ancient's ear with its long yellow beak and then stood back in its dark corner, watching, as still as a statue.

The ancient witch nodded and gestured that they should sit. The umons were outside and apart from the grey bird only the hooded figures of the other moon witches remained, dark and faceless.

The ancient witch began to speak, and his voice was rich and melancholy. 'The ring you wear belongs to the Great O.'

The ouroboros pulsed on Maggie's finger. 'Who is that?' she asked.

'The Great O is the protector of nature and nature itself. Her ring is the most powerful amulet in our world. From whom did you steal it?'

'My Aunt Esme,' Maggie told him. In her head she added silently, *And I'm pretty sure she's not the protector of nature. . .* So then why on earth did Esme have it? But Maggie didn't have time to work that out, because the ancient moon witch was still staring at her and his look was far from friendly.

But then he sighed and shook his head. Suddenly he became even more ancient and weary. 'I see you know nothing.' He clasped his bony pale hands together, as if in prayer and his voice flowed on like a sorrowful song. 'The Islanders, in their deep ignorance, invaded the Great O's sanctum in the Magic Mountains. They trapped her for a while but then she vanished. That is when the sun left us, when the land went dark and the sea turned black. The animals and the birds died. And then the terrible Sadness descended.'

'Is the Great O going to come back?' asked Maggie.

'I do not know, but if she doesn't this world will eventually die.' The ancient witch shook his head. 'It is dying now.' He looked at her sharply again and his voice grew harder: 'You and your animal may pass the dark-time here. Then we will tell you how to find Sun City. But beware, Eldrow is the cruellest and darkest of all the Islanders and he has no reason to show you mercy.'

Two of the hooded witches led them into a small room at the back of the cabin. They gave Maggie and Hoagy water and large flat pieces of grey bread on battered gold plates with a sort of gruel made up of what looked like flowers and a white tubular vegetable. Naturally Hoagy was having none of it, but Maggie wolfed hers down. At first it tasted unpleasant and earthy, but it kind of grew on her. So much so that, as Hoagy looked on with feline disdain, she devoured his portion as well. Though even he succumbed to a little nibble on the bread.

The witches watched them silently as they ate. When Maggie and the cat had finished, they took their plates and threw down coarse dark sacks stuffed with what felt like wool for them to sleep on. Then they left without a word. Hoagy curled up at once and closed his eyes. But Maggie was cold and she lay awake for a while listening to the barking and screeching of the umons who were still gathered by the moonlit lake, until finally sleep overcame her.

She woke with a start in the darkness. It took her a few moments to remember where she was, but when she did she instinctively felt that something was wrong. She could hear a low rustling sound like white noise and there was movement in the main room. Hoagy still snored peacefully beside her, and a large part of her wanted to snuggle up next to him and slip back into oblivion. But she forced herself to get up.

Maggie nudged open the door as quietly as she could and slipped into the main space. In the dim light she could see the moon witches in a huddle, their cloaks flowing together like a single dark mass. On the other side of the room, still motionless in its corner, was the heron. Its yellow eyes locked onto her at once and she felt a connection humming between them in the air. But then just as quickly its eyes flicked away. She only had a moment to wonder why the bird had not alerted the witches to her presence, when she was overwhelmed by another sight.

The solid mass of the witches had parted a little and she saw the ancient lying on his back, his robes discarded to one side, his long white hair trailing along the floor beside him. He was naked and his deeply wrinkled skin was as transparent as a jellyfish. For such a small old man he had a pair of disturbingly enormous and equally transparent feet that two of the other moon witches held up into the air at a forty-five-degree angle to his limp body. Maggie could see his frightening violet eyes were wide open and staring at the ceiling, but he was clearly looking somewhere very far away. The witches' hoods had fallen back and Maggie saw that they too were old with shocks of bright white hair rather like Dot's. Yet beside the ancient they seemed almost youthful.

With great purpose and intensity the two witches pressed at points on the ancient's feet as if giving him a massage. As they did, the ancient began to groan and suddenly colours began to flicker above his head until they burst up like fireworks illuminating the dark air above him, shimmering there like a huge flock of multi-coloured birds moving as one. Maggie just about stifled her gasp, but luckily the witches were too absorbed to hear the tiny 'oh' that issued from her astonished mouth.

For what seemed a long time, Maggie stood rooted to the spot, entranced and terrified in the same measure, watching the illuminations made of every colour swirl and dance above the old man's head. Then the ancient gave a cry. The two witches jumped back and dropped his huge feet onto the floor so that they banged loudly. The glorious swirl of hallucinogenic colours disappeared and the room went very black.

Eventually a lantern was lit and with the utmost

gentleness the witches helped the ancient to sit up and put his robes back on, much as you would dress a tiny defenceless baby. Then they gathered round him once again.

'I have seen but I do not understand,' the ancient said eventually, his voice like a low horn. 'Yes, it is true: this girl is the one who will bring back the light, but I do not see how or why she has been chosen. And she will also bring darkness.'

The moon witches all began to whisper until the ancient raised his bony hand and they obediently fell silent. Maggie's heart was pounding so loudly she was surprised that the witches could not hear it.

'One thing I do know, without any doubt, is that she must not be allowed to leave this place with the ouroboros. The future of all moon witches depends upon it.'

Maggie felt the ring pulsing wildly on her finger – it was burning her skin. She had to get out of here.

The ancient pointed at the door behind which he thought she was sleeping and pronounced in a dreadful voice, 'If we have to kill the girl, we must do so.'

The witches all turned to look and as they did, they saw Maggie standing there. She screamed, but she couldn't get out of the way as they ran at her. Several of them pounced on her at once and she hit the floor hard, feeling as if their thick dark robes would suffocate her. Cold hands held her down by her shoulders and her legs, and then a freezing hand gripped hers like a vice. It began trying to remove the ring from her finger but the ouroboros throbbed angrily and she felt it tighten – it did not want to leave her.

Then somewhere nearby, Maggie heard the sinuous lilting voice of the ancient, 'You will give us the ring.'

Maggie desperately tried to wrench her hand away. 'I promised never to take it off.'

'It must not fall into the wrong hands.'

'Get off me!'

It felt like pliers were ripping at her knuckles.

'You're an alien here,' the ancient continued, 'and aliens cannot be trusted in these dark times.'

To Maggie's horror she saw something glinting in the darkness – was it a knife? She imagined she heard the ring cry out in pain and the sound reverberated around her head.

'No! Please!'

Were they going to cut her finger off? Maggie began to tremble all over with total fear.

Suddenly the grey heron swooped over their heads screeching madly. It looked impossibly huge above them, as if its great wingspan would blot them all out and its wings thumped against the ceiling like drums. There was a moment of absolute stillness when everything seemed to stop. And then she saw the flames.

One side of the cabin was ablaze and the ancient witch was screaming. She realised that his robes were alight. He curled up into a tiny ball and two of the witches threw their cloaks over him, whilst the others used theirs to try and stop the cabin from being overwhelmed by fire. She scrambled up and looked around desperately for Hoagy, but there was no sign of him. She ran back into the side room but he had gone. So she covered her face and dashed through the thick smoke until she reached the door that led outside to the lake. The witches were howling and screaming, but she still could not see the cat.

By her feet she noticed the tiny piece of paper they had carried all this way in the leather case on the floor. She grabbed it just as a ball of brown fur rushed past her coughing and spluttering.

'Maggie!' it screeched.

She ran after him out of the burning building. It was the white-time, but a thick mist hung over the Strange Plains and Maggie could only just see Hoagy in front of her.

'Follow me!' a voice cried.

To her astonishment, she saw Frank right beside her. Without further explanation the umon led them through the dense fog to the lake and splashed into the water, holding his little sack above his head. But as Maggie tried to follow a moon witch appeared from out of the mist like a black crow. He threw himself at her and tackled her to the soft muddy ground by the edge of the lake. She tried to cry out but her mouth filled with dirt.

Frank was already disappearing from view and Maggie just glimpsed his worried face turning back, bobbing above the waterline before she was dragged away, back towards the blazing cabin. She let herself go limp to stop it hurting so much. That was it: they would kill her, or at the very least amputate her finger. She felt numb.

The witch dragged her along in the mud, his grip was like a vice. Smoke filled the air and she could hear the timbers of the cabin crackling like twigs, the screams of the witches and above it all the thunderous beating of the heron's great wings. But then she heard another sound – a crazed high-pitched mewling. She twisted round and from the dense white air she saw Hoagy run at the witch, claws drawn, fangs out.

Spitting and hissing like a wild thing he scrambled under the witch's dark robes and began to tear viciously at his hideous pale skin. The witch cried out in pain and his deadlock grip relaxed enough so that Maggie's ankles fell to the ground and she could scramble to her feet. Copious, disgusting amounts of blood were pouring from the paper-thin wrenched-apart skin. The witch had fallen to his knees.

'Hoagy!' she screamed.

His round one-eyed face appeared from under the cloak covered in deep-red blood, his fangs covered in little snags of the witch's skin.

'That's enough!'

They pelted back in the direction of the shore and were almost in the lake before they saw it. Frank was there too – he'd come back. They all splashed out into the freezing brown water and swam as hard as they could. Maggie looked back but she couldn't see a thing through the mist. They only heard a few cries and shouts from the shore.

'Keep going,' Frank panted.

The water seemed more like thick soup and the swim was incredibly hard. Hoagy was spluttering and complaining like a mad thing, so Maggie let him cling to her back. She had always been a good swimmer, but she'd never done anything like this before. Was she imagining it or did the ouroboros give her the strength she needed? The ring glowed like a beacon on her finger as Maggie swam on for what seemed like miles, unable to see more than a metre in front of her, until finally her feet touched the sludge at the bottom of the lake and she dragged herself and the sopping cat out of the water and onto a bank of flat lilac stones.

They all lay there for several minutes shivering and not speaking. The mist was beginning to lift, and a long way back across the murky lake she could see smoke and flames still rising from the cabin.

Finally Hoagy got up and shook himself out like a madman. 'Swimming in that brown water is the single most humiliating thing that has ever happened to me,' he announced, 'and I don't think I'll ever get all that skin out of my teeth. Pah!' He spat and then flopped to the ground.

Maggie looked at him, so bedraggled and outraged and fat, and burst out laughing hysterically though it hurt every muscle in her body.

Hoagy turned and hissed at her, 'I wish we'd never come. Those foul things were meant to help us.'

Maggie stopped as she realised. 'But Dot told us to go to them,' she said slowly.

'Those insane wrinkled-up little creeps wanted to finish us off,' hissed Hoagy, quite beside himself.

'But why would she send us to them?' asked Maggie quietly.

'I don't care! I want to go back home,' spat the cat.

'Well you can't,' Maggie snapped back. 'Not without me and not without Ida.'

'That's the thanks I get for saving you?' Hoagy hissed at her, looking feral again. He skulked off a few paces away and turned his back on her.

But Maggie didn't have time to worry about him – her mind was whirring. Did Dot want her to die too? She remembered the ancient's awful words about the light and the dark. But his vision must be wrong; like Dot, he had confused her with someone else. She decided not to tell the others what he'd said.

Then she remembered the note. By some miracle the paper had survived, lodged in her jeans pocket. But as she unfolded it, she realised it wasn't made of paper but a brown leathery parchment of some kind. On it was a series of strange hieroglyphic-type letters that meant nothing to her. She tucked it away again.

Frank was sitting up now. He looked very lean and tired.

'What did you do?' she asked him.

'Nothing. It was the heron. He used one of the witch's lanterns to set the cabin alight.'

'But why?'

The umon shook his head. 'It makes no sense. They are allies.'

'But why were you still there?' Maggie asked.

Frank looked at her. 'You're my friend.'

Maggie suddenly felt like crying, but instead she bit her lip very hard until she tasted blood. 'What are sleepers, Frank?'

The umon tilted his head to one side. 'You really don't know?'

'No.'

'They're people the shifters bring here from your world.'

'But why?'

'To take their happiness.'

Maggie frowned. 'What do you mean?'

'Eldrow has invented a way to extract it. They say he first experimented on his sister many moons ago, but she ran away. He uses the shifters because they can read emotions – they can tell how people are feeling – and some can read deep into your mind.' The umon's eyes narrowed. 'They can sense unhappiness, like a hunter senses prey.'

'But wouldn't they want happy people?' said Maggie.

Frank gave an odd little smile, 'When human beings feel happy, it flows through every part of them. But when they have forgotten what joy is, their happiness gets trapped deep inside their minds. And Eldrow knows how to find it. The shifters bring them to him and once their happiness has been taken, they are discarded.'

Maggie was confused. 'But you can't take happiness. It's not a thing. And anyway, you can always make more.'

The umon shook his head. 'That is not certain. Since the sun left and the Sadness came, demand is high: from the lowliest to the highest ranked Islanders – they all want it. They don't care about others' suffering: they are only obsessed with themselves. And yet nothing ever truly makes them happy.'

Maggie felt very heavy. It was like someone was pressing down onto her chest so that she could barely breathe.

'Do you feel happiness, Frank?' she said at last.

'It has never been part of my life,' he answered simply. Frank was looking at her very intently. Then he placed his thin paw on her arm. 'Remember, girl from another place, the only way to beat the darkness is to stop thinking of yourself and to think of others. Remember what I have told you.'

He got to his feet. 'If you want to find your friend you must come with me. I will show you the way into Sun City.'

As before, Frank raced ahead through the trees, his lantern guiding the way. Hoagy and Maggie struggled behind him, the cat occasionally muttering something about dirty great rats under his breath.

Maggie was tired and full of worry. What if Ida's happiness had already been taken and she couldn't make any more? To Maggie it seemed the cruellest thing you could ever do.

After a while they stopped to rest and Frank shared out some of his strange malty loaf. Maggie ate her portion gratefully, but Hoagy had to go and sick his up behind a tree, which didn't impress the little umon.

Maggie was thinking about the mysterious grey bird and the connection she'd felt with it. Why had he helped her?

'Have you seen that heron before?'

Frank nodded. 'The shifter.'

'He's a shifter? But he didn't seem the same as Miss Cane. He seemed kind.'

'Shifters can be good or bad. You only need to know one thing: if their animal form is a bird it means they are true and you can trust them with your life. All others are to be feared and avoided.'

'Do they turn into anything else?'

The umon nodded. 'All shifters have three forms: a human form – this shows their weakness; an animal form, which is their true nature; and an object – this shows their destiny or their fate. They only become their object-form in times of great need, but they can stay like that for many moons.'

'And the moon witches? Are they good or bad?' asked Maggie.

The umon's ears flattened. 'They are neither. But they are close to the Great O, to nature, and this makes them wise. At the full moon they have visions and can see the future. They are healers and it is said they can stop time, though no one knows if that's really true. They used to look down on us umons, but if we are to stop the Islanders from destroying our world we must all fight together. They need us now.'

21

THE PALACE

Maggie's heart leapt as they emerged from the forest and she saw Sun City again. It was so beautiful that it seemed impossible the people there could ever feel sad. Frank led them down the valley hugging the tree line. Then the three of them dashed across the open ground and plunged in amongst the small umon huts. There were no streets here, only dirt paths and the huge eyes of many umons peering out at them as they hurried along.

Close to the city walls, Maggie saw umons loading up a train of linked carts overseen by human guards. The guards wore black gauze-like masks so you could only see their eyes, and they all carried large spears with golden points, whilst small axes hung at their belts.

The trio hunkered down in the darkness.

'If you hide in one of the carts, it will take you into the palace. That is where you will find your friend.' The umon looked at her sadly. 'If you return, I will find you.'

'Of course we'll return,' said Maggie, but Frank had already vanished.

The guards had moved to the front of the train where still more umons were being harnessed, ready to drag it into the city. There wasn't much time.

Maggie looked at Hoagy. 'Ready?' she whispered.

The cat's face was grim but he nodded.

They ran as fast as they could to the last cart. It was much higher than she'd expected and whilst Hoagy jumped in easily it took Maggie a few moments to heave herself over the edge. But eventually she made it and slid down the steep sides. It was dark and spongy in there, but there was a faint pink light and she realised they were sitting on rolls of turf from the Strange Plains.

After a while, a bell rang, the guards shouted and a tarpaulin was dragged across the top of their container. With a jerk, they began to move. A few minutes later, they heard the creaking of gates, voices shouting and the umons barking and howling. Maggie could tell from the change in sound that they were being pulled into a tunnel. After a few seconds they emerged and the cart started up a much steeper incline bumping violently over what felt like cobblestones.

Eventually they stopped inside another darker space and nothing happened for some time. Then suddenly they were pushed into very bright light, rattled swiftly over some kind of grate and plunged back into darkness. There were low mutterings, footsteps and the sound of a door being slammed. Maggie and the cat did not move or speak for some time, until Hoagy finally hissed, 'I'm getting out.'

She heard him tearing at the tarpaulin with his claws and then dropping to the ground. Maggie stood up on the soft turf and breathed in the cold air with relief. But she couldn't see a thing. She could only hear Hoagy rustling about.

Eventually he said, 'We're in a sort of storage place. There are other cart things here. But we've been locked in.'

Maggie groaned. 'What can we do?'

'Can you get down?' Hoagy purred.

Maggie felt her way to the edge and eased herself down onto a stone floor.

Suddenly Hoagy's warm body was beside her, twisting around her legs. 'Hold onto my tail.'

'I thought you told me never to touch it again?'

'Pah! Don't exaggerate.'

Maggie found the cat's tail and held it gently.

'I'll guide you to the door, but if you trip over, do me the courtesy of letting go,' Hoagy instructed.

Slowly they edged forwards. Maggie ran into the occasional obstacle, but they made it, and to her relief, Maggie saw a bright gold thread of light running beneath a wooden door. She pushed at it, but it was locked.

'Pick me up,' purred Hoagy.

Maggie groped around in the pitch black, finally got hold of his fat furry body and lifted him up.

'A little higher. . . lower. . . tiny bit higher. Hold!'

Maggie heard a light scratching noise followed by a rattling. Her arms started to wobble a bit under his not-inconsiderable weight.

'Keep still,' he complained.

'You're heavy, you know.'

'Keep still!'

Maggie tried to think about something other than her aching arms. Until finally there was a heavy click and Hoagy purred like a motor. To Maggie's astonishment the door creaked open a little way and Hoagy fell out of her arms.

'You're a genius,' she cried, and he did not dispute the claim.

Very cautiously Maggie pushed open the door and thick glaring light cut into their dark chamber like a knife. Maggie peered out and saw that the door led onto a passageway built of the same pale stone as the city walls. There wasn't a soul in sight.

Maggie walked up a narrow corridor, Hoagy at her side sniffing at everything manically, until the passageway levelled out. On the left, stone steps led down to an enormous kitchen. It looked about the size of a football pitch with hundreds of pots and pans steaming on open fires and cooks rushing about.

Creeping by unseen they came to a narrow stone staircase a little further along. They climbed up it, grateful for the momentary cover. At the top, a heavy stone door stood ajar, and beyond it Maggie saw the most magnificent room.

Huge round windows like colour wheels were set high in the walls and their yellows, reds, blues and purples were reflected in exquisite quivering repetitions on the smooth white stone floor. Candles the size of small trees rose up into the air and twisting green panels like curled leaves hung on the walls. On the ground a huge sun had been inlaid into the floor in pure gold. And from hidden places in the ceiling a shimmering pinkish-grey glitter fell onto everything and everyone, dissolving as soon as it landed. Some drifted through the doorway and sank into Maggie's skin. Almost at once, she felt a jolt of elation, and all her fear and weariness left her.

In fact, she couldn't understand why she had ever felt anything but a perfect happiness, or what she'd been striving for and worrying about all this time. Life was wonderful, and most of all it was kind. She turned to Hoagy, expecting to see the joy she felt reflected in his face, but he looked as grim as ever. What was wrong with the old mog?

And the music! It was like nothing Maggie had ever heard in her life. It seemed to come from every possible corner like a shimmering gossamer web of sound that made her feel wonderful. It was so beautiful it made her want to cry and laugh and dance joyfully, all at the same time. It rose up, swirled about and into her – a thousand voices, a thousand pianos, drum beats from everywhere, a rippling bass like water, and somewhere a hidden melody that you couldn't quite pick out, but which kept drifting in and out, not wanting to reveal itself, drawing you along.

Through this, figures dressed in gorgeous coloured tunics and gowns moved towards a large staircase, alone or in pairs. And then, cutting through the wonderful music, came a chiming bell. All the figures looked up and quickened their pace.

The bell rang sonorously in Maggie's head and she stepped out from the dark cover of the staircase into the exquisite light and colour. She closed her eyes and it felt like she was floating – she was transparent and the glitter and the light flowed through her. There was, she realised, nothing she wanted to do more than lose herself in this crowd. She started moving towards the grand staircase.

'Maggie?!' Hoagy hissed desperately behind her.

But she had already gone.

Maggie floated over the floor, her eyes wide. The people around her wore the most magnificent gowns she'd ever seen, and armfuls of gold bracelets, and glittering jewels: huge diamonds and opals and emeralds.

Then the boys with the shining golden eyes came towards her, the ones who could turn into the strange orbs. Maggie had not forgotten how one of them had pressed so painfully into her mind, but now, somehow, they seemed like friends. They circled round her giggling and poking at her. Then two of them took her hands and dragged her up the beautiful marble staircase, laughing.

The bell kept chiming hypnotically as the boys brought her to another huge hall whose pillars were decorated in gold suns. To one side a fire roared in an enormous grate. Hundreds of people were already seated, a steady rain of the pinkish-grey glitter falling on them. As Maggie looked around her, the ring pulsated madly on her finger, burning her skin – it was trying to tell her something. But at that moment, she didn't really want to know.

On a gilt platform at the far end of the huge room, another magnificent coloured glass window behind him, sat a man dressed all in white. Maggie stared at him. She felt like she knew him – but where would she ever have met someone like him? He was wonderful. His robe was of such pure white that he seemed to glow, and he radiated a feeling of happiness and goodness. He was tall and very slight, with pale hair and too-large grey eyes that made him look both very young and old at the same time. He was sitting on an ornate gold chair, a low gold table before him. Several servants in black masks stood solemnly about him, but he couldn't stop laughing and smiling.

She wanted to move closer to him but the boys pulled her back and sat her down at one of the tables. Soon Maggie noticed that no one was talking. They only smiled and laughed. And every so often she found herself bursting into laughter about nothing too, but it was the best laughing she'd ever done.

The servants, who also wore masks over their mouths and noses, moved calmly around the tables, and soon Maggie was feasting on a series of strange foods she'd never seen before. But it was all so delicious.

On her finger the ring throbbed very painfully again, and she looked at it with irritation. Why did it keep interrupting her when she felt like this? She tried to take it off, but it was stuck. In fact it felt as if it was getting tighter, the metal squeezing painfully around her finger.

Beside her, one of the boys with the golden eyes was watching her. He took her right hand and examined the ring closely. For a moment everything went hazy. The music and lights blurred and made her dizzy. And Maggie felt the stir of inexplicable unease, but then the boy let go of her hand and started giggling, and the strange feeling left her.

Somewhere above them, the bell began to chime once more and everyone got up. Maggie and the little boys climbed up another flight of stairs and Maggie found herself in a large stone room with an impossibly high black timber ceiling filled with people and lights. Here the music was louder and the beat heavier. It pulsed inside Maggie's brain so that she found herself dancing with everyone around her. But not edging from side-to-side like terrible school discos, not doing lame dance routines, but dancing wildly and madly, with total freedom.

Beyond them, on a separate platform, the man in white appeared again. He was dancing alone, his face full of the same deep joy that Maggie was feeling, his hands flapping and grasping at the air, his magnificent robes dishevelled now, but light and radiance still emanating from him.

Maggie didn't even know how she was moving. Her body just seemed to know exactly what to do and she found herself swivelling around. The boys never left her side but they became a kind of vague presence until Maggie was aware of nothing but the music pulsing through her chest and how happy she was.

22

ALONE IN THE DARK WORLD

Hoagy watched helplessly as Maggie drifted away from him, blissfully unaware that she stood out like a sore thumb with her tangled hair and dirty clothes.

'Humans!' he hissed angrily under his breath. But then he saw something emerge from the shadows of the great hall and his heart began to pound. He smelt it too: that disgusting, acrid smell he had only encountered once in his eleven years and that he would never mistake.

The white wolf moved into the light, its fur glistening, its cold eyes locked onto Maggie as she disappeared up the stairs with some vile little children that had appeared out of nowhere.

Why on earth had he come here anyway? It was the stupidest thing he'd ever done in his life, and they said age made you wiser. He arched his back and hissed scornfully at the whole scene, before disappearing into the dark stairwell.

Hoagy stayed completely still in the dark for many hours until he could no longer hear the music and not even the faintest murmur of voices. Only then did he allow himself to emerge from beneath the stone staircase where he'd been hiding. He was tired and hungry and in rather a grim situation. But mostly his small pink tongue was starting to resemble high-grade sandpaper, so first things first.

He edged down to the huge kitchen. The lanterns were lit, burning the glowing peat cut from the Strange Plains, which gave off its pleasant earthy scent. The long workbenches that ran the length of the enormous space were empty now and scrubbed clean, whilst all over the walls pewter pots hung like glinting shields.

He leapt up onto one of the worktops and strolled down it, his tail high and curling. On the floor at the far end, perhaps for some sort of pet he had not yet encountered, there was a large silver bowl full of water. It was cool and tasted better than anything he'd had in his life. Once he'd drunk his fill, he looked about once more. Cats aren't big on regrets, but the old cat was sincerely starting to wish he'd never met a certain Maggie Blue Brown.

At this very moment, he could have been at Mrs Hacker's, bored out of his mind, yes, but comfortable and no doubt about to tuck into a large bowl of chicken and gravy. In response to these vivid imaginings his stomach rumbled violently. But he had no time to look for morsels because the sound of voices suddenly broke into the silence.

Before he could scuttle out of sight, two large men dressed in shabby tunics appeared in the archway on the far side of the kitchen. Hoagy froze and employed the tried and tested don't-move-and-no-one-will-see-you cat method, but his one eye remained wide and watchful. The men were carrying something.

'This one's heavy,' one of them grumbled as they stumbled down the passageway.

Hoagy saw that a body hung limp between them.

The cat moved silently across the floor and peered round the archway at the back of the kitchen. To his left, some way down, one of the men was opening a heavy wooden door. The boy, because Hoagy now saw that it was a boy aged about thirteen or fourteen, groaned in the other man's arms and he whispered, 'Quick, he's coming round.' They disappeared inside and Hoagy heard a heavy bolt being drawn across.

The cat padded down to the door and sniffed at the gap at the bottom of it. A wildly curious mixture of scents from the unidentified space beyond swarmed to meet his oversensitive nostrils. There was much that was familiar and much that was so utterly strange he didn't know where to begin. But it was useless to stand there.

Tearing himself away from the intriguing bouquet he scuttled back through the kitchen and made his way up to the magnificent hall. There was not a soul in sight. The lanterns were blazing here, too, though a few were starting to sputter out. Through the huge coloured windows the white-time was just starting and Hoagy felt a swell of relief that the endless darkness outside was lifting a little.

He thought about the boy for a moment, limp in the man's arms, but quickly tucked him away somewhere in a corner of his mind. And then he thought of Maggie. What had got into her? Was it some sort of enchantment? He shook his head – speculation was pointless, as every cat knew.

The one thing he did know was that the last time he'd seen Maggie, she'd been climbing the grand staircase. He scuttled up the wide steps and quickly took in the banqueting hall, and on the next floor, a huge empty room with a sunken floor like a ballroom. Then he heard footsteps and his ears swivelled, alert.

Quick as a flash he darted into the shadows, just as two masked guards, their axes swinging from their belts, patrolled past. He waited until their footsteps faded away to nothing, then he sat up and licked his front paws continuously, trying to think. But his thoughts were soon interrupted by a familiar smell.

He hadn't even heard her approach. The wolf had stopped a metre or so away from him in the middle of the passageway, her white fur glowing, so terrifyingly real that he felt like he couldn't breathe. She was massive and when she sniffed the air he knew at once that she'd sensed him. He had no time and therefore no choice. He counted to three and scrammed.

The wolf yelped in surprise and swiped at him so fast that she nearly made contact. But he just managed to dip out of the way and hurtle down the stairs. He didn't dare look back, but he thought he could feel her hot breath on his fur. At the bottom he hit the marble floor at such speed that he skidded across it like it was an ice rink then fell back down the dark stairwell. But although he started to run almost before he had landed, she was still right behind him. For a huge beast, he had to admit – she could really move.

He ran back through the kitchen with no idea of where to go. All he knew was that there was a locked door on the left, so he swerved to the right and kept running. The passageway went on upwards but there was a turn to the left. He risked it and skidded round the corner. As he did, he looked back to see how close the wolf was. Then the ground gave way beneath him, his stomach lurched and he fell through the air.

He hit cold hard stone and looked up winded and confused. He was outside the palace in the freezing air. He looked up and saw an open trapdoor above him. A second or two later, the wolf's huge white head peered out of it trying to work out if she could make the jump. But it was too far. For a moment their eyes locked onto one another. Then he ran.

A terrible howl issued from the wolf's mouth. Over his shoulder, Hoagy saw the orbs drifting down. There were people in the streets now and he used them as cover as he ran through their legs, his desperation to get out of this godforsaken place stronger than anything he'd ever felt. He ran and ran until he saw the little tunnel that went through the walls and led to the umon shantytown beyond. He raced into it.

The city gates were open and bursting out of them he saw guards in front of him, their faces covered with black masks, their tall unforgiving spears rigid in their hands. But they were busy with a small cart that was trying to get into the city and he managed to skirt round them. But then he tripped over his own exhausted paws, fell and hit his head on the stone. After a few moments he felt himself being dragged along the ground. Then there was nothing.

PART THREE

23

MAGGIE IN SUN CITY

When Maggie came round after the first ecstatic revels, she felt hollowed out and her head throbbed like someone had enthusiastically scraped out the inside of her skull. She could hear two voices: a man's that she didn't recognise and another that sent shivers down her spine. She opened her eyes and found that she was in a large stone room decorated with richly coloured drapes and illuminated by flickering lamps.

Sitting on a chair a little way from her bedside was the same pale-haired man from the revels, but now he was dressed in black. Around him the six orbs hovered in a protective halo and Miss Cane stood behind them all, keeping her distance just by the door.

'And she came alone?' the man was saying. 'No one helped her cross?'

'No one,' Miss Cane replied, licking her long fingers in a way that utterly repulsed Maggie. 'Or at least, we cannot discover who it was.'

'What did the Children find?'

'Nothing. They can't get into her mind at all. We have never encountered one like this.'

At that moment, Eldrow had turned to look at Maggie. She pretended to be asleep but perhaps he noticed her eyelids fluttering because his voice suddenly changed. It became gentler. 'If it's not too inconvenient, I need you and the Children to stop ripping her apart.'

Miss Cane's snarled. 'But I know this one. She came here to rescue a sleeper. She is trouble and we must end her.'

'A child who can pass between worlds alone? No, no, she is special. Besides, she reminds me of someone. Someone I used to care about many moons ago. Don't you like her?'

'Not in the least,' growled Miss Cane.

The man laughed loudly then his voice became harsher, 'Why don't you get out of here?'

Maggie must have drifted off again because the next time she woke the man was still there, but to her intense relief Miss Cane-the-wolf and the orbs had gone.

He smiled down at her. 'My name is Eldrow and this is my city.'

Maggie sat up in fright and tried to move away from him – this was the man that would show no mercy, who was full of darkness.

But he spoke very kindly to her. 'I'm so glad you're here,

Maggie Blue. Not only are you a special, wonderful child, you have brought me a great treasure.'

That was when Maggie realised with horror that the ring was no longer on her right hand. It was on Eldrow's, forced over the thick knuckle of his little finger where it did not belong. With a sickly lurch in her stomach, she knew that she had failed utterly: she had lost the ring and she had not found Ida.

She sat up abruptly and reached for it. 'Can I have my ring back?'

Eldrow smiled. 'I'm only borrowing it, Maggie.'

'But I promised I'd never take it off.'

'Who did you promise?'

'No one,' Maggie said, feeling confused.

He laughed. 'Who gave it to you, Maggie?'

'No one. I found it in the woods.'

Eldrow smiled. He played with it on his finger in a way that made Maggie feel slightly sick. 'I've heard it gives you special powers? Is that true?'

Maggie shrugged, 'I feel a bit stronger when I wear it, that's all.'

'I see, I see.'

As Eldrow spoke Maggie heard a voice: *take me back . . . take me back . . .* Maggie looked around confused. She put a hand to her temples . . . It was like an inner sound wave that rippled through her, a private thought deep inside her . . . She heard it again: *don't leave me . . . don't leave me . . .*

It was the ring. It did not want to be with this man – that was all that she understood. She remembered how it had pulsed so angrily on her finger when she'd been at the huge party and she had ignored it.

But Eldrow was smiling at her. He radiated light and happiness, and he was looking at her as if she was the only person who mattered to him. He held out his hand, and without thinking Maggie took it. It was firm and warm. He helped her out of bed and up onto her feet. Maggie looked down at herself: her jeans were torn and she was covered in mud from the lake and the woods. Her hair was matted and filthy; her nails were black. She felt ashamed.

Eldrow seemed to understand. 'Don't worry. We'll look after you,' he said and put his arm around her. 'But why have you come to us, Maggie?'

'I'm looking for my friend, Ida Beechwood.'

'Ida?'

'You know her?'

'But of course I do. We brought Ida here because she was deeply unhappy. Her parents don't love her properly and she was feeling very low.'

Maggie nodded: she knew that was true, after all.

He smiled again and it was as if all Maggie's troubles fell away. Her shoulders dropped and she relaxed.

'Many people don't understand me, Maggie,' Eldrow said. 'But I give people happiness, that's what I've dedicated my life to. Ida is beginning her new life in a place called the

City of Flowers. And she is blissfully happy. You will see when you meet her again. Do you believe me?'

And suddenly Maggie did believe him. Eldrow was the best person she had ever met.

After that first meeting, everything was like a dream. Maggie slept in a beautiful room in one of the palace's four turrets. From one window she could see out across the city, and beyond its walls the endless dark forest. And from the other, the pink-violet blur of the Strange Plains that glowed mysteriously when the light fell away.

Each white-time her maid Una brought her a small coffee and a sweet bun that tasted better than anything she'd ever had in her world. Next a troop of obliging umons came in carrying water heated in Eldrow's private chamber and filled her bath. After she'd washed, Una brushed and plaited her long hair, and helped her dress.

In the mirror she still had the same very pale skin and too-large eyes, but she didn't look pathetic any more, and she didn't look poor. That wasn't possible with the beautiful clothes Eldrow had given her, long dresses, tunic tops and flowing trousers in rich colours, and as many gold bracelets and necklaces as she wanted. And there was something different in her expression. It was hard to describe, but it came from the fact that, for the first time, she knew the world outside held nothing but kindness for her, from knowing that she was special.

Eldrow had granted her the freedom of the city, and the orbs and Miss Cane were not allowed to so much as touch her. Each time Eldrow held his revels, she was the guest of honour, and she and the ruler of Sun City danced together with that mad happiness she had only ever felt here, in this world.

Every day she wandered through the palace and the streets of Sun City looking at the shops selling beautiful coloured glass tankards and trinkets, and little vials of the pinkish glitter. She was dazzled by the huge golden suns that adorned the buildings and the gold that dripped from the wealthier inhabitants who travelled through the streets in ornate wooden carriages drawn by teams of panting umons.

Wherever she went she was greeted by warm waves and smiles. The ordinary people of Sun City, those who wore the simple tunics and did not attend the revels, seemed a little worried if she tried to talk to them. But she never felt lonely. She talked to Una sometimes, but mostly she talked to Eldrow.

Eldrow – Maggie just liked saying his name to herself sometimes. From the moment she'd seen him, he had seemed familiar to her, as if she knew him from another time or place. But maybe that was how it felt when you finally found your best friend, when you found someone who completely understood you.

He was nothing like the man the moon witches and Frank had described. He was very gentle. His huge grey eyes were the colour of the sea in winter and full of kindness. He was tall and very thin, slightly stooped, and Maggie guessed he was about forty. During the revels he was full of light and mad energy, but at other times he was quiet and thoughtful. He told her it was a privilege just to know her, that no one had ever crossed between worlds without the help of a shifter before. He told Maggie she was special and that people in her world just didn't know how to appreciate her.

She felt like she glowed in his presence. And she confided in him about everything: her mum's illness, her dad leaving, how Ida had picked on her at school and yet her strong feeling that they were friends. And Eldrow listened attentively to every word she said. But then she realised that she no longer really cared so much about those people anyway, just as they didn't care about her, and soon she stopped talking about them altogether.

Every day Eldrow came to see her and they were driven through the streets or went to his garden on the palace roof to look out over his great city. Occasionally he would take her into his library and read her stories from the huge illuminated books there. It was true that the orbs barely ever left his side, and Maggie felt they were always watching her, but they usually kept their distance and she began to get used to them.

And not only was Eldrow kind, he was a genius. He had invented the network of pipes embedded within the walls of the palace that allowed music to be heard in every room. By stopping certain valves you could control where the sound went. And he had his own troupe of musicians who played strange wind and string instruments Maggie had never seen before. And he'd invented an electric train for his own personal use.

But best of all he had singlehandedly cured the great Sadness by inventing glitra, the pinkish-grey powder that fell on everyone during the revels. Eldrow explained that it was the reason Sun City was the wealthiest and most magnificent city on the whole of the Island.

He placed the glitra on his tongue constantly from a small gold box he always had on his person. And he let Maggie have a small vial of it to sprinkle on herself whenever she wished. When it first touched your skin, it was absorbed and moments later you felt the most amazing surge of joy. It was true that the first burst quickly dimmed, but you still felt wonderful. Maggie had never felt such happiness before, and her old life drifted away from her like an unmoored boat pulled away by the tide.

24

THE ROOM

Maggie woke earlier than usual, just as the white-time was starting to encroach on the darkness. It was hard to keep track of time but she thought it was about a week since her new and wonderful life had begun.

She got out of bed and watched as a couple of streets away a lantern keeper scrambled up a ladder to refill the peat. The orbs hung above the palace like six small moons, keeping an eye on the city. All was calm. So why did she feel so agitated?

She got up and sprinkled a little glitra on herself from the bowl she kept on her dressing table. She felt the chemical surge of joy at once, but for some reason it didn't alleviate her sense of foreboding.

She went back to the window. There had been no revels that dark-time and most windows were covered with blinds to block out the light. But a few streets across, she saw a strange sight.

Several children dressed in black tunics were out on one of the flat rooves playing a silent game with a red ball. One child stood in the middle like a statue while the others threw the ball around the circle they'd made. Then occasionally the statue-child lunged to try and steal the ball. But it was all done in total silence. Maggie watched them, mesmerised.

One small girl no one ever threw the ball to had given up and stood looking out over the rooftops. Suddenly she spotted Maggie staring at her. The girl waved and Maggie raised her hand without thinking. Then the others came to see what she was looking at. Feeling shy, Maggie stepped away from the window so that they couldn't see her any more. She got back into bed, but stayed wide-eyed until Una came in with her breakfast.

Eldrow had not been to see her for two white-times, she didn't know why. She felt lost without him. Walking through the beautiful streets of pale stone and being greeted so nicely by everyone seemed a bit empty now. And when she climbed up to the beautiful roof garden, without Eldrow there she soon felt bored of that, too.

Listless, she dragged herself back to her room and lay on the bed staring at the ceiling. Una hurried in when she called and offered to do whatever she liked. But it occurred to Maggie that Una was a servant and she had to pretend to like her. The thought depressed her and she sent the maid away.

For the first time in days, Esme drifted into her mind.

Her Aunt Esme in West Minchen . . . neither the person nor the place seemed real anymore. And did her mum still call every Thursday? Maggie's heart jolted. She didn't want to think about Cynthia. She couldn't stay in her room any more so she got up and went downstairs to see if anything was happening.

The great hall was empty except for the occasional scurrying servant. Across the shining marble floor she noticed a door. Maggie frowned: she had the weirdest feeling that she'd been through that door before, but she couldn't remember when or why.

She crossed over the vast shiny floor and slipped into the cool darkness, down the steps to a huge kitchen. It was not a revels day and so there were only a few cooks down there, attending to bubbling pots. They smiled at her vaguely as she lolled against one of the worktops.

She wandered over to the other side. Finally, here was somewhere she'd never been before. There was a small archway and beyond it a stone passageway that ran alongside the kitchen. To the right, the passage rose up slightly. To the left, Maggie saw a small wooden door. She walked towards it.

At first it looked like the door was firmly shut, but as she got closer she realised it was open just a crack, and a moon-like crescent of golden light shone behind it. Excited to have found something new, Maggie pushed the door open a little more and slipped inside.

The first thing she was struck by was the heat – it was suffocating in there – and heavy condensation dripped from the walls. Set on a low table on the opposite side of the narrow room were several glass containers, like miniature fish bowls. A delicate thin white tube fed into each one, and a grey residue that shimmered in the low blurry light was accumulating on the inside.

There was a weird sound, too, a distant low gurgling like at the dentist when they put that plastic tube in your mouth to take away the fluid – what was this?

The tubes disappeared through holes bored into the floor and flowed down into a space below. Maggie looked for a way down and sure enough there was an open hatch and a long ladder at the far end that dropped into a brighter white space below. She got onto the floor and peered down.

This room was considerably larger, with a high vaulted ceiling and walls painted bright white. Huge glass containers, giant versions of the ones on the table, sat in a long row and into each, one of the delicate bone-like tubes disappeared. Various smaller ladders and boxes were packed neatly to the sides. And inside each glass container, something was crouched and alive . . .

She heard her clothes ripping before she understood what was going on. Something had grabbed her. She screamed as she was dragged back along the hard stone floor and into the dark passageway. Then the heavy door slammed shut behind her.

Maggie lay there for a moment, her head throbbing where it had been bumped along the stone. Beside her the wolf was slowly shifting back into Miss Cane. The glossy white fur became the long pale hair, and the snout somehow morphed into the woman's sharp porcelain face.

Since Eldrow had held her back that first time, Miss Cane always spoke to Maggie in the same patronising voice she had used at Fortlake.

'Believe me, Maggie,' she simpered now, 'you don't want to know what's in there.' And she began to lick her fingers in that repulsive way she had.

Maggie stood up. Her beautiful scarlet dress had been ripped beyond repair. 'I'm going to tell Eldrow you attacked me,' she yelled, surprised by how angry she sounded.

But the wolf-woman only laughed; she threw her head back and cackled. 'Go ahead, Maggie. Go ahead. You're the best of friends, after all.' Then she went away down the corridor, seeming to glide over the stone flags.

Despite her show of outrage, Maggie felt relieved that the wolf had dragged her out of there and shut the door. She didn't want to know what was in those containers.

And when Eldrow walked in to her room the next white-time, she felt such a surge of happiness to see him again that she forgot all about it: her unease, Miss Cane's violence, the weird room. Nothing else mattered when he was with her.

25

THE CAT STRIKES BACK

When the cat came round, it took him a moment to realise that he was underground. He leapt up and scratched madly at the walls. Soil fell over him, got into his eye, his fur and his mouth, and panic surged through him, until a high-pitched screech stopped him mid-claw. Frank was standing nearby, his eyes wide with fright, his paws raised to protect himself. Hoagy stopped his mad scrabbling for a moment and realised he had not been buried alive; he was in a narrow tunnel.

He didn't know if he had been waiting for him or if it had been pure chance, but the creature must have rescued him from outside the palace walls and somehow dragged him down here, into a little network of tunnels. Not a cat's favourite spot, but at least it was too small for that stinking wolf to get into. For now, that was all that mattered.

In the tunnels he was able to sleep and regain a bit of strength. Frank would pop in with water and food every so often then disappear again. He was a kind rat, Hoagy had to admit, and he'd never met one of those before. Hoagy tried to explain a few times that he needed to get back into the palace, that Maggie was in there and that she wasn't safe, but Frank barely responded and Hoagy wasn't too sure if he understood.

Hoagy only knew one thing for certain: he had been in this world too long – far too long. Maggie Blue had wandered off to some weird hypnotic panpipe music, and that was it – he was stuck. If he didn't find her and drag her back to that portal, he had no idea what would become of him.

And Hoagy hated this dark world more than any amount of mewling could express. He hated the freezing cold, the lack of any decent daylight, and more than anything he hated the weird array of smells his nose was constantly assaulted by. He longed to be at home breathing in the polluted suburban air and prowling around his territory.

By now wars would be being waged over his three streets, and local pretenders to his throne would gleefully be speculating that he'd finally crawled under a bush to die or that his substantial furry body had met with a fast-moving vehicle. This thought alone made him inwardly rage. Plus the fact that he hadn't had anything decent to eat for what felt like a decade. This awful dark loaf the rats ate was the end, it really was.

After several days of recovery, Hoagy woke from a delicious snooze and found Frank there beside him. He beckoned him to follow. The cat padded along behind him until they came to a shaft that rose two metres or so up towards the dark sky. The little rat climbed it nimbly whilst Hoagy managed to leap up halfway then scrabble up the rest into the darkness. He found himself back above ground, on the outskirts of the umon town that clung to the walls of Sun City. Half a mile away or so, the endless forest loomed up and a sliver of new moon hung in the dark sky.

After a moment, he spotted the large grey bird lurking in the shadows, its beady yellow eye trained upon him. He looked around, half-expecting to see a hoard of wrinkly old moon witches rushing towards him, too. But no such apparitions appeared. He considered running, but where could he go anyway? So he decided to watch and wait.

Frank went over and the heron bent its thick grey neck down to its level. The two seemed to consult for a moment. Then before he knew what was happening the bird was running hard at him. Hoagy froze in terror. It took off just before it reached him but then its powerful talons grabbed the scruff of his neck and dragged him off the ground.

Too shocked to even miaow, Hoagy held his breath as he was lifted high over the wall and dense streets of Sun City. The heavy beating of the bird's great wings raged in Hoagy's horrified ears, but no one seemed to notice their ascent. The bird kept cleverly to the shadows. It circled then landed very gently on top of one of the palace turrets. Hoagy fell from its beak with a disgusted mewl. The heron glared at him, tapped its beak on the roof then lifted itself back into the sky.

Hoagy watched it glide silently away then leapt up onto the turret walls and looked about him. The heron must know the palace well because it had chosen the least well-guarded spot. Below them, in the brightly illuminated gardens, several masked guards patrolled up and down. Whilst on the other turrets, Hoagy could see at least one man standing guard. But here there was no one. And the orbs were not hanging in the sky.

The cat heard footsteps from below – perhaps the bird had merely picked a moment when the guards changed over. Hoagy slunk into the darkest part of the roof and pressed his body against the cool stone. Sure enough, a guard emerged from a narrow staircase. Before the man had a chance to sense another presence, the cat slid silently down the dark stairs.

Hoagy found himself in a long passageway. He walked past endless closed doors, his nose twitching like mad, until he finally caught the girl's scent, faint but distinctive beneath a heavy perfume.

He followed it along the passage until he saw a glow of light from under a door. He got his courage together, pushed at it with his paw and peered into the room. There was one lantern flickering low by the door and in its dim light he saw Maggie, but hardly in the circumstances he had feared.

She was asleep in a huge bed. The room smelt of flowers and on the floor in front of an ornate mirrored dressing table were the remains of a rather good-looking meal. First things first – it was longer than he cared to remember since he'd wrapped his chops around anything decent. He sniffed at the plate tentatively for a moment then proceeded to wolf it down. The meat bore some relation to chicken and the few odd-looking vegetables were perfectly edible. When he'd licked the plate clean he leapt up onto the bed and nipped gently at her hands.

'Maggie,' he hissed. 'Wake up.' She stirred then started. 'It's Hoagy.'

'Hoagy?' She fumbled around, sat up and lit another small lantern by her bedside.

He considered her. Her hair was brushed, her face washed, in fact she looked happier and more refreshed than he'd ever seen her. Finally he saw recognition in her eyes. She frowned a little.

'Oh, Hoagy,' she said. 'Where have you been?'

'I've been down a hole.'

'What are you talking about?'

'Let's get out of here,' he purred.

Maggie rubbed her eyes, still half-asleep. 'Why?'

'Why?' Hoagy retorted in disbelief. 'Because we need to escape.'

'But I'm happy here,' the girl said.

Hoagy half-closed his one eye. 'Don't you remember what the ancient moon witch told us about Eldrow?'

Maggie shook her head. 'He was wrong. So was Frank. Eldrow is the kindest person I've ever met.'

'What's going on, Maggie?'

The girl couldn't help smiling and her voice was proud as she spoke. 'Eldrow says I'm special because I can cross between worlds. Apparently no one else can do that. He says it's a privilege to know me. And honestly, all the stuff we've been told about him. It just isn't true.'

Hoagy noticed her bare right hand. 'Where is the ring?'

'Oh,' Maggie flushed a little, 'Eldrow's borrowing it.'

'And what about Ida?'

'No, no, no,' Maggie said smiling, 'we were wrong. Eldrow brought her here to make her happy.'

'You've seen her?'

The girl shook her head. 'Not yet, but I will soon. She's living in a place called the City of Flowers. And she's really happy.'

Hoagy's eye narrowed to a slit. 'Pah! And you believe that?'

'Why shouldn't I?' Maggie retorted. 'Her parents don't love her. And I know how that feels.'

Hoagy shivered as if a mouse had run over his litter tray. It was her eyes – her huge eyes that were grey like the sea. They had grown cold, as if the chilliness of this wretched place had infected her.

'Eldrow's different,' she continued, 'he really cares about me. No one else does.'

'I think you're confused,' Hoagy purred gently.

'Why? Because I'm happy?'

'Well, you've clearly forgotten about me in your wonderful happiness.'

The girls flushed. 'No, I – I was just confused when you woke me. Of course I didn't forget you. I've been worried sick. Why don't you rest with me for a while? We'll figure out what to do afterwards.' She patted the covers. 'Lie down on the bed and sleep.'

Whether she remembered him or not, this girl was the only person who could get him back to West Minchen, and Hoagy needed to keep his cool. But it was difficult. He purred urgently under his breath, 'You're in danger, Maggie. Eldrow is not your friend.'

'And you are? You only came here because Dot told you to. And she sent us to those mad moon witches.'

'He's not your friend,' the cat said again. 'There is something rotten about this place.' And he sniff-sniffed the air as if to confirm it.

Maggie's cheeks were burning now. 'Maybe it's you!'

The cat felt his heckles rise uncontrollably. 'Or maybe it's *you*!'

'Just because I've found a real friend you—'

'I couldn't care less whether you've found a friend or not!'

'Exactly!' the girl shouted, triumphant.

The cat sighed. Suddenly he was sick of it all. You were better off sticking your paw in the fire than trying to help a human being. Isn't that what the wise grandcats had always told him when he was a kitten? He had made the mistake of caring and the thought made him even angrier.

So he hissed at her violently, the full fang and spitting job. 'Fine! I'll find my own way home. You stay here with the psychopaths.' He leapt down from the bed and scuttled to the door.

He heard her calling, 'Hoagy! Come back!' but he was already out in the passageway and running hard. He knew it was the stupidest thing he'd ever done in his life – he needed her to get home – but a cat had some pride.

Or maybe not, he thought, as he made his way back to the roof. This is what his life had come to: he was now hoping some stinking grey bird would come and pick him up – him! If anyone from West Minchen had seen him, he would have had to go into immediate retirement.

Outside the guard was fast asleep, his head tipped back against the stone, snoring heavily. So the cat risked moving slightly into the light, hoping against hope that the heron would be watching.

He didn't hear it coming until the huge wings were beating right on top of him. Then his paws were flailing in the air and they were gliding silently over the walls. This time, they went as far as the edge of the great forest before

241

it finally set him down in the black sea of leaves. Hoagy rolled around in them to try and get the bird scent off him whilst the heron watched him with a look of disdain. Though frankly he was probably just projecting. Did birds even have different expressions?

A moment or two later Frank appeared from amidst the undergrowth. 'Is she alive?'

Hoagy sat up and licked his front paws for a few moments. When he spoke his voice was dripping in sarcasm. 'Oh yes. And she's terribly happy. She doesn't want to leave.'

'They're caring for her?'

'Apparently she's very special,' hissed Hoagy.

'But why? Why is she valuable to them?'

'Pah! Who knows. But she's forgotten all about us, of that I can assure you.'

The rat shook his head. If possible he was paler and more worried-looking than ever. 'She is in great danger.'

Hoagy shrugged and then nodded at the silent bird. 'And why is this great lump of a bird so interested?'

'He wants to know where the ring is.'

'Ah ha.' The cat's eye went to a slit. He addressed the bird, 'And you can tell those wrinkled-up little witches, too – the girl no longer has the ring. She's given it to Eldrow.'

The bird remained as passive as before.

Then the rat said, 'He will take you back through the portal. He is a shifter. He can cross.'

The cat's ears pricked up and his tail rippled with pleasure suddenly. 'He can? This bird can take me back to West Minchen?'

'I don't know that place. But he can cross.'

The unofficial code of all felines may never have been committed to paper, but its content was fairly clear: do what's best for yourself, know which side your bread's buttered on, don't look a gift horse in the mouth. And Hoagy was a feline, after all.

He looked at the heron and for the first time in many days a smile broke out all over his furry face. He breathed a huge sigh of relief: finally, he was going home.

26

THE CITY OF FOLK

Maggie couldn't sleep after Hoagy had gone. Instead she lay staring up at the ceiling, trying not to feel bad. If only he'd stayed with her. But he was always so stubborn. She'd tried to help him, hadn't she?

Her thoughts were disturbed by the sound of crying. But no one cried here. She went over to the open window and listened. But it was unmistakeable: the sound of desperate inconsolable sobbing and it was coming from one of the small stone buildings just beyond the palace.

Far below in the street she saw a dark ribbon moving towards the sound. Then the guards banged aggressively on several doors with the ends of their spears and shouted warnings out into the street. Above them a few shutters opened and worried faces peered out.

The crying stopped. It was as if the person was holding their breath, and a tight silence hung in the air. After a few more threatening shouts, the guards marched away, the faces began to disappear and the windows were shut tight again. Maggie heard a quiet whimpering that carried to her on the still air. Then finally that stopped too.

Beyond the city, Maggie noticed that dark purple clouds were gathering. In the distance, there was a crack of thunder and a violent pulse of lightning jagged into the sky. There was a moment's pause then the ice and rain began hammering down, extinguishing many of the lanterns, until a curtain of dark water obliterated her view of the city.

'Maggie Blue?'

She turned and found Eldrow standing in her room. She hadn't heard him come in.

'I have a surprise for you.' He put his arm around her shoulder and squeezed hard. 'We're going on a journey.'

Once the storm had passed, they set off. They travelled in Eldrow's private train: three connected cars made from the dark wood of the forest that moved on a grey ribbon of metal that split off in different directions across the valley floor. In the first carriage, four of the Children morphed into orbs and positioned themselves in small silver dishes connected by a tangle of silver wires. Eldrow pressed a switch and they began to glow. After a few minutes, the engine turned and the train was propelled silently along the track.

The other two carriages were very small but

lavishly furnished. Eldrow and Maggie travelled in one, the remaining Children and servants in the other. But instead of their usual over-excited manner, the two boys were silent. They peered through the narrow window adjoining the carriages and their glowing yellow eyes were trained on her at all times. They seemed to be waiting for something – Maggie wasn't sure for what.

The little caravan moved smoothly along the valley floor passing close to a small clear stream a little further down. The terrain, though not lush, was covered in long pale grass peppered with small black and purple flowers. But soon the air became damp and stale, and the landscape changed.

They came to a huge area of man-made fields. Enormous lights strung up on long wires shone on a weird black crop that flowed out as far as the eye could see. Amidst it, umons were scything the black stalks whilst others collected it into bundles and carried it on their backs to carts. Masked guards watched them silently, the golden tips of their spears glinting in the artificial light.

The only other sign of life was a series of low white structures that appeared every so often in the distance. There were no trees and no birds or animals. And as they rounded a big curve in the valley, Maggie could make out the hills whose sides had been sheared away for the rich peat. But soon the dark-time fell and she could only sense their jagged shadows.

They had been sitting in a long silence when Maggie spoke. 'Is the City of Folk near the City of Flowers?'

Eldrow glanced up. 'No. It is inland and we are going to the sea.'

'Will I be able to see Ida soon, though?'

Eldrow shook his head, as if in disbelief. 'Do you think of anyone but yourself?'

Maggie's voice faltered a little. 'What do you mean?'

His eyes glittered. They were darker and stormier than she'd ever seen them before. 'I mean perhaps you could think of me for a change?'

'B-but I do,' stammered Maggie.

'You do? Really? Why is it then that you always want more? Haven't I given you enough that you would dare to ask me for more?'

'I didn't mean it like that.'

Eldrow shook his head in disgust. 'Ida hates you, doesn't she? You told me so yourself. Why would she want to see you?'

Maggie felt like she'd been punched. His voice was cold and harsh. He'd never spoken to her like this. She looked down and didn't move. Amidst the whirl of her thoughts she could hear the ring calling to her. She had not heard it for days, *Release me . . . release me . . .*

Eldrow clapped his hands violently together and the two servants rushed through the connecting doors. They began turning their seats into small couches to sleep upon.

When they were finished Eldrow lay back on his bed without even looking at Maggie, and instructed that the lanterns be extinguished. Darkness fell around them and Maggie had no choice but to lie back, too.

He was soon asleep, but Maggie stayed awake for a long time watching the two Children, who had morphed into orbs and moved noiselessly alongside the train like guards as it glided towards the sea.

When she did sleep, she had awful vague dreams about the shapes she had seen in the huge white room. In the dreams she kept trying to get closer to them but whenever she did a fine film of mist would come over her eyes. Finally, she managed to get right up to one of the glass containers and she saw what was inside. . .

She woke up screaming, but couldn't remember what had frightened her so much. It was the dark-time still, but Eldrow was already up and he was watching her. The scream from her nightmare faded from her lips and for the first time, she felt afraid of him.

As the white-time crept in, the servants brought them coffee and fruit. Maggie gasped as they rounded a corner and she saw the sea in the distance. Or at least she thought it was the sea: she couldn't be entirely sure because it was a pulsing sheet of grey-black. And beside it, a sprawling city made of the same pale stone as Sun City rose up, the light from it creating a golden haze in the sky.

Eldrow's mood seemed to have lifted and he smiled brightly at her. He came over and sprinkled a little glitra on her, before dropping a generous dose onto his own tongue. Maggie felt the powder sink into her skin and at once her mood began to lighten.

'We are here to consult Almarra,' Eldrow said, 'the wise woman of Folk.' He pointed to a tall thin tower in the distance. 'She lives there with her attendants and she has a strong desire to meet you, Maggie. I have told her how special you are.'

Maggie wanted to ask what it was all about, but she didn't dare upset him again. In her brain the ring would not shut up, *Release me, release me, set me free . . .* She looked at it glinting on Eldrow's finger and noticed that his skin was badly burnt where the gold touched him. The ring hated him. How she wished it would stop talking to her. How she wished she'd never seen it in her life.

As their train came to a halt, several servants, young women wearing black dresses with large stiff skirts and hoods covering their hair, met them as they stepped from their carriage. One took Maggie by the hand and she found herself being led into a dark tunnel that ran under the city. Eldrow and the orbs followed with the rest of the dark-clad women behind.

They all began to climb a narrow spiralling flight of stone steps that went round and round and up and up until Maggie's legs were hurting and she felt dizzy. But the young woman never let go of her hand and kept up her own steady pace until she was almost dragging Maggie behind her.

Finally they reached a small circular level with a door leading off it on one side, and a drawn curtain on the other. Fresh cooler air flowed into the space from diamond holes cut into a dark timber roof. Maggie breathed in – it was the sea air and for a moment she felt happy, like she was back at home.

Eldrow stood beside her and without a word slipped his hand around her waist and squeezed her tightly. Perhaps it was his way of saying sorry for how he'd been on the journey, but he said nothing. The orbs hung around them, buzzing quietly.

Then the door opened and a calm voice said, 'Welcome to the City of Folk.'

A very tall, spindly woman, dressed in a long black cape, had emerged. She must have been over two metres tall with long red hair that fell over her shoulders. She held out her long hands to Eldrow who let go of Maggie and knelt before her.

She touched his forehead and said, 'Let me see it.' Eldrow held up his hand and she examined the ring. 'It burns you?'

'It's nothing.'

She bent in very close, quite fascinated, and muttered to herself as she did. 'It is . . . it really is . . .'

A high-pitched wail started up in Maggie's head. The ring did not want to be touched by this woman either. But then she let go and the wailing subsided.

Eldrow and the woman exchanged a strange look and then she turned to Maggie.

'Maggie,' she said, 'come with me.' And she held out a long spindly hand adorned with beautiful rings.

She led her onto a balcony overlooking the sea. It was crammed with luscious plants and flowers, and the smell was almost overpowering. There were orchids and lilies and roses, and many other flowers Maggie had never seen before. Warm lamps hung over everything and there was the constant sound of water trickling.

'We have a system that extracts salt from the sea water so we can tend them,' the woman said softly. 'Though,' and she shrugged her bony shoulders nearly to her large ears that stood out at right angles from the side of her head, 'they always die after a few moons anyway. They do not like it here.'

But Maggie was looking beyond them now, out to sea. In the middle of the black ocean storms were raging. And further down the curve of the coast Maggie could see a huge mountain range.

The woman followed her gaze. 'Beneath those mountains the Elders are constructing the City of Gold. If this world dies, we will be able to survive there for many moons.'

'You think this world is going to die?' Maggie said.

The woman nodded and smiled sadly. 'If the Great O does not return.'

It was what the moon witches had said, thought Maggie.

The woman lit what looked like incense and poured Maggie tea from a huge gold pot. It was sweet and it warmed her up.

'I am Almarra, the sage of the City of Folk. People come to me to ask advice – they think I can see the future, however much I tell them I can't.' She smiled. 'But I do see things others don't. Eldrow has told me you have that gift, too. And that you are rarer than the rarest orchid. And now I have met you, I know it is true.'

The scent from the incense drifted into her mind and the woman's voice made Maggie feel better. It was a relief to be away from Eldrow and the orbs. As if reading her thoughts, Almarra said, 'I hate those shifters that hang around him, too. That is why I sent them away, so we could talk in peace. But the Children are loyal. So is the wolf. And that is what Eldrow values more highly than anything else, Maggie. Loyalty.' Gently she rearranged Maggie's hair and her fingers were cool and soothing. It reminded Maggie of something her mum used to do years ago when she was very little.

'You must forgive him if he sometimes gets angry. It is very rare for Eldrow to bestow love. And he truly loves you. You remind him of his sister. But she betrayed him.'

'What did she do?' Maggie asked.

Almarra's small eyes grew wider. 'She fell in love with a shifter. Such cross-relations are forbidden, but instead of repenting she ran away. She fled to the Strange Plains.' Her long fingers still ran through Maggie's hair. 'People cannot survive there very long if they are without an animal guide; there is no north, south, east or west. They get lost and disorientated, they start to hallucinate, and most die of hunger and thirst. They never found her and Eldrow was heartbroken.'

Maggie felt a chill go through her. She didn't like this story.

The woman took both her hands and looked her right in the eyes. 'We have many enemies in this world, Maggie. Those who don't want the light to return. Or those who do not think we are capable of bringing it back. But believe me when I tell you that whoever gave you the ring is using you. They do not care for you as we do.'

So that's what it was about, thought Maggie wearily. It was always the ring.

'Who gave it to you?'

'No one. I found it.'

Almarra smiled sadly. 'That can't be true, can it?'

The incense was in Maggie's eyes and nose. She felt slightly faint. 'Why not?'

'If you care for Eldrow as much as he cares for you, you will tell us who gave you the ring. And why. He has done so much for you. He's the only one who truly cares for you and you cannot imagine how important this is, for all of us.'

It was true – Eldrow had done more for her than anyone ever had. And he loved her. All Dot had done was send her into the clutches of some creepy wrinkled-up witches that wanted to kill her. But still Maggie hesitated. He had frightened her before.

'Maggie,' the soft voice persisted. 'You can save our world, Maggie. It's your destiny.'

She remembered what the ancient had said – about her bringing both the light and a terrible darkness. Maggie didn't want that to be true. Maybe if she told them what they wanted, she wouldn't have to be part of it any more. They'd find the Great O and bring her back, and everything would be OK.

'We don't want to hurt anyone. We just want to know where the Great O is. We have been waiting for a sign for so long and now we have it. We're depending on you, Maggie.'

Maggie sighed. 'My aunt had the ring, but someone else told me to take it.'

'And who was that, Maggie?'

'Dot.'

'Dot?' Almarra smiled. 'That's a strange name. Who is she?'

'She's no one, just a friend of my aunt's. She's an eccentric old lady and she knows about weird stuff. That's all. She told me to take the ouroboros because it would make me stronger. And she told me never to take it off.' Maggie instinctively lowered her voice. 'And also, the ring doesn't want to be with Eldrow. I can hear it; it talks to me.'

'You can hear the ring speak?' Almarra was staring at her intently. Then she nodded. 'I understand. But what does Dot look like? Where does she live? We only want to talk to her.'

So Maggie described Dot's mad white hair, her tiny wheelchair, and then the house on the corner a few streets from the high street with the turret.

Almarra hugged her close. 'You will go down in Islander lore as the one who helped us bring back the light.'

Maggie relaxed. She felt like she'd done the right thing for once. They just wanted to know if Dot knew anything. And she obviously did. Hadn't she told her to take the ring? She sat back, exhausted suddenly, and looked out over the strangely beautiful dark sea. With the pale white sky above, it was like looking at two giant squares on a chessboard.

Almarra squeezed Maggie's hand. 'Stay here. I'll be back soon.' And she was gone.

Maggie peered over the edge of the high walls. Below her she could see the inhabitants moving about, whilst the rocky black beach stretched up the coastland and far off wild storms still raged over the ocean.

*

Almarra was gone for a long time. And after a while Maggie felt the same stirrings of unease as when she had woken and found Eldrow looking at her. She pulled back the curtain a little and peered out. Two orbs hung in the air just outside the door opposite, and one of the sombre young servant women sat on a chair quietly sewing a huge mound of black material.

Just then there was a loud clattering from somewhere below. The servant woman sprang up and the orbs instinctively drifted down to see what was happening. Maggie took her chance. She pushed back the curtain, scuttled over to the door opposite and pushed it open.

She found herself in a large empty room where there was another balcony with a curtain pulled across. She saw the outline of two figures standing beyond it. Maggie crept over and tried to listen against the swirling wind.

Eldrow was speaking in a low, urgent voice. '. . . I have been tormented by awful dreams – of the Magic Mountains falling into the sea in flames, of the land all burnt, Sun City in ruins, everyone ended. They are so vivid that when I wake it takes me a long time to realise that they are not true.'

'The girl says she can hear the ring speak,' Almarra said. 'She says it doesn't want to be with you.'

'Do you think I care what it wants?' Eldrow let out a cry and clutched his hand. He panted for a few moments with the pain.

Almarra laughed. 'It burns you?'

'What of it? It's the most powerful amulet in our world and no harm can befall the wearer. Aaaah.' Then he muttered through gritted teeth, 'Besides, it's getting better – I'm taming it.'

'You prefer that it hates you.'

They both laughed. 'Perhaps.'

'And the girl?' Almarra said after a moment. 'Why did you bring her here? It's not your usual method of information extraction.' Her voice was gently mocking.

'She is so like my sister, down to her every movement – it confuses me.'

'You care for her?'

'I care for no one!' Eldrow snapped. 'But there is something odd, do you not think, about her appearing to me like this. She brings the ring; she claims to cross alone; the Children cannot read her.'

'You think it's a trap?'

'That's why I brought her to you.'

Maggie saw Almarra, in silhouette, put her hands together like she was praying. She stayed still for some time. When she spoke again, her voice was deadly serious. 'The girl troubles me. You must watch her like a hawk. She has strange powers, but she seems without guile. My spies have told me of a moon witch prophecy that says this child will bring light to the Island. But why should we listen to them? They run on superstition and make-believe, and they are no friends of ours. But I cannot tell if we should protect or destroy her.'

'Protect or destroy her,' Eldrow repeated thoughtfully.

A dark figure suddenly appeared beside Maggie and she gave a small cry of surprise before she could control herself. The voices stopped abruptly. Terror constricted the servant woman's face and she gestured wildly at her huge skirt. Maggie understood at once and scrambled under the dark rustling dome just as the curtain drew back.

The young woman's legs were trembling as Almarra stalked over. She was like a spider, Maggie thought.

'Why aren't you guarding the child?'

'I'm sorry, ma'am. I thought I heard you call for me.'

Maggie was so close that she could have reached out from under the thick material and grabbed Almarra's spindly legs. She held her breath.

'Get back to your post.'

She curtsied. 'Yes, ma'am.'

The curtain was drawn across again. Maggie crawled like a cat under the skirt as the woman edged out of the room.

They shuffled across the circular stone hallway. Through the layers of gauze, Maggie could just make out the two orbs back at their post. The young woman bowed her head towards them then drew the curtain back and closed it behind them.

Maggie rolled out from beneath her skirts and stood up. 'Thank you.'

The woman said nothing and Maggie saw that her dark eyes were full of fear. Somehow a flow of understanding passed between them. She seemed to be silently wishing her good luck. She pressed Maggie's hand and then fled.

Maggie looked out at the cold dark sea, but she barely saw it. Eldrow wasn't her friend. He had only cared about her enough not to torture her for the information he needed; it was only the ring that he wanted.

Her cheeks flushed with shame. She had fallen for it, just like with Ida, just like with Hoagy. She thought of Almarra's words, 'I cannot tell if we should protect or destroy her.' But instead of fear, she felt rage.

So be it. Her life as a special, happy person was over – it had never existed. She had no friends. She was a loner, just like her mum. But there was no way these creeps were going to decide whether she lived or died. Maggie took a deep breath – red was rushing through her so fast that she felt like she might explode. She had to calm down and she had to think. She only knew one thing: she could no longer rely on anyone but herself.

Soon afterwards, she heard footsteps behind her, but when she turned to see Eldrow and Almarra beside her, she adopted such an innocent happy expression that they could not imagine the anger that was churning inside her.

27

IDA

The dark empty landscape passed by them vast and unseen. Two of the orbs hovered in the carriage with her, so Maggie kept a blank smile on her face. The happiness she'd felt here, the elation from the glitra, suddenly didn't seem real. When it wore off, she realised, there was only a deeper emptiness left behind.

Eldrow was asleep and in the gloom she saw the ring glinting on his finger in the faint light thrown by the orbs. For once it was not calling to her, as if it too slept. She felt no compulsion to try and take it back. It had found the right home. She would be glad never to see it again.

She thought about Frank for the first time since she'd woken up in Sun City. Was he still waiting for her outside the city gates? 'The only way to beat the darkness is to stop thinking of yourself and truly think of others.' That was what he had said to her. But she hadn't listened.

Truly think of others . . . Was it possible that she'd never really thought of anyone but herself? She'd only ever seen her mum as someone who didn't understand her, who made her life difficult . . . And she'd been so obsessed with being friends with Ida and then so full of the idea of rescuing her that she hadn't thought much about who she was, or why she'd been so sad the day she was taken.

And Hoagy – she almost started crying just thinking of his old fat furry body. She missed him. But the orbs must not see that she was upset and she must not wake Eldrow.

The cat had lost weight, and he'd looked so tired and old when she'd seen him. Was he her friend? She didn't really know any more. But he was here in this dark world because of her and she'd turned him away. He might be dead by now. The thought was unbearable.

And behind it all was the white vaulted room with the things inside, the living crouching things that flowed into her mind again and again, however hard she tried to shut them out.

A heavy rain was falling when they finally got back to Sun City. A cortège of umons picked them up in a hand-drawn carriage, and Maggie nearly fell asleep as they jolted from side to side up the steep cobbles towards the palace.

As they entered the great empty hall, Eldrow gave a nod and the Children morphed into orbs and drifted up to the ceiling like scaly helium balloons, leaving her and the great ruler of Sun City together.

They walked up to the second floor and stopped beside the enormous ballroom that now stood in darkness, a vast empty space. Eldrow put his hand on her shoulder and instead of joy, Maggie felt dread. Only a few hours before he had calmly been discussing whether she should live or die – it clearly didn't matter much to him either way. The ring whispered away in her head, but Maggie wasn't listening.

Eldrow smiled down at her, but his smile was cold. 'You have proved your loyalty to me, Maggie.'

Maggie smiled back at him as sweetly as she could and said, 'Can I visit Ida now?'

His eyes glittered dangerously. 'You remind me so much of someone who was dear to me, Maggie. We were close, so very close. But she disobeyed me. I don't want to see you make the same mistake. You won't, will you? Not after everything I've done for you?'

Maggie shook her head. She tried to look calm but her heart was beating wildly. She forced herself to go on, 'But I just want to see Ida again, just once.'

That was it: in one swift movement he was upon her. He slammed her against the wall and grabbed her neck so that she found it hard to breathe. 'Don't ever say her name to me again!' Then he let her fall to the floor and walked away down the passage until his stooping black form disappeared from view.

Maggie tried to get up, but she had no energy at all. She

lay on the stone floor, staring at the ceiling and listening to the sound of the rain plummeting down outside. She felt too numb to be anywhere close to tears: she was blank. But she knew now: it was all a lie. If Ida was still alive, she was not happy and she was probably not in the City of Flowers, if that place even existed. Maggie knew she must do what she had come here to do.

After a while, Maggie forced herself to get up. She felt like a robot as she trudged up to her room and closed the door. She knelt down and opened the heavy wooden trunk at the bottom of her bed. Tucked away inside she found her old West Minchen clothes. They had been carefully washed and pressed, and she felt a sense of relief as she took off her robe and all her heavy gold jewellery and put on her old T-shirt and jeans.

She couldn't find her coat or trainers anywhere – it was possible they had been deemed too disgusting to keep. So she had to put the soft green slippers she'd been given onto her bare feet. Then she tiptoed to her bedroom door and peered out.

Sure enough, an orb was hovering just outside. She went over to her dressing table and rang the bell. A few moments later, a very sleepy Una appeared.

'I would like a bath,' Maggie announced.

'At once?' Una asked, confused and rubbing her eyes.

'Now!' Maggie screamed.

The maid started with surprise, and ran out. Eventually, four umons arrived with huge vats of boiling water balanced on their backs. Then a fifth arrived with cold to cool it off. The maid lit the lanterns and Maggie instructed them all to leave.

She made sure her bedroom door was slightly open. But instead of getting into the bath, she opened her wardrobe and threw all her beautiful clothes and gold jewellery onto the floor, making as much noise as possible.

It wasn't long before the orb had drifted down to watch her. She turned round as if shocked. 'What do you want?'

The orb merely buzzed closer to her. Steam was rising from the bath.

Maggie took a few steps back. 'Leave me alone.'

But the orb only came closer. She moved to the other side of the bath until the orb was hovering right over the water. It was almost touching her face. She felt its malice flowing out, and the anger she'd felt sitting on Almarra's balcony looking at the black sea came back to her so strongly she was afraid of herself. But there was no time for hesitation.

She lunged forwards, placed both hands on top of the orb and pushed it into the hot water with all her might. It was surprisingly solid and electricity pulsed painfully into her skin. The orb shrieked like an animal in pain and there was a horrible singeing smell. Maggie ran.

She ran down the great staircase, across the deserted hall and then down to the kitchen. At the archway, she turned left and saw the door. It was wide open and golden light spilled out into the dark. There was nothing else to do, but go inside.

The heat was almost suffocating. Maggie moved across the narrow space to the ladder that led down to the huge white room. She felt calm; there was no turning back.

She climbed down the rungs, blinking into the bright white light. Maggie could not hide from it now: she forced herself to look. And she saw that there were people inside the containers: the 'sleepers', human beings trapped in glass prisons.

Closest to her a dark-haired boy, maybe a couple of years older than her, was sitting but slumped over, his long slender hands limp at his side. His skin was grey and covered in a sheen of sweat, and a streak of dribble leaked from one side of his mouth.

In the next container along, another smaller boy with glasses lay on the floor splayed out on his back. His eyes were wide and staring but he wasn't moving. Maggie hurried past him, afraid to look.

Next a woman in a once-smart blue suit, now greasy with filth, rocked backwards and forwards on her haunches, muttering to herself. Maggie wanted to scream: this was unbearable. But then she saw Ida.

She was curled up in the foetal position, her curls dark with grease and pushed away from her face, which was slick with sweat and dirt. She still wore the hideous green uniform of Fortlake Secondary with its bogus Latin crest, but now it hung around her body like a sack. Her skin was yellowish and she had deep bruises beneath her eyes. A sinister pale tube trailed out of her skull. So this was Eldrow's idea of happiness?

Maggie saw how the long tube went from the upper floor into the top of the container and then into the back of Ida's head. Peering round she saw that a tiny hole had been made at the base of Ida's skull just by her ear and the tube had been inserted into this hole. In a flash she remembered Dan the Tree, the weird mark he had shown her in the woods.

Just then, a sopping wet boy appeared at the top of the ladder hissing and screaming, his gold eyes flaring like a deranged cat. And someone violently grabbed her arm.

'Silence!' Eldrow screamed, and the shifter backed away, though its eyes still glinted with hate. 'Well, Maggie,' Eldrow said, his hand holding her so tightly she could feel her skin starting to bruise, 'I've been meaning to give you the tour for some time.' And he laughed.

She tried to turn round so she could see him, but he held her there like a helpless animal. 'So, you've finally found your friend,' Eldrow's voice continued, heavy with sarcasm. 'And the wonderful glitra you've been enjoying? This is how we make it. Who knows, maybe you've even enjoyed a little of Ida's happiness?'

Maggie thought she might be sick. She felt his hand

shove her and she fell against Ida's glass cage. She pressed her hands against the glass. Its surface was very hot, almost too hot to touch.

'Ida?' she said softly.

Ida's eyelids fluttered and she moved slightly, as if she sensed someone was looking at her. Finally, after struggling for some time, she managed to prize open her eyelids. And then they shot open. Maggie span round, but it was too late. Two orbs rammed into her, shock surged through her body and she slumped to the ground.

28

HAPPINESS

The back of Maggie's head hurt. She moved a sweaty hand over to it and drew sharply back in panic. Something was sticking out of the back of her head. She curled up on the hard slippery floor. There was no energy left in her body, her mind, or her soul. She was a vacuum. Yet something still bothered her, like an itch. There was someone there, someone near her. She needed to open her eyes.

When she finally managed it, she saw an animal was watching her from behind thick glass. It was trapped in a dirty glass cage. It was a cat, a cat with one eye and beside it there was another creature: a scruffy grey thing with a long tail and a scrunched-up pink face. She said something and the sound of her own voice confused her as if she had never heard it before.

The creatures looked afraid; they looked tired and afraid. But they were familiar to her. She put a hand up to the glass. It felt warm and slippery – she was very hot. Then she understood – *she* was inside the cage, not the cat. On the other side, the cat raised its paw, so they would have touched were it not for the barrier between them. Then to her absolute astonishment, it spoke.

'Maggie, you have to get out of here.'

It knew her name, which she would have struggled to remember just then. She knew the cat from another place and time. The name came to her lips before she realised what was going on, 'Hoagy.'

The cat broke into a deep sonorous purr and its claws extended and retracted against the glass. Maggie felt the pain in her head again, stronger this time.

'Can you pull that thing out?' he said and nodded at the back of her head.

But Maggie didn't feel she could do anything. There was nothing in the world for her, so she might as well stay here where she didn't bother anyone, where she could sink into her own uselessness.

The little grey creature spoke. 'Girl from another place, you have to get out.'

Maggie found the strength to speak, 'Please, just go away.' As she said it, she knew she didn't really want them to go away.

Hoagy started purring loudly and his tail flexed irritably at the same time. 'The rat rescued me outside the city walls. We decided to come and find you together. To speak

269

frankly, I could have been home by now. So stop feeling sorry for yourself. We need you to get up.'

Maggie groped around in her head. 'What's happened to me?'

The grey creature looked grave. 'You're a sleeper. They're taking your happiness.'

Maggie's heart stuttered as a flood of memories came back. She moved her hand back to the same sore spot again and tentatively felt the smooth slender thing attached there. It felt like soft bone, sturdy but flexible. But even moving it a tiny bit caused her awful pain and she cried out. Tears filled her eyes.

The cat spoke calmly, 'You've only been here a few hours. The rat thought they might bring you here. He crawled in through some pipes and found a way to get me in. We saw what they did to you. The wolf was here, and the psychopath and his six little friends. But they've gone now. They won't have taken too much happiness from you yet. So stand up and pull that thing out of your head. Do you understand? Then you can get out.'

Maggie tried to stand, but she was very weak and her feet slipped on the bottom of the huge glass bottle. Eventually she staggered up using her hands against the condensation-heavy sides. Beyond her she saw the other big glass bottles just like the one she was in. They stretched out like a mirror reflecting on itself, except they were not reflections. There were other people inside them, other sleepers.

In the bottle closest to her, a man with receding hair and an overgrown beard was slumped against the side. His head, which currently lolled forwards, also had a pale tube coming out of it from a tiny hole cut just behind his left ear. He wasn't moving.

The same long delicate white tube, like tarnished ivory, ran from the man's head through the top of the bottle and up into the wall. Tubes from other glass jars did the same. Maggie couldn't bear it. She bashed her hands against the thick glass sides wanting to breathe clean fresh air, to be out of here. But she was only making herself tired.

She took a deep breath and tentatively felt for the tube at the back of her own head. Again she winced in pain at the slightest contact. Hoagy was looking at her. He didn't move a muscle, his one eye didn't even seem to blink and Maggie felt like he was trying to give her strength. She looked once again at the half-dead man in the bottle beside her. She had to get out.

She closed her eyes: five . . . four . . . three . . . two . . . On one she wrenched at the tube with all her might. A terrible noise sounded in her ears, like a wild animal screeching in pain, and just before she blacked out she realised it was the sound of her own scream.

When she woke the pain was unbearable, there was blood all around her, and a deafening alarm was ringing. Gradually she understood that Hoagy and the umon had pushed one of the ladders down into her bottle and their paws were dragging her up it.

As she got to the top, a masked guard ran into the room wielding his axe. He lunged for them. Maggie fell down the other side of the bottle, while Frank leapt at the guard and bit deep into his leg. The man crumpled up in pain on the floor. Then, while the going was good, Hoagy turned and sprayed tomcat pee right in the guard's face so that he screamed and put his hands up to his eyes.

There was the thunder of more footsteps above them and closer still, the confused moans and cries of the other sleepers, disturbed from their awful slumber. Frank grabbed Maggie's hand, she managed to stand up and he pulled her away. She looked back for a moment at her glass cell and saw the dangling tentacle of the tube that had been stuck into her head covered in blood and little scraps of flesh. She would have been sick but for the speed with which the little umon propelled her across the floor, Hoagy running close behind them.

The umon dragged Maggie into a hidden corridor off which there were a series of small stone cells. He pushed her into one.

'I used to serve here,' he hissed.

In one corner there were several ladders, bits of the tarpaulin-like material they'd covered the train carriages with and stacks of metal pans and cups. Frank threw some of the tarpaulin over Maggie and then the cat and the umon slunk into the shadows behind her amongst the ladders, their bellies pressed against the floor.

Beneath the heavy material Maggie's breath sounded very loud as she listened to the guards rushing into the room beyond them. There were shouts and shrieks over the moans of the sleepers. Suddenly a guard looked into their cell. Through a gap in the tarpaulin, Maggie saw him clearly: he had a long distinctive scar visible on his cheek above his mask and strange yellow eyes. She stayed as still as she could.

Please go away, please go away . . . she said over and over in her head.

He seemed to be looking straight at her, but he didn't come any further into the room. Then he ran out. 'No one!' Maggie heard him shout. And she heard his footsteps run away again.

She rested her head back against the cold stone and breathed out in relief. She could still hear cries and pounding feet. The whole palace was on red alert. But after a while, the sounds became more distant.

They crept back into the white room. It was empty and Frank raced for the exit, but Maggie ran back looking for Ida. When she saw her she thumped on the glass, but the crumpled green pile didn't move. Maggie banged on the glass as loudly as she could and screamed, 'Ida!'

The girl stirred and her eyes opened but then they rolled back in her head. Hoagy was beside her. But Frank was already halfway up the ladder to the upper floor.

'It's too late,' he barked anxiously. 'The guards will come back. The whole city will be looking for you soon.'

'We have to get her out,' shouted Maggie.

'There is no time!' screeched the umon.

Maggie felt red surging through her and with it, a little more strength. 'She's coming with us!' she screamed back.

Frank looked startled, paused for a moment, then twitched his snout and ran back. Maggie picked up one of the ladders from the side and Hoagy nimbly climbed up and jumped down into Ida's container. Maggie slid down beside him and shook the lifeless girl.

Meanwhile Hoagy began to gently bite at the hideous tubing coming out of Ida's head. It was clearly tough stuff and he struggled to even make an indentation, but eventually it started to tear.

Ida stirred and her face creased up in pain as Hoagy chewed and bit. Finally it broke and as it did, the awful deafening wailing of the alarm started up again, like fifty bells being rung together right inside your head. Ida passed out again.

Hoagy began to lick Ida's face with all his might with his rough little tongue. At last Ida stirred and sat up, but nothing flickered behind her half-dead eyes.

Maggie got right into her face and shouted, 'Ida! It's Maggie Blue.' There was no response. 'It's the Bruise! You hate me, remember?! You have to get up!'

Frank was running around frantically now in circles,

like a dog chasing its tail. 'There's no time, there's no time. We'll be ended!'

Hoagy started biting Ida's legs again, harder now. She wailed but still didn't move. Then, in his new favourite manoeuvre, the cat turned his bum towards her and delivered a smarting spray of pee in her direction, though he was careful to avoid the eyes. Ida coughed and gagged, but it seemed to wake her up a bit. She shook her head to try and escape the stench, her face frowning in confusion and disgust.

Maggie managed to pull Ida to her feet, then grabbed the top of the ladder and seesawed it into the container. She pushed Ida up it, let her fall down the other side then she slid down beside her. But as she pulled the limp girl up onto her feet and dragged her towards the exit, something else caught her attention. One of the sleepers, the inhabitant of the bottle next to Ida's, was watching her intently from behind the thick glass. He was staring at Maggie, and there was a flicker of recognition in his eyes.

It took Maggie a moment to piece together the drawn cheeks and desperate sunken eyes with the ragged corduroy trousers and sensible gold-rimmed glasses. And then Maggie realised she knew him too. Despite his grey skin and withered form, her geography teacher seemed filled with a taut sinewy energy different to the other sleepers, and sweat dripped rapidly off his tired distressed face.

Maggie went up to the glass. 'Mr Yates?'

Maggie thought about how happy he'd been that day Miss Cane met him after class, how she had flirted with him, no doubt to lead him to this awful place, and she felt she hated Miss Cane-the-wolf more than any other person or thing she had ever known.

'There is no time!' Frank screamed again behind her, quite beside himself now.

Mr Yates grinned at her, an awful empty grin. Looking at him was like looking down into a deep black hole – it was terrifying. So she turned away, grabbed Ida's hand and ran, pulling Ida along with her.

Stumbling and panting they dragged Ida up to the boiling hot upper floor and then into the stone passageway. The shouts were louder here, but Hoagy recognised the place at once. He led them to the open trapdoor he had fallen through, and Maggie and Frank peered over his shoulder. It was about a two-metre drop, but there was now a huge wooden crate full of discarded food beneath the hole. It emitted a putrid stench that wafted eagerly up towards them. Hoagy purred with glee.

Ida had dropped onto her hands and knees and was crawling off, so Maggie grabbed her arm and with a last quick glance at Hoagy, just pushed her out. Ida squealed as she fell and landed in the nasty mess below. Hoagy and Frank dived in after her. But as Maggie got down onto the ledge the cart began to move beneath her. She pushed herself out and just managed to catch the side of the cart, hitting her back on the edge painfully. She stifled her howl of pain and slid off the edge into the putrid pile of food.

She found Ida, Frank and Hoagy half-submerged in stinking garbage, the latter looking deeply unimpressed by circumstances, an errant slice of some weird purple vegetable unwittingly perched upon his head. He was about to speak, but Maggie put her finger to her lips.

The cart was attached to a team of umons and an old driver was geeing them on, seemingly oblivious to the late arrivals to his cargo. Trundling into the bright illuminated streets of Sun City they could hear the shouts of guards and from the rectangle of sky afforded them by the wooden cart, Maggie saw the orbs skim rapidly down into the streets searching for their prey.

There were maggots writhing on her skin in the rotting food making it hard not to gag, there was blood seeping out of the wound at the back of her head where she'd wrenched out the tube. But all Maggie felt was triumph; a wild adrenaline-filled joy to be leaving this dark and hideous place.

29

CIRCLE OF LIGHT

Their descent suddenly became steeper and then they jerked to a stop. Ida made a little cry, but it was muffled down in the container as shouts rang out and the umons pulling them barked. Then they heard the heavy city gates creak open and the cart moved out onto rougher uneven ground. The sky darkened above them and they were thrown roughly from side to side.

Finally, after what felt like many hours, they came to a halt and Maggie peered over the edge of the cart. Now the only light came from the driver's lanterns. The umons sighed and Maggie could see steam rising from their bodies in the chill air as the driver dismounted slowly.

Maggie saw him press something at the bottom of the cart and suddenly she was catapulted into the air. She screamed as she was thrown into an even bigger cesspit of rubbish. The old driver paused at the edge of the tip for a moment or two. But he must have thought he was hearing things because he soon got back onto his cart and plodded away.

The cat's peevish voice rang out in the darkness. 'This really is the height of glamour.'

Maggie started laughing with relief, but quickly stopped as she got a mouthful of something that was moving. She spluttered and spat. 'Can you see Ida?'

'No. She's probably just nodded off again.'

They searched around for her in the darkness until Hoagy spotted her, limp and passive, a cabbage on top of her head. Frank emerged too and they all dragged Ida out onto the bank.

Shards of white-time light were just beginning to pierce the darkness and they saw they were in a wasteland, flat and dull, with only the recently disturbed soil of other dumping grounds in mounds around them. The white-time was paler than usual and the land seemed to stretch for ever beyond them to the flat horizon. Sun City was nowhere to be seen.

At least no one would be looking for them here, thought Maggie.

Frank paced up and down. 'We must return to the place between worlds.'

'But won't they go there too?' asked Maggie.

His snout twitched. 'For now they think you're still in Sun City. But they won't for long. We must try and get there first.'

Maggie dragged Ida onto her feet, but she was determined to move on her hands and knees, so she just let her crawl along beside her.

She thought about West Minchen and it seemed completely unreal. That people were getting on with their normal lives, driving along the street, buying food in a shop, going to work . . .

Maggie wondered if Esme had been relieved when she realised she'd gone. Had they told her mum, had there been an assembly for her at school, had her dad come to London? No one would be surprised she had run away. It was expected of her. Anyway, she didn't have a home to go back to. There was nowhere in particular she was meant to be. She looked at Ida, and despite the girl's desperate state, she still felt a flicker of envy.

Abruptly the land curved round and fell away in front of them. And after a few more minutes of traipsing it flowed down slightly and a little stream suddenly appeared.

'Drink,' Frank instructed.

Maggie and Hoagy gulped down water and forced a few handfuls into Ida's mouth, but the umon was already pacing up and down impatiently, his face drawn with worry.

'We must be moving.'

Maggie splashed water on her face and tried to rinse her hair quickly. The cold water woke her up and without warning, the image of Mr Yates' face flashed into her mind. But he had been too far gone – there was nothing she could have done. *Except get him out of there* a quiet voice said in her head. But she couldn't save everyone. *You could have saved him,* the quiet voice replied.

Maggie shook her head – she couldn't think about him now. If Eldrow caught them, then she and Ida would be taken back to the huge glass containers. And then there would be nothing, just the awful dull pain in your heart that made you want to die. She shivered. She would do whatever it took to get them home.

They hurried on in silence. Ida occasionally stopped crawling and slumped over, but carried on like an automaton as soon as anyone gave her a little shove. She said nothing, looked at nothing and there was no expression on her thin weary face.

By the time they dropped down into the dead leaves of the forest, exhausted and hungry, it was the moment just before darkness fell. There was no sound or movement coming from the black trees, but Maggie felt afraid.

Ida whimpered softly beside her, but she didn't move.

'Do you think they took all her happiness?' Maggie whispered, but Hoagy didn't answer.

Frank was up on his haunches sniffing the air. 'We must take the tunnels. They can't reach us there.'

'Underground?' Maggie's heart began to race. 'But . . . but I can't.'

The umon ignored her and set off into the trees. Maggie, Ida and Hoagy followed until Frank stopped and began stomping on the ground. Finally the earth fell away and he beckoned Maggie over.

'You go first then I will lower the girl down.'

Slowly Maggie got down onto the ground and hung her legs over the dark drop. 'Is it far?' she asked.

'Go!' Frank hissed in her ears and his webbed paw pushed her down into the narrow darkness.

It was the same soft pile of soil and leaves as the other hole, and after a few moments, Hoagy landed elegantly beside her. They pressed themselves against the earth walls so that Ida could fall safely, which she did, like a rag doll.

Then Frank nimbly climbed down using tree roots as handles. He dropped down beside them.

'We have built a secret network of tunnels all over the Island. Shifters are terrified of being under the earth, and the guards cannot fit.' He eyed Maggie and Ida appraisingly. 'You two will just make it.'

He opened his little rucksack and in a now-familiar routine, sliced off four pieces of the strange malted loaf with his pearl knife.

Maggie fell upon hers like a wild beast and even Hoagy forced his down, although he had to make a huge effort to control his bodily convulsions so he didn't just throw it up again straight away. Ida just let hers fall to the ground and looked blankly ahead, seemingly no more perturbed by the confined tunnel than she had been by the vast empty plains or the dark forest.

Frank cocked his head and listened intently. 'It's quiet,' he observed to no one in particular.

'Perhaps they've given up?' suggested Maggie.

He shook his head. 'No.'

'Couldn't they just let us go?' said Maggie.

'No one disobeys Eldrow,' Frank replied. 'That is punishable by ending.'

He scratched himself violently then got on all four paws and led the way into the dark tunnel. Ida went next, then Maggie, both on their hands and knees, and Hoagy brought up the rear.

Underground the air was thick with soil and the walls pressed tightly around her. Maggie tried to control her fear as they crawled along, but almost at once, she began to panic. What if the tunnel collapsed and they were buried under all that earth? She couldn't turn round; she could only keep onwards. She could feel Hoagy's narrow hot breath just behind her.

It's OK, just keep going, she told herself, *it will be over soon. Just keep going . . .*

But it was so hot in there, she felt like she couldn't breathe.

Then they started to take right and left turns round narrow corners until Maggie was utterly confused and she knew she could never find her way back. Ahead of her, Ida kept plodding along like an obedient dog, clearly nothing in her head. But, despite her best efforts, Maggie's thoughts were starting to get out of control and she felt like the dusty soil was filling up her lungs.

'Hoagy?' she whispered, her voice catching with fear.

'Hmmm?'

'Can you remember the way back? I mean, if we had to go back, could you remember how?'

'Of course,' came his confident reply. 'Cat-nav, remember?'

Maggie crawled on a little more reassured, but then she wondered if it was true. Maybe he was lying. Maybe cat-nav didn't work underground. And didn't he sound a little scared, too? They'd taken so many turns by now. There was no way back. And the thought of it, and how far under the earth they were, how dense and thick the soil was above them, how it could all fall in upon them at any moment, made her want to choke again.

She gasped for breath. Her head pulsed and she couldn't see straight. She started crying and her breath came in short sharp bursts of panic.

Frank turned. 'What happens back there?'

And Maggie tried to answer, 'I . . . I . . . I . . .' But she never got the words out because just then the ground began to slope upwards and Maggie felt, with unbelievable relief, a cooler breeze flowing down to them from above ground.

Just before they came out into the air, Frank turned to them. 'Hold on to me, girl from another place. You must hold the limp girl, then the feline. We have to walk without the light.'

They did as he said, then the umon extinguished his lantern. Clutching his paw, Maggie could tell that the little creature was hyper-alert and tense. His whole body twitched with anxiety as he led them along in the dark, his head flicking constantly from side to side.

All around them the forest was eerily quiet. No lanterns flickered through the trees and no orbs hung above the tree line. But Maggie could feel him trembling. As they walked he looked back to her and she could just make out his pale worried face.

'Will you take me back to your world, girl from another place?' he whispered. 'I can't stay here. They will end me.'

Maggie squeezed his paw. 'Of course. We'll look after you.'

'Thank you, friend,' he said. But his voice sounded sad.

When they arrived, Frank made them wait for ages crouching in the black leaves. But eventually he let them creep forward. The umon lit his lantern and sure enough, there it was: Maggie's bedraggled blue scarf still tied to the gnarled arching tree.

Ida sat down and slumped against a tree, and Hoagy began to retch, his body undulating into a rhythm until finally, with a great *bleurgh*, he vomited up the malty loaf. Then he began cleaning himself frantically. Meanwhile Frank prowled around the perimeter of the trees, muttering softly to himself.

Only Maggie felt relief. She'd done it. She'd come to the dark world and rescued Ida, just like she said she would. She would go back to her world and get kicked out of school and then she didn't know what would happen to her. But at least she would know she'd done this. That she'd been Ida's best friend without Ida even knowing it. In some ways, wasn't that the best kind of friend you could be?

She sat a little apart from everyone else, closed her eyes and cleared her mind of everything: the lake glittering beneath the glorious moon, the umons swimming, the ancient's wrinkled face; Sun City, its pale walls and magnificent palace, Eldrow in ecstasy, his long arms flying from side to side, his head flung back; the bottles, the awful bottles with the sleepers slumped inside; the tube with little bits of her flesh sticking to it, Mr Yates and his desperate eyes. No, no, no – she especially wanted to forget him.

Slowly she let it all slip from her mind until something in her head seemed to open up like when a feature is about to start at the cinema and the screen widens. Then there was nothing left in her mind except a sense of light and a humming white noise. She smiled.

She imagined the window was right in front of her, shimmering, fuzzing at the edges in its mysterious way, a wall of light in the pitch-black forest. Slowly she began to be aware of a different kind of air flowing over her. It was not the damp chill of Everfall Woods – it was different. A sterile heated air, an indoor air – it confused her.

But when she opened her eyes, she saw it all the same: the quivering rectangle of light. And as she drew closer, almost in a trance, to reach out and touch the jittery electric edges, that strange soft rubber she must prize slowly apart with her fingers, she imagined she could hear a strange tinny music, a sort of glockenspiel wittering an inconsequential tune.

But then another flickering of light distracted her from somewhere in the corner of her eye. Irritated she glanced away from the portal and saw a row of bright lights slowly forming a circle all around her. She stepped towards them but she still didn't understand.

There came a terrible scream. She saw Frank on the ground, not moving, a bloody gash on the side of his head. She looked around for Ida. The orbs had pinned her down and she lay beneath them like a zombie, not fighting, not struggling. Hoagy was nowhere to be seen.

The lights moved forwards a little and Maggie saw at least twenty guards, their faces hidden by black masks, their axes and spears raised. They surrounded her in a circle blocking the way to the portal. And coming through their ranks now were the same two dreaded figures that had haunted her fevered glass-bottle dreams: Miss Cane with her long glinting white hair, and Eldrow, his once-gentle features now distorted with rage.

30

A KNIGHT IN SHINING TINFOIL

Before Maggie could think what to do, several masked guards rushed at her, shoved her to her knees and tied her hands behind her back. When she looked up at Eldrow his eyes were terrifying, like the storms she'd seen raging over the black sea. Miss Cane stood beside him, though still a safe distance from the ouroboros on his finger, her sharp teeth bared, ready to pounce.

'What are you doing here?' Eldrow said very softly.

His voice chilled Maggie to the bone. She looked over at Ida. The orbs had morphed into the six little boys and two of them were sitting on Ida's fragile body, their golden eyes glowing. A trickle of blood seeped to the ground from the back of Ida's head where the end of the eerie white tube still stuck out. Maggie could feel her own wound pulsing.

'You betrayed me!' Eldrow screamed suddenly.

Maggie jumped at the violence of his voice. 'I'm sorry, I'm sorry.' Even stronger than fear, she felt shame at how badly she had let everyone down. She pressed her nails into her palms until they hurt.

She glanced round. Beyond the line of masked guards, she could still see the portal hanging calmly in the thick air. She knew Miss Cane could pass through it and that the orbs could at least see it, but could anyone else? Could Eldrow or his guards? If she could just get Ida there and push her through, she would have done something. But it was impossible. The portal might as well have been a thousand miles away.

Eldrow loomed closer to her, his voice was a threatening hiss. 'Nobody wants you now, Maggie.' He paced around her and prodded her painfully at the top of her chest with his strong sinewy index finger. 'You're useless to everyone. Your mother is in the dark place, in despair, but you can't help her. You cannot even make her smile, not for one moment. She hates you.'

He was behind her now, his voice winding into her ear. 'And your father? He abandoned you – that's how little he cares.' He laughed. 'And yet you are so desperate for someone to love you that you came here to rescue a girl who doesn't even like you and never will.'

Maggie closed her eyes and let his voice wash over her. She had no resistance to him any more.

'But you forgot all about the girl, didn't you, Maggie? You forgot her and everyone else when you thought *I* cared for you, when you thought the ruler of Sun City loved you. But why would I ever care for someone as pathetic as you?'

It was true. She couldn't pretend to herself any longer. No one liked her, not even her mum and dad. Esme had tried, but it was no good. She'd never had a real friend. Wherever she went, other people, normal people, didn't want her there. A strong pain began to radiate out from her heart.

Eldrow's face was very close to hers. 'And now everything must end for you,' he said softly, almost sadly, 'because no one disobeys me. Ever.'

Maggie kept pressing her nails into her palms as hard as she could. She clenched her teeth together and scrunched up her eyes as tightly closed as they would go. She was holding herself together and then from somewhere deep inside her head she heard a voice . . .

Release me and I will save you.

It was the ring!

She opened her eyes. Miss Cane was still standing motionless near Eldrow, her terrible green eyes fixed upon Maggie. Then suddenly, as if she could wait no longer, she morphed into the wolf and rounded on Maggie, snarling aggressively in her face. Maggie fell back in shock and cut her hand on a sharp stone lodged amidst the black leaves on the ground behind her. She felt a trickle of blood start to seep out and the wolf's snout twitched with interest.

'Enough!' commanded Eldrow, but there was amusement in his voice. 'There's still something I want to know.'

The wolf hunkered back and Eldrow motioned to the guards to pick Maggie up. As they did, the rope tying her hands caught against the stone. She felt the material tear a little and a spark went off in her brain.

'Who helped you cross, Maggie? I don't believe you did it alone. If you tell us, your ending will be merciful.'

Maggie fell to her knees, this time of her own accord. 'Please forgive me. I know I'm not worthy of you. I've made a terrible mistake. But I understand now that Ida is worthless. I've only ever felt truly happy with you. Please forgive me.' And Maggie opened her big eyes as wide as they could go. 'Please take me back. I miss you.'

She heard the wolf snarl behind her and the Children morphed back into orbs and hovered towards her. She had to find the strength to hold them back. Almost at once she felt the invisible probes begin to dig into her mind, the painful unpleasant ache, and the white haze began to descend around her.

But the voice kept on: *I am with you. I will never let you go. You are stronger. . .*

Maggie looked into Eldrow's eyes, and suddenly she forgot all about the orbs, and the guards and even the wolf faded away. She began to feel calm, and the more she looked into his twisted-up angry face, the calmer she felt. After a few moments, something clicked in her brain, that strange feeling when knowledge rose up so certainly to her.

And suddenly she could see him. She could see and feel his self-pity and despair – it washed over her in a powerful wave. And Maggie gasped because what she felt the most, more than anger, more than hate and pride, was fear. Eldrow was a quivering mass of fear. He was lonely and he was afraid.

Looming above her, Eldrow was motionless, shocked and fascinated, as if he too was only just learning how he felt. Somehow he knew that she could see him and for a moment he didn't know how to react. She mustn't anger him now. She let her mind go blank.

Only good things, she thought, *only positive things, no hate, no anger, no red.*

So from her heart, for real, not pretending, she transmitted feelings of happiness and love towards the unhappy twisted-up man. She imagined love flowing from her to him like a wave, an invisible pulse straight into the centre of his bitter unhappy self. It was like colour flowing into a sea of black.

But as she did, with a small part of her mind, cold and clear, she rubbed the rope against the sharp rock behind her, over and over again. She could feel the orbs still pressing at the edge of her consciousness, but somehow, she didn't know how, she could keep them back. And she could feel Eldrow shocked by the emotion she was sending him. And still he didn't move or react.

The masked guards edged a little closer, alarmed and

confused by this impasse. The orbs, too, drifted nearer, unsure of what was happening. Only the wolf didn't move a muscle. She remained alert, watching and waiting to attack.

Maggie felt the rope come apart – her hands were free. But she didn't react. There was very little time – it had to be now.

'Come on, Maggie,' she said to herself, 'you can do it.'

Very suddenly, so that no one would have a chance to understand what was happening, Maggie jumped up, ran straight at Eldrow and hugged him as tightly as she could. Astonished, he allowed her to do so. In fact, he hugged her back.

Maggie could hear the voice screaming now, *Release me . . . release me . . .!*

She reached down, took Eldrow's hand in hers and squeezed it, as if comforting him. The orbs moved quickly towards her, aware something was happening, sensing her rising panic. Eldrow began to unclasp his hand and move slightly away from her. There was no time to delay.

In one quick movement she took hold of the ouroboros. It expanded and yielded to her touch. She slid it off Eldrow's little finger and then, with every ounce of strength she had left, she pushed him. Quickly she slipped the ring onto her own finger and the snake ate its tail again so it fit her perfectly. It glowed and she felt her mind clear and a new strength and energy flow through her.

Eldrow writhed around on the black leaves screaming, 'End her! End her!'

In a flash the wolf was upon her, its claws digging into her flesh, poised to rip into her throat. And there is little doubt that Miss Cane-the-wolf would have happily obliged her lord and master if there hadn't come, just at that moment, from amongst the dark trees, a most terrible sound.

It was a war cry; a guttural, primitive shriek that shook the black leaves on the trees and seemed to stop time. An enormous man wrapped from head-to-toe in tinfoil, rushed out from the trees. He ran straight for the wolf and in his hand he held a roughly made wooden club.

The wolf barely had time to react before Dan the Tree was upon her. He struck her with the club right in the stomach and the wolf howled in agony. Then Maggie saw something in his other hand: a small dagger with a bright golden blade. As the wolf lay stricken, he plunged it into her, aiming for her heart, but the wolf swerved out of the way so that it only grazed her side.

Dan the Tree fell and as he got his bearings again, the wolf darted away from him. The shiny foil was wrapped round his limbs and secured with black tape. His glasses had been newly mended with the same tape. And on his head he wore a hard plastic white hat, like builders wear, with a light attached. His eyes were wild.

The orbs had immediately formed a protective wall around Eldrow, who watched the scene unfolding with a sort of manic excitement. The masked guards had also woken from their trance and ran at the huge man with their axes raised. But Dan the Tree fought as one possessed, his dagger and club slashing out wildly, hacking down the guards who fell away wounded, and swinging madly at the orbs when they attacked him until he caught one with a heavy blow.

The club knocked the orb to the ground and then the huge man was upon it with the dagger, right into its centre. The orb gave a terrible howl of pain. Yellowish fluid seeped out from its inner sphere, there was a flash of bright light then the orb disintegrated into a fine powder and sank into the ground. Steam rose up briefly then died to nothing. The other orbs screamed and rushed up into the air. Beneath them, Miss Cane-the-wolf still crouched on the ground, blood seeping from her side, trying to collect her strength.

Beyond the chaos, Maggie could see the portal, an unmoved observer to everything happening around it, only waiting, shimmering and expectant. She moved towards it, but guards immediately surrounded her, their axes raised. She could only see their dark blank eyes and there was no pity there.

'End her!' she heard Eldrow scream again.

But then the beating of heavy wings sounded in her ears. Everyone looked up. A huge black shadow hung in the sky, it tilted its body downwards, its long beak like a spear, and flew straight towards Eldrow.

There was a tremendous thud as the heron slammed into the man's body. His black form crumpled to the ground. At once every guard ran to attack, their axes raised, but the bird was already in the air again. The orbs rushed up to it, but as they did, Maggie heard another sound – a hissing, like white noise. She looked up.

Above her she saw black figures standing in the trees like statues. And then they jumped, descending from the branches like black petals. They fell onto Eldrow and their dark heavy cloaks smothered him. He screamed, but they were all over him, their long spindly fingers like suckers against his skin. Maggie gasped – the moon witches!

Now every orb and guard piled into the melee. And Maggie suddenly realised – the witches thought Eldrow had the ring; they were going for the ouroboros. This was her chance.

She rushed over to Frank, but he was gone, his little pink face resting, peaceful now, on the ground. Ida was still lying nearby where the orbs had abandoned her. She was still breathing but she was unable to support herself and slumped back over when Maggie tried to get her up. Maggie lifted her, but even with the ring flooding her with new strength she could only manage a few paces before she had to drop her to the ground. The girl was like a dead weight.

The ouroboros pulsed on Maggie's finger, instructing her, trying to tell her what to do. She understood. She took the ring off and plunged it onto Ida's emaciated thumb then she slapped her hard in the face.

'Wake up!'

Ida's eyes shot open as if she'd been given an adrenalin shot. There was still no recognition or understanding in her eyes, but she was awake and fear dilated her pupils. She wanted to live.

Maggie dragged her over to the portal. Still holding Ida, she reached out for the corner and felt the electric current flood through her; it was like a comfort blanket now. She turned and looked desperately around for Hoagy somewhere amidst all the madness behind her.

'Hoagy! Hoagy!' she cried out. But there was no sign of him. She had to keep going.

Behind them, the battle raged. Moon witches kept falling like an endless black rain, even as their comrades lay dead on the ground, or curled up into tiny black balls and scuttled into the forest like beetles. Not far away, Dan the Tree had lost the club, but still he fought and slashed wildly and dangerously with the golden blade at the guards. But Maggie could tell he was starting to tire. There wasn't much time.

She began to rub the two edges of the worlds together. Her mind was far from clear, but somehow it worked. Behind her, she heard a cry go up from Eldrow. The current increased and her whole body started to shake. She was about to jump through when the wolf sprang at her and dug its fangs deep into her shoulder, holding her back, its growling filling her brain.

Maggie screamed in agony and fell to her knees. She managed to hang on desperately to the edge of her world with one hand and onto Ida with the other. But the pain was getting too much. She would have to let go of everything soon. The wolf's harsh white fur brushed against her face and she felt her fingers beginning to lose their grip. She was going to pass out.

Suddenly a lump of brown fur threw itself kamikaze-like through the air from a tree branch right at the wolf. Distracted, the wolf's jaws released Maggie and in one swift swivelling movement used its claws to rip open the body of the cat. Blood spurted everywhere and the brown heap of fur landed in a pile at Ida's feet.

But the release of the wolf's jaws had given Maggie a tiny chance.

'Get him!' she screamed, and Ida, like the little auto-maton she'd become, grabbed the limp bleeding cat in her arms. With her last bit of strength, Maggie threw her body into the glimmering space, Ida and the cat tumbling in with her.

As she fell, the wolf tried to rip into her body once again when a gold dagger appeared up and through its sternum in one swift movement. As they disappeared back into the white nothing, she saw the wolf's face contort and then its whole body slump. Behind it was the glowing triumphant face of Dan the Tree. The guards rushed to attack him and now his task was complete, he collapsed to the ground.

Before she blacked out, Maggie thought she saw one of the orbs. Did it touch Ida as they crossed over? Was it coming through? But then it and everything else in the dark world was gone, and they were falling, falling . . .

31

LOST

Two girls and a cat landed in a heap on the white shiny floor of the huge suburban shopping centre, hot air blowing onto them from some obscure source. All three were filthy and covered in blood, but only one seemed to be alive.

After a few moments that one opened her eyes and lifted her head into the sterile unnatural air. Her black greasy curls were plastered to the side of her sunken cheeks; she was so thin and feral-looking that she was like a wild animal lost beneath the artificial lights. She stood up and it seemed like she must collapse. But then she started to move . . . a few trembling steps.

The girl barely gave her fellow travellers a glance, nor did she notice the blood on her hands and clothes, as she began to run, her filthy bare feet slipping across the tiles. She ran like a startled deer, purely from instinct, past groups of people who looked at her strangely, but other-wise did not impede her.

She was pushing at the brass-framed glass 'EXIT' door before the first scream came. But the girl didn't imagine it had anything to do with her, nor did she care if it did. She pushed open the heavy door and disappeared into the cold fresh air.

Meanwhile, shoppers at the Renters Way shopping centre were starting to gather around the disturbing scene. And for far too many moments, nobody did anything except stare, except for one man who got out his phone and began to film.

An alarm was sounding the length of the endless upper floor and after a few minutes, two first responders in green uniforms pushed their way through the crowd. They found, lying there unconscious, a girl of about twelve or thirteen bleeding profusely from a deep bite mark in her right shoulder. Her face was ghostly pale and her long hair was dark with dirt and so tangled that it had started to matt into thick coarse lumps.

The strange thing was that the deep bite mark could not have been administered by the, presumably, dead cat who lay motionless beside her, its stomach ripped open. The girl and the animal's blood pooled and mingled together on the pristine white floor. The first responders treated Maggie as they waited for the ambulance whilst security guards tried to encourage the onlookers to disperse without much success.

One woman pushed through the lingering crowd and rushed over to the injured feline. It was obvious that there wasn't much hope, but she took off her silk cat-print scarf anyway and wrapped it tightly around the poor desperate body to try and stem the bleeding. Then lifting it as gently as she could in her arms, she too hurried for the exit.

A week later, Maggie, whose own disappearance was never a story, and who was only mentioned in passing in the *West Minchen Bugle* as the 'injured teen', was propped up on several pillows on Esme's bed wearing the nice fluffy slippers Esme had bought for her since she'd got back. She was watching a documentary about twins and whether they were psychically linked, when the buzzer to the flat went.

Maggie started. She was afraid of being on her own now and Esme was out. The buzzer went again, shrill and insistent. She heaved herself out of bed, wincing with pain, and shuffled to the door.

She pressed the button. 'Hello?'

'It's Detective Hammond. Could I come in for a moment?'

Maggie felt a stab of anxiety. She didn't want to talk to anyone, especially not him. She buzzed back, 'I'm on my own and I'm not allowed to let anyone in.'

But then she heard Esme's voice in the background. The intercom buzzed off and the outer door opened in the hall.

This time they'd had to tell her mother about her

disappearance, and Lion had been forced to come to London. In fact, when she'd woken up in hospital, he'd been at her bedside.

Quite naturally everyone wanted to know where she'd been, what she'd been doing, and what in the hell had bitten her on the shoulder? And as Maggie couldn't answer any of these questions in a way that would satisfy them, she just kept saying she couldn't remember over and over again, which didn't please anyone at all.

Her father had gone again a few days ago having given her one hundred pounds Christmas money and making her swear she would never run away again. But Esme had been kind, so kind. And when she'd first seen Maggie lying on her hospital bed, she'd burst into tears and given her a big hug. Maggie promised to tell her everything about what had happened as soon as she could face it, she just didn't feel like it now.

Sometimes when she closed her eyes she saw Mr Yates' terrifying eyes staring out at her from behind the grimy glass, or the moon witches dropping from the trees like heavy ghosts, or she felt Eldrow's deep swirling fear washing over her.

Mostly she thought about Frank, who had been so brave and kind to her and had lost everything. And Hoagy whose lifeless body had disappeared from beside her and whom no one seemed to have even noticed. Who no one even remembered clearing up and putting in a bin.

His absence made her heart ache and that was why she had been waiting for her aunt to return. But now, although Esme came in clutching the photocopies and a packet of plastic folders, first she would have to speak to the awful inert lump that was Detective Hammond. He shuffled in wearing dirty trousers and an old coat. His skin was grey and saggy, and he smelt of old cigarettes.

Esme made sure that Maggie was nicely propped up on some cushions and then went to make coffee. The detective didn't even bother with niceties about her health. He just got straight to the point and he spoke as if he barely had any time.

'Did you know that Ida Beechwood reappeared on exactly the same day as you?'

Maggie nodded. 'I heard that.'

'Someone found her walking along a main road near the motorway and they took her to hospital. She has exactly the same round incision behind her left ear – like the one you have.'

Instinctively Maggie's hand went to the bandaged-over tender spot and she felt a lurch at the memories it provided.

The detective pressed on. 'But she says she can't remember anything,' here his eyes narrowed, 'just like you. You're sure you don't remember anything?'

Maggie shook her head.

'Also a man called Daniel Arbol, the man who lived in the woods down there, mental health problems and so on.

He's been around for years. No one's seen him since the day you got back.' Detective Hammond leant in closer and Maggie realised he was obsessed with the whole thing.

'What about Miss Cane?' she asked. Would he at least admit he'd been wrong about her?

Hammond coughed and sat back. His voice became more formal. 'We have ascertained that she used fake references and possibly a fake identity to gain her position at Fortlake School, but as yet we've found no connection between Ida's disappearance and Miss Cane's sudden removal from the area. We're still trying to ascertain her whereabouts.'

Maggie felt a flicker of anger for a moment that he couldn't say he should have listened to her. But . . . she let it go. What was the point? No one could have stopped Miss Cane from doing what she wanted to.

She stared at him, willing him to get up and leave. She had a hunch he was becoming one of those people who get too far into online conspiracy theories.

He tried again. 'Can you remember where you went?'

Maggie shook her head.

'I don't understand why you won't say anything!' the man burst out suddenly.

Just then Esme clattered in with the tray, but Detective Hammond was already on his feet. He looked down at Maggie. 'If anything does come back to you, let me know. You have my number.' And he walked out without a glance at Esme.

After he'd gone, they drank the coffee in silence until Esme said, 'I'm sorry I didn't believe you about Miss Cane. I should have listened to you. It just seemed . . . a bit far-fetched.'

Maggie shrugged. 'I know. It's OK.'

'What is the hole in the back of your head, Maggie? Do you remember?'

But the question made Maggie feel like crying and she just shook her head. So they didn't talk about it any more.

Instead, once they'd sealed them all in little plastic folders, Esme wrapped up and went out into the cold to stick up the posters of Hoagy's beautiful fat face with the word 'LOST' in huge letters above it and Esme's number below. Maggie didn't hold out much hope, but at least it felt like she was trying, that she hadn't given up on him.

32

THE PARTY

And so, for days Maggie stayed at home and saw no one. Esme dressed her wound and changed her bandages; she slept and watched stuff on her laptop. She didn't want to go out and she even refused to take her mum's Thursday-night calls.

She lay on the sofa for most of the day, the phone right next to her, in case anyone called about Hoagy – though no one ever did – and watched the different types of day drift past: the freezing sleet, the rain, the dull grey sky and occasional bright winter sun.

When the phone did ring, it was usually Esme's friends, a shaky old lady or gent asking about string quartets or poetry evenings. But then one afternoon it was a voice she knew.

'Maggie? Is that you?'

Maggie immediately felt afraid, and a hundred thoughts she'd been trying to keep out of her mind rushed back.

'Can you come and see me?'

Maggie's whole body was tense, but she tried to keep the fear out of her voice. 'I don't want to.'

Dot was trying to sound calm too, but her voice was tight. 'I heard that Ida came home. You must have been very brave, Maggie. I didn't think it was possible.'

But Maggie was not in the mood for flattery. 'Why did you tell me to go to the moon witches?'

'Because I knew they would help you.'

'They tried to kill me!' Maggie realised she was shouting.

'Maggie, that's impossible.' Dot sounded genuinely shocked. 'They are peace-loving.'

'No, they're not! And the ancient witch had this vision about me: he said I was going to bring back the light, but—'

'*You* bring back the light?'

'It's not true, obviously. And he said I would bring darkness, too. When I wouldn't give them the ring, they attacked me.'

Dot's throat sounded constricted. 'Did they get the ouroboros?' she managed to ask.

'No, we escaped.'

Dot gave a big sigh of relief. 'Good. Good. I'm sorry, I . . .' She broke off. 'Tell me, was the moon full when the ancient had this vision about you?'

Maggie could still see its extraordinary luminescence in her head. She didn't think she would ever forget it. 'It was the biggest most beautiful moon I've ever seen.'

308

There was a long silence. 'Then I don't know.'

Was Maggie imagining it or did the old lady sound afraid?

'Nothing is clear to me any more. I am a moon witch, Maggie, if you have not worked that out already. But I'm in exile. I no longer speak to my brethren. Still, I thought they would help you if I asked. All I do know is that what the ancient sees at full moon is never wrong.'

'But it's got nothing to do with me,' Maggie burst out. 'Everyone's looking for someone called the Great O because *she's* going to bring back the light. Not me!'

'And they won't find her.'

Maggie was shocked. 'You know where she is?'

Maggie suddenly remembered that she'd told Almarra and Eldrow about Dot, that she had told them how to find her. She was about to say something but Dot cut into her thoughts and her voice was harsh.

'Where is the ring, Maggie? You must bring it to me right now.'

The ring! It was all anyone ever cared about. Red pulsed through Maggie. 'It's gone!' she snapped. 'It's lost for ever.'

The tension in Dot's voice had turned to anger. 'Don't lie, Maggie.'

But Maggie was angry too. 'I'm not lying. I don't have it.'

'I don't believe you.'

'That's your problem then,' Maggie snapped.

This time the silence was so long, Maggie thought Dot had simply hung up. But then she started to speak.

'My world, the dark world as you call it, is in the end times. If we cannot stop the Islanders then everything is over. They rip the earth apart for gold and for peat, they damage the portals to bring what they desire from other worlds. Then they blame the floods and quakes and tsunamis on the Great O. They steal other people's happiness, yet they can't work out why they are so miserable. They are sick at heart.'

'The moon witches don't seem much better,' Maggie retorted.

But Dot ignored her. 'Even after the Great O sent them such a terrible warning: the sea black, no sun, no animals, no birds, terrible droughts, they won't change, they can't understand that they are not the centre of the universe.'

'But if the Great O is so powerful, why doesn't she just destroy them or get them to do what she wants?' asked Maggie.

'Exactly what a human would suggest!' Dot snapped. 'Nothing is that simple. Everything is connected. Don't you see?'

'But who is she?' asked Maggie. 'What does she look like? No one seems to know.'

'That is because the Great O is everything and nothing. She has no form but she is every form, endlessly mutable – the ultimate shape-shifter. A super-shifter!'

Maggie sighed. 'Great. That's really cleared things up.'

'Some things are mysterious, Maggie. In fact almost everything about the universe is, whatever humans want to believe. Why can I hear the universe humming at the full moon? Why are the trees allowed to speak once every thousand years? I don't know. And I don't need to know.'

'But you must have some idea of who she is?' Maggie persisted.

'Think of her like a goddess of nature or Mother Earth. She is a higher power, far above us, yet she is subject to the earthbound. Everything we do affects her. She has been weakening for many moons, for millennia. And since she vanished from her sanctum in the Magic Mountains she has lain dormant, in hiding. But now she is waking up, and that is because of you.'

'This has nothing to do with me!' Maggie cried, truly exasperated now. 'Don't you get it? I don't care whether your world lives or dies – it's the most awful, hideous place I've ever been to. I brought Ida home and now I just want you to leave me alone.'

'But you are connected to the dark world, Maggie, whether you like it or not. I don't understand how, but you are not a normal schoolgirl from Norfolk. The ring—'

'All you care about, all anybody cares about, is the stupid ring! You didn't tell me what could happen and I nearly died. And Hoagy did die – he's dead! Did you know that? He was my only friend. And Frank, too. And you don't care. And I hate you! I hate you so much!'

Maggie was shaking. Emotion and pain had surged up and burst out of her without warning. But Dot's voice still came down the wire, expressionless and flat now.

'I don't know why my brethren attacked you. I don't know what you suffered. I only know one thing: the Great O has chosen you, Maggie, and there is nothing you can do about it. There is something in you that she needs and she will take it. You cannot escape your fate.'

'Try me!' Maggie screamed and slammed down the phone.

She was trembling all over and when it rang again she grabbed the wire and yanked it out of its socket.

When Aunt Esme got home later that night, she found Maggie crouched on the floor hugging her knees to her chest and shivering in the dark. But Maggie would not say a word.

And Esme was surprised the next day when Maggie angrily refused to go and visit Dot. But like so many things at that time, such as the fact she hadn't got her beloved ring back, she let it slide without explanation when she looked at the girl – still so pale and tired, some dark sadness stirring behind her huge eyes.

Esme heard her most nights, screaming in her sleep. She would get up and go through to make sure she was OK. But even when she was sobbing, Maggie never woke up from her nightmare, and Esme thought it bad luck to disturb her. Instead she held her hand and waited by her side until the dream had passed and Maggie slept peacefully again. Then she crept back to bed.

One grim wintery day a few days before Christmas, they were having a late breakfast when the phone rang. Esme got up to answer it and after a few moments of listening, said, 'Of course. Wait a moment. I'll get her.'

Then she covered the mouthpiece of the old black phone and said gently, 'It's your mother. I think you should speak to her, don't you?'

Maggie pushed her chair back, walked slowly over and took the phone. She was afraid that she was going to start crying, but after a moment she managed to speak in a normal voice.

'Hi, Mum. How are you?'

'Oh, you know. Not very good.'

There was a long pause where neither of them wanted to risk saying anything else. Maggie could sense Aunt Esme was very still behind her, listening.

'I'm sorry I disappeared, Mum.'

Her mum replied in her old voice, her normal voice, 'It's OK, love. I often wish I could disappear too, just for a bit. But you're OK? I mean in your head too? Nothing bad happened?'

'No, Mum. Nothing bad happened. I'm OK.'

'Good.'

'Mum . . . Am I really from Norfolk?'

To her astonishment, her mum laughed. 'Yes, Maggie. You were born in Norfolk.' She hesitated. 'But there are things you don't know. One day, when I'm stronger, I'll tell you. I promise.'

It would have to do for now. There was more silence and in it Maggie screwed up her courage. Even though she knew she'd get a load of grief for it, she wanted to try.

'Mum, I just wanted to say, don't ask me how, but I think I understand, I mean at least I think I understand a bit why . . . why you couldn't get out of bed, or take me to school, or go to the shops or cook or anything. And why you sit and listen to the radio all day. I'm not trying to say I know how bad it is, but I think I get it more now. And . . . and the feeling . . . I think it will go. You will get better.'

She broke off, feeling a little breathless waiting for the angry sarcastic response, but none came. Instead there was only silence down the line. They just hung on the line together for what felt like ages, sharing the weird space the telephone makes between people.

Finally her mum spoke, still in her old soft voice. 'Thanks, Maggie. I appreciate it.'

She hung up immediately, but for once Maggie didn't feel like punching a hole in the wall or smashing a glass. She listened to the dial tone for a bit then replaced the phone gently.

*

Maggie couldn't stop thinking about Hoagy. No one knew what had happened to his body after he had crashed onto the cold floor of the shopping centre beside her, blood pouring from his insides. She'd blamed Dot, but really she felt like it was her fault. It weighed heavily on her as if something was pressing against her lungs, so that occasionally she felt like she couldn't breathe.

Esme tried to cheer her up by asking her to put up the Christmas decorations for her annual festive drinks party. Unfortunately her aunt's dreary selection of decorations was hardly likely to arouse festive cheer as they featured some sad, balding tinsel, a few homemade cardboard Christmas trees from a craft workshop about twenty years ago, and a selection of limp paper stars and cracked baubles. Once arranged on the tiny faux Christmas tree, which Esme balanced on the piano beside the stuffed owl, the effect was fairly depressing.

But Esme did receive a lot of cards, which they strung up around the living room. Esme had a lot of friends, far more than her parents, because she was a good person, Maggie decided. She helped others and she didn't judge them too much.

On the evening of the drinks party, Maggie helped move the furniture, clean up and set out the glasses and nibbles, but she hid herself away as soon as Esme's crumbly mates started to arrive. Although Esme had told her she could use her room, Maggie had taken up her usual spot, wrapped up in a duvet in the pink bath. Next door, she could hear the constant traffic of the weak-bladdered guests going in and out of the toilet, but she still preferred to be here.

After a while she heard the shrill ring of the archaic house phone. Eventually someone picked up or else the caller rang off. But a few moments later, footsteps approached the bathroom door. Somehow she knew it was Esme and that her hand was hovering at the door, about to knock.

Maggie closed her eyes, *Please go away, please go away, please go away* . . . she said in her head. And to her great relief, after a few moments, she did.

Much later, when the party was breaking up and Maggie was drifting in and out of sleep in the bath, she was woken by the sound of the front-door buzzer. She assumed it would be a taxi or someone there to pick up a guest. But then she heard voices exclaiming and, some time after, Esme's footsteps once again at the door. This time there was a knock,

'Maggie? There's someone here to see you.'

Maggie instantly slid down deeper into the bathtub. 'I don't want to see anyone.'

'I think you'll make an exception in this case.'

'Who is it?'

She could tell from the sound of her voice that Esme was smiling. 'Trust me. You'll want to come and see who it is.'

As always, curiosity got the better of her and Maggie reluctantly hoisted herself out of the tub. Her hair was unbrushed and she only wore an old long T-shirt and pants ready for bed. But determined to make no effort, she put on her cosy slippers and dressing gown, and shuffled into the living room.

The first thing she noticed was a tiny woman with set white hair standing in the middle of the room by the sofa. The remaining guests had made a sort of respectful clearing around her. As Maggie came in, everyone turned to look at her.

The second thing she noticed was that this same tiny white-haired woman was wearing a bizarre turquoise tracksuit with a huge white cat sewn onto the sweatshirt-style top. Maggie scowled. Why would Esme get her up just to meet one of her weird friends?

But then a familiar voice rumbled close by, 'I'm over here.'

Maggie spun round and saw one large eye observing her coolly from deep within the sofa cushions.

'Hoagy!' Maggie fell on her knees and wrapped her arms around the warm old cat.

Despite all the bystanders, she started sobbing into his thick soft fur. And she only stopped when she felt a curt tap-tap on her shoulder, claws out.

'Pah! You're getting my stitches wet.'

Maggie sat back and once she'd wiped away her tears,

she saw the same old self-satisfied features staring at her calmly. Though maybe he did look a little different, a little older, a little more tired. And he had a new battle wound, his most impressive yet: a huge jagged scar that ran down his partially shaved belly from close to his throat almost to his tail. And both his back legs were in bandages.

Tears started running down Maggie's face again but the old cat put his paw on her hand, no claws this time.

'We made it, girlie. I knew we would.'

There was no question that Mrs Valerie Hitchcock was the last-minute guest of honour. It was nearly eleven, but Esme brought out a dusty bottle of champagne from somewhere. Maggie thought they should probably check the best before date, but she didn't want to dampen the party spirit. She was even allowed a small glass of it herself, replete with ice cube.

Whatever their former feuds, Hoagy was clearly forgiven and in his new fragile state Esme fussed over him in a way Maggie could never have imagined, fetching him leftover salmon and a tin of mackerel, and personally serving him on the couch whilst rubbing his ears in a way that made his eye almost disappear with pleasure.

Then Esme, Maggie and the remaining party stragglers sat down to hear Valerie's story. How she'd wrapped Hoagy up to try and stem the bleeding. That when she'd got to her car, she'd realised he wasn't breathing and had actually performed human to cat mouth-to-mouth resuscitation.

How there was an emergency vets close by that immediately operated on him. And, finally, how he had spent the last two weeks recovering as the most pampered resident of Mrs Hitchcock's Hendon cat menagerie.

She might never have realised someone was looking for him, but her niece lived in West Minchen and had seen the posters. Otherwise she had planned to keep him.

'I'm surprised you wanted to come back,' whispered Maggie, as Mrs Hitchcock ran through further details of how she had tended to Hoagy night and day.

But to her surprise the cat's tail flicked with irritation.

'Excuse the parlance,' he hissed under his breath, 'it's not a phrase I normally approve of, but quite frankly that woman is as mad as a bag of cats. All those mogs she keeps have lost the plot too. It's like *Apocalypse Now* down there. They're all nuts!'

Maggie rolled her eyes at him.

That night, Hoagy stretched out on the sofa and Maggie lay on her duvet on the floor covered in blankets. After all the excitement, the old cat nodded off almost at once and his soft shallow breath soothed Maggie into a dreamless sleep for the first time in many nights.

33

CHRISTMAS EVE

And it was Hoagy who finally persuaded her to leave the house.

'Spending the rest of your life in this pathetic excuse for a flat is a fate worse than death,' he purred from his spot on the sofa. 'As soon as I'm healed, I'm getting back to my patch. No one is going to stop me reclaiming my territory, I can tell you that for nothing.' He glanced over his shoulder at the glass case on top of the piano. 'And that owl is really starting to freak me out.'

After this bold pronouncement, he immediately fell asleep – he was still very weak. But Maggie sat and thought about what he'd said. It was true: she couldn't stay hidden here for the rest of her life. If she stuck to the main streets and didn't go near the woods, maybe it'd be OK? At least she knew Miss Cane-the-wolf would not be bothering her. But what about the orbs . . . what about Eldrow . . . what about the moon witches? Her best hope was that they had all finished each other off in that huge fight. It was what they deserved, she thought bitterly.

So she went out with a scarf hiding most of her face, and her long hair tucked into a woolly hat. At first, she started at every noise, imagined she was being followed by everyone she saw and was usually back at the flat after five minutes. But gradually she got more confident: maybe the dark world would let her go after all? And she found she liked walking round the streets, using the quickly fading winter light to peer nosily into people's homes, or gazing up at the moon that showed itself palely against the cold blue sky.

Then one day she found herself walking towards Dot's place. It wasn't exactly involuntary. She wanted to take a look at it – she didn't know why. When she thought over their last awful conversation she had this nagging feeling that something had been very wrong, that Dot had been afraid.

She turned the corner and saw that it was still there: the end house with the curious turret. She walked up to it. Nothing had changed. Cars went by occasionally and a small boy in a hoodie was kicking a football against the side of the house from the street again and again, the *thump-thump* pulsing like a dull heartbeat in the chilly air.

Maggie sighed – why had Dot betrayed them? She'd thought she was a friend, or at least an ally. Maggie still had the tiny note – the miniscule strip of paper with the strange hieroglyphics spelling out something she couldn't understand, something, she now realised, about her. She'd found it in the pocket of her jeans when they'd returned her things to her as she left hospital.

Reluctantly she walked up the path to Dot's front door. The curtains of the large room with all the books and herbs and her snooker table were drawn. Was she asleep?

Maggie pressed the bell and she heard it ring out in the silence of Dot's flat. It felt deserted. But she never went out, did she? Maggie shrugged. Whatever – she didn't even know why she was here.

For some reason she didn't understand, her eyes filled with tears. Somehow, in her heart, she didn't think Dot had meant to hurt her. But there was so much she didn't understand.

She turned for home, so deep in thought that she didn't notice the little boy who'd been playing football. He stopped kicking his ball up against the side of Dot's house to watch Maggie walk away, and his eyes glowed yellow in the pale wintry light.

After that, Maggie didn't leave the flat for a couple of days. But then it was Christmas Eve and she thought she'd better get Esme and the cat a gift or two. So she set out once again, her face entirely covered by a scarf, her hair tucked out of sight. And this time she took the added precaution of wearing a pair of Esme's huge sixties sunglasses.

She went into Moss Hill, the posh area where all the nice shops were. The streets thronged with last-minute festive shoppers and the roads were clogged with traffic. She had the money from her dad in her pocket, so she splashed out and bought Hoagy a tin of the finest mackerel and a DVD of *To Catch a Thief*, and for Esme she opted for two sherry glasses, some fancy tea and a mug saying 'World's Best Auntie'. It was cheesy, but she thought Esme might appreciate it. She had been so kind to her since she'd got back.

She didn't have anything to do after that, so she sat down on a bench outside the fancy organic food shop that was heaving with people and watched a group of Christmas-jumper-wearing carol singers who were running through the festive classics. This frighteningly enthusiastic choir was just launching into 'Good King Wenceslas' when Maggie heard someone call her name. She hunkered down into her coat and pulled her scarf further up over her face, her heart racing. But it was too late; she'd been spotted. There was a person standing right in front of her.

She wore a dark blue coat and a pair of brand-new cherry Doc Martins. She was much skinnier than before and her face was pale. But she was still beautiful.

'Maggie.'

Maggie pulled off her ridiculous sunglasses and tried to act nonchalant. 'Oh, hey.'

Ida sat down beside her and Maggie noticed her

concerned-looking family hovering nearby. For several moments she didn't say anything, and Maggie had the feeling she was working up the courage. Finally she broke the silence.

'My parents said you went missing too?'

Maggie shrugged. 'Kind of.'

Ida suddenly blurted, 'Can you remember what happened to you? I can't. Can you tell me what happened?'

'It's OK,' Maggie said quietly. 'Don't worry. You're OK now.'

But Ida shook her head vehemently and the words tumbled out. 'I'm not. Something happened to me, but I can't remember what it is. Everyone thinks I'm mad, though they won't say it. Do you understand? And I feel so sad. And I have this weird hole in the back of my head, like a wound. I don't even know how it got there. Nobody does.'

Maggie felt sick at the thought of it, but resisted the urge to put her hand just below her hairline and feel her own scar.

Ida hurried on, eager to get the words out. 'And I have these weird dreams, every night. And you're in them. In my dreams you always save me from . . . I don't even know what it is. Something dark, something that is going to suffocate me . . .' She was nearly in tears. Mr Beechwood was about to come over, but Maggie saw Ida's mum hold him back.

'Ida. I promise you, everything is OK now. Nothing bad happened to you. And you're safe. Do you believe me?'

Ida nodded, but her eyes still looked full of anxiety.

Maggie took a deep breath and then she took both of Ida's hands. 'Listen, I know you never wanted me as a friend, but I am your friend,' Maggie managed a little smile, 'whether you like it or not. I'll look out for you. If you need me, just let me know.'

This seemed to calm her. Ida squeezed Maggie's hands and looked down. 'Thanks.'

Then Maggie heard a quiet voice, one she had not heard for many days. It began to play in her head like a secret record. Maggie dropped Ida's hands suddenly and her heart began to race.

And now Ida was looking for something in her pocket. Then, making sure her family couldn't see what she was doing, she took out the ouroboros. Its deep pinkish gold glittered in the cold winter light, still beautiful, but Maggie felt cold with fear.

'The other day I woke up and I did remember one thing,' she held the ring out to Maggie, 'that this is yours.'

Maggie put up her hands as if protecting herself. 'No, no, it's not. It's not mine.'

In her head the voice was calling out to her, *Take me . . . take me . . . I need you . . .*

Maggie closed her eyes. She had hoped never to hear that sinewy sweet voice again.

When she opened them again Ida was looking at her, her thin face full of concern and confusion. 'Are you OK?'

Maggie nodded. She got herself together. 'Do you have a safe in your house? Your dad seems like the kind of guy who'd have a safe.'

Ida nodded. 'Yeah, in his study.'

'Do you know the code?'

'I could find out.'

'Put the ring in a box and put it in your dad's safe. And don't touch it. And don't tell anyone it's there. OK?'

'OK.'

Maggie hoped it was the right thing to do. If no one wore it, maybe no one would come to any harm? And no one would ever think to look—

'But why . . . ?' Ida began.

'Darling?'

They turned and saw Philip Beechwood was standing almost beside them, his face tight with anxiety. He seemed far less confident now. He made a jerky let's-go gesture with his arm.

Ida turned back to Maggie. 'I have to go.' But she still hesitated a moment. 'I know you did something to help me. Look, I know I wasn't that nice to you before . . . but I'm . . . the thing is . . .'

Without warning she leaned in and hugged Maggie very tightly. Her thin body felt very warm in her arms, but Maggie was so shocked she could barely hug her back. Ida pulled away and looked at her, emotion flickering over her face.

'So . . . see you in school next term,' she said and managed to smile at her.

Maggie couldn't detect any cruelty in the smile, not even a slight smirk.

'Yeah, OK,' said Maggie.

'We'll sit next to each other, yeah?' said Ida.

Maggie shrugged. 'If you like.'

'Great. Well, Merry Christmas and everything.'

'Yeah, you too.'

Maggie watched as Ida ran back to her family, then disappeared into the holiday crowd. Against all the odds, she'd done it; whatever happened next she'd brought Ida home. And Maggie felt something she hadn't truly felt for a long time: happiness.

THE END

TO BE CONTINUED IN
MAGGIE BLUE AND THE WHITE CROW.

ACKNOWLEDGEMENTS

Thank you to Lisa Williamson, Bella Pearson, Sandra Dieckmann, and to Hoagy the one-eyed cat. And thank you to Nick for always believing in me.

GUPPY
BOOKS

Guppy Books is an independent children's publisher based in Oxford in the UK, publishing exceptional fiction for children of all ages.

Small and responsive, inclusive and communicative, Guppy Books was set up in 2019 and publishes only the very best authors and illustrators from around the world.

From funny illustrated tales for five-year-olds and magical middle-grade stories, to inspiring and thought-provoking novels for young adults, Guppy Books promises to publish something for everyone. If you'd like to know more about our authors and books, go to the Guppy Aquarium on YouTube where you'll find interviews, draw-alongs and all sorts of fun.

Children's literature plays a part in giving both young and old the resources and reflection needed to grow up in today's ever-changing world, and we hope readers of all ages enjoy the story they find here.

Bella Pearson
Publisher

www.guppybooks.co.uk